DEATH'S FIRST KISS

My High School Odyssey: Book 1

William Butler

Followed Dreams Publishing
PO Box 1391, 400 NW Gilman Blvd, Issaquah, WA 98027

Library of Congress Control Number: 2023910074
ISBN: 979-8-9863218-1-3
https://williambutlerauthor.com/

To my mother, Judy, who showed me what a strong woman was, and laid the foundation for all my successes in life.

Chapter One

Catalyst

Evan slammed the door shut as he raced out of the apartment, not bothering to lock it behind him. Using the guardrail for stability, he hurtled down the stairs from his second-floor landing, jumping the last half and sprinting toward his locked bicycle.

Crap! Of all the days to wake up late, why did it have to be this one? He thought to himself as he frantically freed his bike, throwing his leg over the seat and pedaling away as fast as he could.

In less than a minute, he was out of the apartment complex and racing past the convenience store at the corner. A glance at his father's old watch told him he had less than fifteen minutes to get to school or miss the morning's English exam.

It was only four weeks into his third year of high school, but today was his second major exam of the year. His English teacher, Mr. Hanson, was one of the strictest teachers on campus, and if he were late, he'd be locked out of the class, further damaging his already tenuous grade. If it hadn't been for a phone call from his friends, Oliver and Katie, a few minutes earlier, he would still be home, blissfully sleeping and screwing up his chances for college.

As he rounded the last corner to school, he glanced at his watch again, the hands reading 8:08.

"Shit!" he hissed under his labored breath.

The irony of the situation—that he'd stayed up late last night studying for this very test—was not lost on him, though at the moment, he couldn't remember a single thing he'd crammed into his head.

His thoughts briefly floated to the results of his first test two weeks prior, where he had initially earned himself a respectable 81% but was marked down two points to a 79% because of poor penmanship. To add insult to injury, a less than encouraging note of "You can do better than this" had been scrawled across the top in bright red ink.

Evan pumped his legs as hard as he could, ignoring the growing stitch in his side and his aching muscles. The school was finally in sight, and for a moment, he felt a surge of hope that he might make it when he heard the early bell ring. The bell meant that he only had five minutes to get to class.

Evan lowered his head and pushed himself even harder, arriving on campus a few minutes later. With athleticism born of desperation, he jumped from his bicycle and sprinted toward class, cringing at the sound of metal crashing into metal as his bike careened into the chain-link fence behind him.

As he sprinted around the last corner to his English class, he didn't dare slow down, taking it at full speed, leaning in heavily to maintain as much momentum as possible. Then, CRASH!

Pain exploded across his shoulder as he struck

something hard, throwing him to the ground as a numbing sensation spread across his chest and down his left arm.

As he stumbled, he was lightheaded and confused, unable to fully grasp what had just happened. The only clear thought was that he still had time to get to class. Scrambling desperately, he steadied himself and sprinted away.

As he ran, Evan glanced over his shoulder to see what he'd hit. He got a brief glimpse of a girl with bright-silvery hair and a long dark skirt on the ground, having been thrown to her knees.

"Sorry!" he called out over his shoulder as he bolted toward the door to his English class which was finally in sight.

As he ran the last few feet, the numbness retreated, leaving in its wake a sharp, stinging pain that helped to clear his addled mind. As the pain intensified, he was ashamed that he hadn't stopped to check on her, hating himself for not ensuring that she was all right after such a violent impact. But there simply wasn't time.

The bell signaling the start of class began to ring as Evan arrived, throwing his foot into the doorway just as the teacher pulled it closed.

Mr. Hanson glared at Evan as he panted heavily, sweat pouring off him.

"You're late, Mr. Morgan," the teacher said before opening the door just wide enough for Evan to enter.

"Thank you, sir," Evan said as he slithered in, relief surging through him as he walked to his desk, flopping into his seat a moment later.

"That was close," Oliver chuckled quietly as Evan mopped the sweat from his forehead and ran his fingers through his light-brown hair.

With the door closed and locked, Mr. Hanson walked to the far side of the room to his desk, where a small stack of test packets sat.

"With Mr. Morgan's dramatic entrance behind us, we can get started," he said. "Everyone clear your desks. Miss Lopez, will you please hand these out?" He held out the packets toward the brunette, who sat directly in front of the teacher's desk.

As Maria began handing out stacks of tests to each row, Katie glanced back at Evan, scowling over her glasses at him.

Katie had been Evan's first friend in Riverview, having met in elementary school when he'd moved to town in the middle of his third grade. He still remembered her long, braided chestnut hair and oversized round glasses from back then. They had become immediate friends and had remained close ever since, though she had cut her hair much shorter in their freshman year. Evan loved her caring, sensible personality and the flashes of fiery passion that leaked out when he or Oliver did something moronic, which they occasionally did just to annoy her.

As Evan smiled back with a thumbs-up, Katie grimaced as she shook her head before turning her attention back to the impending test.

As the last remnants of the numbness fled, Evan's chest and arm pulsed in vibrant pain. He looked back at the door, wondering who he had run into and why she was carrying a backpack full of bricks. Was she okay? Did she need help?

An unexpected knock at the door caused him to jump as a sense of dread shot through him. Had someone witnessed what had happened? Was he about to get in trouble for assaulting someone? Or worse, had she been seriously hurt?

With a loud grumble, Mr. Hanson crossed the room again, glancing briefly around and easily identifying the one missing student.

"You know the rules, Mr. Simmons," he said loudly enough to be heard through the door. "If you're late on test day, you must wait until the exam is over. You can make it up after—" he said as he pulled the door open, stopping mid-sentence.

Evan's heart sank when, instead of a lanky, blonde boy, stood a young woman with bright-silver hair and a dark skirt—the very person he'd crashed into moments earlier. Her arrival and Mr. Hanson's stunned silence drew the attention of everyone in the class.

After a brief pause, Mr. Hanson regained his composure. "Yes? I'm in the middle of class," he said brusquely.

Without a word, the girl handed him one of the crumpled pieces of paper from the disheveled pile in her hands. Mr. Hanson hesitated, pausing another moment before grabbing the offered paper and taking a step back. As Mr. Hanson read, it seemed to Evan that the girl's arrival had momentarily frightened the teacher, though the thought seemed ridiculous.

She was undoubtedly one of the most striking-looking girls Evan had ever seen, and he couldn't help but stare at her while she waited for Mr. Hanson's response. Her hair was surprisingly long, sweeping behind her and reaching well past her waist, flowing around her in a cascade of bright silver. Her skin was a pale, creamy color with soft, rounded cheeks and steel-colored eyebrows. At first, he thought she had pale-green eyes, but as the teacher shifted, Evan realized they were silver, with the green color reflecting Mr. Hanson's shirt.

Beyond her unusual appearance, there was a mysterious, intriguing quality to her that called to him, though perhaps he was just feeling guilty for earlier. While he was sure they'd never met, he couldn't help but feel that something about her seemed oddly familiar...

When he'd finished reading, Mr. Hanson grunted as he opened the door for the newcomer. "Very well, Miss Blackmore, come in. Everyone else, turn your tests face down and do not begin until I tell you to do so."

The room remained unusually muted as Mr. Hanson walked the new student to the front of the class.

"Attention, everyone!" Mr. Hanson said unnecessarily, as every eye was already glued to the pair of them. "We have a new student joining our class today. She recently moved to Riverview, and I expect everyone to help her get settled. Miss Blackmore, would you please introduce yourself?"

Evan appreciated the apparent fascination the class had with the newcomer. He, himself, was burning with curiosity as to who she was and why she had come to his little corner of the world.

A low level of murmuring slowly spread among the other students though the mood was strangely antagonistic, with a few whispers reaching his ears of "What's wrong with her?" and "Why did she have to join our class?" and "He better not put her back here." A chill breeze ran through the room as if the cold reactions had become tangible.

He couldn't understand everyone's apparent revulsion and took a closer look to see what could generate such immediate animosity. He briefly considered her volumes of bright, silver hair but quickly dismissed it. While it was unquestionably unique, it wasn't unusual for students around campus to dye their hair unnatural colors. There were plenty of girls and a few boys sporting bright red, green, or blue hair. Her choice of clothing didn't present any reason to object either. Fall had arrived, and while it wasn't freezing yet, her blue turtleneck sweater and long-black skirt were similar to many other students' clothing choices.

It was true that she was oddly pale, but not to the point that it should freak everyone out. Her colorless eyes gave her a vaguely ethereal look that he would have thought others would have found intriguing rather than disturbing. The combination of skin tone, pale eyes, and silver hair gave her an oddly monochrome appearance. Evan briefly wondered if she had been sick recently, perhaps explaining why she was starting school four weeks into the semester.

After a few moments, he gave up trying to guess why everyone seemed so ready to reject her and contemplated mass insanity.

As the seconds stretched out, the girl remained perfectly still, hands folded in front of her. Her head was down, avoiding eye contact with everyone. Slowly, the murmuring grew in volume as another chill swept through the room, and she took a wary half-step back. Evan felt something stir. He wanted to come to her defense and had the crazy notion of standing up and putting himself between the uncomfortable, vulnerable girl and the strangely threatening class.

"Quiet down," Mr. Hanson said tersely. "Go ahead, Miss Blackmore," he said as he reached over and gave her a light, encouraging push forward.

After a quick intake of breath, she quietly addressed the class. "My name is Hana," she said. "Hana Blackmore. I, um, hope we can all get along."

The mood of the room continued to darken with a student from the back calling out, "Yeah, right!" accompanied by several quiet chuckles.

"Enough of that!" Mr. Hanson said, eyes searching for the culprit as Evan looked around.

The class immediately quieted, and after a moment, Mr. Hanson motioned to an empty desk at the front of the room.

"You may take that seat, Miss Blackmore."

As she sat down in the chair, it heartened Evan to see his friend Katie lean across and quietly introduce herself to the newcomer. It relieved him that not everyone in the class had it out for Hana, and he was unsurprised that it was Katie who was the first person to greet her with a smile. With Hana's back turned to the others, the murmuring quieted as Mr. Hanson retrieved several papers from a desk drawer and deposited them on her desk.

"We are taking an exam this morning on the themes and significance of foundational U.S. documents and historical literature. You can sit and review the class syllabus during its duration," he said. "I do not tolerate interruptions during tests, so please remain quiet, and if you have questions, keep them to yourself until the test is complete."

Hana nodded, picked up the syllabus, and began reading.

Relieved that the drama around Hana was over, Evan turned his attention to the test as Mr. Hanson announced they could begin.

As he took the test, Evan felt optimistic as the answers came easily and readily. When he arrived at the end of the test, the clock told him he had nearly ten minutes to spare—enough time to check his answers and rewrite anything that was too sloppy.

A few minutes later, Mr. Hanson spoke up. "All right, class: pencils down and packets closed."

The clock on the wall said they had only a couple of minutes before the end of the period, so the rest of the students gathered their belongings in anticipation.

"Before you leave," Mr. Hanson said, bringing the class to order again, "I need a volunteer to show Miss Blackmore around school today."

Considering the negative reception Hana had received earlier, Evan wasn't surprised when only a single hand went up. Despite being bewildered over their reaction, he decided he wasn't about to let this opportunity slip by and raised his hand. He still felt awful about crashing into her and hoped that Mr. Hanson would pick him so he could apologize. It would also give him an opportunity to show her that not everyone in class was an idiot and that at least someone was glad that she'd come to Riverview.

With the faintest of glances in his direction, the teacher turned back to Katie, who had been the first to volunteer. "Miss Pascal, you have Mrs. Roberts next, correct?"

"Yes, sir!" Katie said with barely contained enthusiasm.

"Good. Will you please show Miss Blackmore around?"

"Yes, sir!" Katie beamed.

The bell rang, and the class became a flurry of noise and motion as the other students packed up and headed to their next class. Evan shoved his things into his backpack and made his way out of the classroom, disappointed to have missed his chance to apologize. A moment later, Oliver joined him, and they headed toward history.

Oliver was Evan's best friend and had been since middle school. The two of them had conspired at the end of last year to pick most of the same courses for the semester and had sat next to each other for each of their morning classes.

"Why didn't you raise your hand to show the new girl around?" Evan asked as they walked. "You never miss a chance to make a good first impression before a girl has the chance to get to know you."

"Meh, she's not really my type," Oliver shrugged.

"I didn't know you had a type. I always thought that if she was breathing and willing to give you the time of day, that you were game."

"That offends me, sir!" Oliver said with mock indignation. "I happen to have very particular tastes, my good man." He laughed at his own joke.

Evan laughed along with his friend, surprised at Oliver's lack of interest. He had never known them to disagree when it came to girls and couldn't fathom why *anyone* wouldn't be entranced by Hana Blackmore.

As he settled into his history desk, Evan wondered if Hana would appear in any of his other classes. However, when lunch arrived several hours later, he walked alongside Oliver to their usual lunch spot behind the science building, disappointed at not having seen her again. Oliver was quick to pick up on Evan's diminished mood.

"Hey, man, what's wrong?" he asked as they settled down on the small strip of grass under their favorite tree. "Forgot to bring a lunch?"

"As a matter of fact, yes. I didn't have time to grab anything." Evan groaned as he flopped down on the grass, lying on his back and stretching, causing the soreness in his shoulder to flare up and begin throbbing again.

"I figured." Oliver smiled while pushing over half of his tuna salad sandwich and a little bag of carrot sticks.

"So, what happened this morning?" Oliver asked. "We waited as long as we could before Katie called."

"I'd fallen asleep while studying for the test today..." Evan yawned. "I usually do that stuff at work, but I was swamped last night, so I tried to cram when I got home. I must have dozed off."

"Your boss still out of town?" Oliver asked.

"Yeah, for another two weeks." Evan groaned as he sat back up, resting on his uninjured elbow and taking a small bite of the sandwich. "So, it's just been me and the other part-timer, Vicky, covering the bookstore. I've had to put in a lot of extra hours lately."

"I don't know how you do it," Oliver said through a mouthful of tuna and mayonnaise. "Working at the bookstore, and school, *and* taking care of your sister. I can see why you're having a crappy day."

"It's a lot of work; I'll give you that. But that's not what's bothering me."

"Oh? What's up?"

Evan set the sandwich down and took a gulp from his water bottle before answering. "You know the new girl in English? Hana Blackmore?"

"The creepy one with the silver hair?"

"She's not creepy, but yeah, her."

"What about her?" Oliver smiled slyly. "Don't tell me you have a crush on her already?"

"No, that's…" Evan sputtered, "listen, I ran into her this morning, right before Mr. Hanson let me in."

"Dude," Oliver said. "You stopped to hit on a girl as the bell was ringing? Bold!"

"No, you idiot. I *literally* ran into her. I knocked her down and everything. I bet that's why she was late."

"Dick move," Oliver said, shaking his head. "Why'd you do that?"

"It wasn't on purpose! I was running to make it in time for that test, and as I came around the corner of Building H, she was right there! There wasn't time to dodge or anything!"

"Uh-huh," Oliver mumbled through another bite.

"I wanted to stop and help, but there wasn't time. If I'd stopped, I wouldn't have made it."

"Do you know if she was hurt?"

"I'm not sure," Evan groaned. "I hit her really hard. I think I ran into the books in her backpack though, because when we hit, it felt like I ran into a brick wall. I was too busy trying not to fall down to see exactly what happened to her, but when I looked back, she was on the ground." He rubbed his forehead. "I feel awful."

"As you should." Oliver's tone was flat and no-nonsense. "What are you gonna do about it now?"

"I don't know," Evan shrugged. "Apologize?"

"Well, there you go then. When you see her tomorrow, just walk up to her and say you're sorry for being a dumbass."

"Yeah," Evan said, but he couldn't help but feel

troubled. He still recalled when he'd moved from Chicago and how scary it had been joining a new class in the middle of the year. The sight of her introducing herself to the class with her face looking down and wringing her hands tugged at his heart. Knowing that she was also likely aching in pain while up there because of *him* made it even worse.

The next morning, Evan awoke in a pool of sweat with his covers piled in a wad at the foot of his bed. The screeching of metal-on-metal rang in his ears. The nightmare was so real he could taste his fear, acrid on his tongue, pulse pounding in his chest and ears. He could still smell the odor of oil, asphalt, and blood as if he had survived the crash only seconds ago. As he sat up and ran his hand through his damp hair, pulling it out of his eyes, he looked around the room in the early morning light to reassure himself that it had only been a dream.

Alongside his bed was the corner desk he used for studying with its two shelves filled with action figures and pictures of his family. Across from it was Ellie's pile of tennis racquet's, balls, and their overflowing clothes hamper. On the other side of the room from him was Ellie's captain's bed where she still slept soundly, all wrapped up in her blanket, oblivious that her older brother was awake, heart still racing. He was home, safe and warm, and more than a decade removed from lying in a cold street, bleeding to death.

It had been years since he had dreamed of the car

crash that had killed his parents, and while he had been plagued by nightmares for a long time afterward, he couldn't recall the last time he'd had one. As his breathing began to slow, relief spread through him that it was just a memory. But it had felt so real: his sense of fear and panic, the jolt as his father swerved as he fought to keep control of the car, and the look of terror on his mother's face right before they hit.

His mother's face... a face he hadn't seen outside of pictures in so long. Echoes of her voice skittered on the edge of his memory, though he could only barely recall what she sounded like. He could envision the countless hugs she'd given him but couldn't dredge up what it felt like to actually touch her. He had a faded, vague memory of his dad laughing loudly while holding a spatula as they grilled a backyard dinner, where he could still smell the grilling hamburgers and onions but couldn't remember the sound of his father's laugh. They were gone, taken in an instant in a freak accident that no one and nothing could have prevented. Suddenly his relief at waking from his dream fell away, and a part of him wished he was still in the dream, reliving the last precious moments he'd ever had with his mother and father.

The clock on his headboard told him it was nearly an hour before his earliest alarm would go off. He considered trying to return to sleep but didn't want to risk sliding back into the nightmare. Though seeing his parents again almost made it worth it. After several long minutes, he pulled himself out of bed, mindlessly grabbing his clothes for the day and shuffling toward the shower.

As he worked quietly, fragments of that day continued to swim into his thoughts. Unwelcome memories of the car tires screeching, the explosion of glass, and the sound of metal wrapping itself around metal swam into his mind. As he lathered himself, he brushed across the bruise on his shoulder. The sudden stab of vibrant pain reminiscent of the car crash years earlier pushed him even further into that dark memory. Suddenly it was too real, and the fear, pain, and loss, from that moment overwhelmed him. Tears began to flow as his chest constricted. The loss of his mother and father felt like a vice around his heart, stealing his strength as he sat down in the flow of hot water. It took a long time to calm down again, and when he finally emerged from his shower, his skin was red and his eyes swollen.

When he arrived at the normal corner with his friends, they immediately picked up on his mood.

"Hey, are you okay?" Katie asked after Evan mumbled a weak 'good morning.'

"Uh, yeah, sorry," Evan said with a shrug. "Just had a bad dream last night, and it's left me a little out of it."

"What, were you attacked by zombies or something?" Oliver asked with a chuckle.

"I wish," Evan said. "It was about my parent's car accident. And was less like a dream and more like reliving the whole thing."

"Oh, I'm sorry, man," Oliver said apologetically.

"It's fine," Evan said as he smiled weakly. "Don't worry about it."

The rest of the morning passed without Evan registering much of what was happening around him, going from class to class with little awareness. When his day wrapped up at the end of study hall, Evan was relieved it was over. He hadn't been able to shake the uneasiness he'd felt all day and worried that his grief could ambush him again at any moment.

"Ready to go home?" Katie asked after the last bell of the day rang.

"Sure." Evan shrugged as he grabbed his backpack.

"Would you like to come over to my place?" Katie asked as they left the school grounds. "I have your favorite: root beer."

"I appreciate it, but I just want to go home and go to sleep. I'm exhausted."

"Are you sure? We have vanilla ice cream too. I can make you a root beer float."

Evan considered her offer briefly before shaking his head. "Nah, thanks, though. I'm just going to go home, hug Ellie, make dinner, and go to bed."

"Okay," Katie said with a smile. "but if you change your mind, you know where to find me."

"Thanks," Evan said as he smiled back. "But why do you even have root beer at your house? I thought you and your parents didn't like the stuff."

"Oh, it's left over from the last time you came over," Katie chuckled. "It's not like the stuff goes bad or anything. Or that anyone would be able to tell from the taste."

Evan laughed for the first time that day. Later, when they separated from each other on their respective routes home, Evan's pocket buzzed as Oliver texted him:

Oliver: Hey man, want to get online later and

murder some zombies or something?

Evan: Not home yet...

Oliver: ok then, WHEN YOU GET HOME, do you

want to do stuff?

Evan: Not really.

Oliver: R u sure? Might make you feel better to take down a boss or two…

Evan: Thanks, but I'm good. I'm feeling better and just want to veg a little at home and go to bed early.

Oliver: Alright then. See you tomorrow

Evan: See you.

As Evan walked home, he found himself smiling, knowing how his friends would go out of their way to make him feel better. Even if Oliver's suggestion was the same thing they did nearly every night. It was comforting to know they cared.

The visions from the morning had finally faded into the background, and he enjoyed a relaxing evening at home before going to bed early. It wasn't until he was fading off to sleep that he remembered that he still hadn't apologized to Hana.

By the time Wednesday arrived, Evan's life had returned to normal: getting up at the usual time and meeting Katie and Oliver for the walk to school as they always did. With no frantic rushing or haunting memories. More importantly, he was determined to follow Oliver's advice and approach Hana that morning before the start of class. He would introduce himself and offer a heartfelt apology. He was mildly concerned that doing so might ignite some rumors from the other students, but he wanted to put Monday's events behind him and ease his guilty conscience. At least he could stop worrying about it, if nothing else.

The three of them arrived early and took their regular seats. As they waited for class to begin, Oliver regaled Evan with a heroic tale of his latest conquest in his favorite video game, Arena Combat, from the night before. Evan listened with only half an ear, watching as each student arrived, waiting for the bright mane of silver hair that would announce Hana's arrival. With only a couple of minutes remaining before the bell rang, she finally appeared.

Evan perked up and watched as she crossed to her seat. He was hoping she might look in his direction and wore his most charming smile just in case. Unfortunately, she arrived at her assigned seat without once having glanced in his direction. He continued to watch her as she sat down, and for one brief moment, when she turned to hang her bag on her chair, she looked up, and their eyes met.

What had been a neutral, reflective expression on her face changed at that moment. His hopes of making a good impression died as he watched her eyes narrow and her lips purse before she turned away, obscuring her face with a surplus of bright silver hair.

A cold chill ran down Evan from that brief glare. His blood felt cold as goosebumps erupted on his arms, and his stomach twisted into knots. Her glance made him retreat further into his chair, feeling the depths of her loathing of him. It felt like he'd fallen, fully clothed, into the deep end of a pool and couldn't remember how to swim.

"Dude, you okay?" Oliver asked as Evan dropped his head into his hands and groaned.

The bell rang, saving Evan from having to respond as Mr. Hanson called the class to order, though Oliver kept peering over at him with a quizzical expression.

When English wrapped up, Hana gathered her things in a flash and was the first one out the door, staring straight ahead the entire time, pointedly looking away from Evan's side of the room. Apparently, it was still too soon to apologize. Hana was clearly furious with him, and he could hardly blame her. He knew how difficult it was to transfer to a new school, and he couldn't fault her for hating him after he knocked her down on her very first day.

At least she didn't seem inclined to confront him over the incident, so he hoped that perhaps, in time, he might have an opportunity to explain himself and make amends.

It would be fine.

Chapter Two

Study Session

It wasn't fine.

Despite his plans to put it behind him, Evan remained distracted and preoccupied with how he'd wronged Hana Blackmore and couldn't yet make up for it.

The following Tuesday, Mr. Eldridge walked between the rows, handing out the results of the previous day's practice chemistry exam. As he got to Evan's seat, he placed the answer sheet face down on the desk and tapped his finger on Evan's desk.

"Not great, Evan," Mr. Eldridge said. "I recommend you study before the exam; you still have time; the actual test is on Friday."

The teacher moved on to the next desk as Evan reluctantly turned over the piece of paper.

It wasn't the worst score he'd ever had, but a 74% made him anxious. He knew that he was on the edge of slipping from a B to a C. Chemistry wasn't his best subject, sure, but Evan had goals.

He was just thinking that he needed to get some help when the teacher paused at Oliver's desk.

"Would you please stop at my desk after class? I'm starting to get worried for you," Mr. Eldridge said with a note of genuine concern in his voice before moving on and offering further encouragement to others as he went.

Oliver glanced at his score and groaned.

"Crap," He grumbled with a grimace. "I'm going to be in so much trouble."

"What did you get?" Evan asked.

Oliver turned his answer sheet so Evan could read it. A large "59" was written in bold red ink with an added note: "Not your best work. I know you can do better!".

"If my mom sees an F on my test, she's going to be pissed," Oliver said. "I'm going to get grounded."

"Yeah," Evan said teasingly, "she'll probably take away your GameBox."

Oliver groaned again. "How'd you do?"

"Not good." Evan showed Oliver his answer sheet.

"What are you talking about?" Oliver asked with widened eyes, "I would kill for a 74!"

"It's not an F, that's for sure. But I need to get at least a 96% on the test, or I'll have no chance at getting an A by the end of the semester."

Oliver rolled his eyes, "You still dreaming of running off to college after high school?"

"Of course."

"Well, good luck with that," Oliver said. "Too much effort if you ask me. I'll just be happy to graduate."

Evan understood why Oliver had given up on any dreams of college he may have had. He was the third of four children, only one year younger than his twin sisters, both of whom were good students as well as stars of the school's basketball team. Their grades weren't good enough for full scholarships, but they would likely get a modest offer based on their athletics.

Oliver's family knew they would need to come up with a good portion of the money for college tuition by the start of the next school year for each of them.

Oliver's parents had divorced in the middle of his freshman year, and finances were stretched tight in his household. His father had promised to help fund the kids' college education, but it was doubtful that they could afford to send three kids to college within two years, even with his help.

The divorce had been messy and especially hard on the kids. It took more than a year for his parents to fully separate and the household drama to settle down. Evan remembered how distraught his friend had been, relaying tales of yelling, broken dishes, and tears. The latter half of Oliver's freshman year and most of his sophomore year had seriously suffered from it. Evan was still surprised that he hadn't been held back.

Oliver's grades ensured that he wouldn't be receiving any scholarships unless he could be awarded one for playing video games.

Oliver stared at his answer sheet in anguish. Evan wasn't certain if his friend was more upset at the grade or the idea of losing access to his video games.

When the bell rang, Oliver had a brief discussion with the teacher while Evan hung back. A short while later, as the two of them shuffled out of class, Oliver looked over his shoulder at Evan. "Do you think Katie would let us cheat off her Friday? She has Mr. Eldridge right before us, so she could give us the answers!"

"Not a chance." Evan knew the answer immediately. "Though I'm pretty sure she would help us study."

"Yeah, you're right." Oliver sighed in defeat. "It'd be a lot easier if she gave us the answers, though."

"Yeah." Evan looked back at his paper and the disappointing grade. "I'll ask her today."

Evan's opportunity to ask Katie for assistance came later that afternoon. At the end of the previous year, he had signed up to be a student volunteer for the last-period study hall, expecting it would help him with his schoolwork and keep him focused. He shared that duty with several other students, including Katie, who greeted him with a huge smile when she arrived.

Seeing her at the door to the library, Evan remembered their first meeting, nearly ten years earlier, after his parent's accident. It was right after he and his younger sister had moved to Riverview to live with their Aunt Madeline. Katie had been the first person to befriend him when he transferred into her class in the middle of the school year.

While the pigtails were gone, and her choice of clothing had evolved over the years, her bright, friendly nature remained as brilliant today as when they'd been eight years old. Her natural warmth had drawn him in at a time when he'd desperately needed it, and she had welcomed him readily. They had remained close friends ever since.

In addition to sharing classes with her throughout most of his school life, he frequently spent time with her on the weekends. She was a regular guest at his house and a particular favorite of his younger sister, Ellie. Evan surmised that it likely had something to do with the fact that Katie wasn't much taller than his ten-year-old sibling, having stopped growing near the end of middle school.

In the past year, he had seen less and less of her as their social circles drifted apart, but he was confident she'd be willing to help him prepare for the upcoming test.

"Hey, Katie, how's it going?"

"Hey, Evan," she said as she stored her backpack and jacket under the library desk. "I'm good. How are you?"

"Not great, actually."

"Aw," she said. "What's wrong?"

"I bombed the chemistry practice exam," he said.

"Oh." She smiled her familiar knowing smile. "You know there's something you can do about that, right?"

"Have you give me the answers right before class?" He teased, unable to resist the temptation.

The smile on her face vanished, replaced by a deep scowl.

"No! Idiot!" she said brusquely, turning away while busying herself with rearranging the items on the countertop. "You could study. Like everyone else. And you should know better than to ask me to help you cheat. Geez, you sound just like Oliver."

Evan couldn't help himself from laughing out loud, causing several heads to turn in his direction while the librarian glared.

"Actually," Evan said quietly, "I wanted to ask if you'd help me study for the test. We have a few days, and I'd really appreciate the help."

"Of course," Katie said without hesitation. "You could have just said that. Jerk." She playfully punched him in the arm. "I'm busy today and tomorrow, so how about

Thursday after school?"

Evan's spirits lifted. With Katie's help, there was a chance that he'd ace the test instead of watching his grade slip even further.

"Perfect. I'll call out of work too, so we'll have all night."

"All night? Just how bad *are* you at Chemistry?" Katie giggled while elbowing him in the arm.

Later that night, as Evan lounged on the couch next to his sister watching television, he pulled out his phone and began texting Oliver:

Evan: Hey man, I wanted to let you know that I asked Katie about giving us the answers for the chemistry test

Oliver: No way, really? Did she say yes?

Evan: HA! You wish.

Oliver: If she's not going to give us the answers, then why are you bothering me

Oliver: I'm busy

Evan: Sure you are, you're just playing video games

Oliver: Am not

Oliver: Do you think all I do is play video games?

Oliver: That hurts

Oliver: You wound me sir

Evan: Sorry

Evan: So what are you doing?

Oliver: Looking up a walk through guide for a

video game

Oliver: I'm stuck

Oliver: :P

Evan: LOL

Evan: You're an idiot

Oliver: True, true

Evan: Anyways...

Evan: I talked to Katie, and she agreed to help me

study for the test

Evan: Want me to ask if you could join us?

Oliver: Yeah, sure. If it's just us, we'll prolly just

play games and not get any studying done

Evan: Probably... one sec then

With a couple of quick taps on his phone, Evan added Katie to their chat:

Evan: Hey Katie, are you busy right now?

Katie: Not really, what's up?

Evan: Oliver wanted to know if he could join our

study group

Oliver: Yes, please. Evan will buy you an ice
cream!!

Evan: Why do I have to buy her ice cream? Pay
your own bribes!

Katie: Lmao

Katie: Sure, he can join.

Oliver: You know it would be a lot easier if you
just gave us the answers

Katie: ABSOLUTELY NOT OLIVER ANDREW
BRANCH!

Oliver: Ok then, just help studying

Katie: Now I'm tempted to tell you "No."

Evan watched the exchange in amusement. After several seconds of no updates, Oliver pleaded his case with a crying emoji:

Oliver: :~(

Another couple of seconds passed before Katie finally responded:

Katie: Fine, but you better be serious about
studying or I'll kick you out.

Oliver: Ok, I'll behave. I promise.

Katie: Thursday. If you're both in, I'll bring Sarah

and we can make it a group thing.

Evan: Sounds great! Thanks Katie

When Thursday morning arrived, and Evan was getting ready for school, his phone chirped, announcing a new message:

Katie: Hey there

Evan: Good morning

Katie: I'm sorry, but I caught something. I won't

be at school today.

Evan: That sucks. Are you ok?

Katie: I'm all right. Just a mild fever and a cough.

Evan: I'm sorry. I hope you feel better soon

Katie: Me too, but it means that I won't be able to

help you study today.

Katie: Don't worry though. I've recruited

reinforcements.

Evan remembered that Katie had mentioned bringing Sarah. He hadn't hung out with her much but knew she regularly had the highest scores in any class they shared. Katie had bragged before about how she had several advanced placement courses and would likely be the valedictorian of their class. It may not be as fun as working with Katie, but he was certain Sarah could help him prepare for the test.

Evan: Oh cool. Thanks!

Katie: No problem

Evan: And when you're feeling better, I will take you out for some ice cream

Katie: Sure. It's a date!

Katie: I'll tell everyone to meet up at the library after school.

Evan: Thanks again Katie. You're a lifesaver

Katie: My pleasure. :)

That afternoon, when school let out for the day, Evan and Oliver met outside the library where they had agreed to meet up with Sarah. While they waited, Oliver took out his phone and began playing a video game. It wasn't long before she arrived with her younger brother, Kyle.

Sarah was primarily Katie's friend, having met in their freshman year and becoming fast friends. Evan felt a little guilty that the only real things he knew about her was that she was super smart and that her grandparents had immigrated from Jamaica.

Of all his extended circle of friends, Sarah was the

most stylish, and Evan had always admired her eye for color. Today she was wearing an ocher-plaid skirt and matching top, her jacket tucked under one arm. The colors complimented her umber skin tone and long, ebony hair nicely.

Kyle was her younger brother by two years and had just started his freshman year at Riverview. Kyle's choice of dress was far more casual than his sister's, with jeans and a t-shirt under a forest green jacket, his corkscrew hair mostly covered by a green and gray beanie.

"Hi, Sarah," Evan said. "Hey, Kyle."

"Sup," Oliver grunted without taking his eyes off his game.

"Hello," Sarah said while her bother simply nodded.

"Thanks for helping us out today," Evan said. "We're all set if you're ready, though I guess we should decide where we're going."

Sarah looked around with a confused expression on her face. "What about Hana?"

"Hana?" Evan asked in surprise. "Hana Blackmore?"

"Yeah, Katie invited her," Sarah said, her tone matter of fact. "Apparently, she's pretty good at Chemistry, so Katie asked her to fill in. She didn't tell you?"

"Uh, no. She didn't mention it." Evan's cheeks felt a little warm. "Does Hana know that she's going to be helping us today? You know, Oliver and me?"

"I don't know. Katie just told me she'd be coming too."

"Great." Evan sucked in a breath.

Evan's stomach tightened at the thought of facing Hana. *There was no way that she would have agreed to help them study if she knew he would be there, right?* He couldn't imagine exactly how she'd react when she found out, but he was certain it wouldn't be good. He vividly remembered their disastrous first encounter and the blood-freezing glare she'd thrown at him days later.

As they waited, his nervousness grew. After a minute, he considered canceling the session altogether. He could tell the others he wasn't feeling well, and with the acrobatics his stomach continued to do, it wouldn't be a lie. As he was about to call everything off, Sarah raised her arm and pointed beyond him.

"There she is."

Evan spun around so quickly that he nearly lost his balance. As he stumbled and regained his footing, he thought he heard Sarah suppress a laugh behind him.

A moment later, Hana joined the four of them.

Sarah took the initiative and began introductions. "Hana, this is Evan, Oliver, and my little brother Kyle." She motioned to each person as she named them.

Evan braced himself for the outburst that was sure to come. At the very least, he expected a cold, chilling glare like last time, but to his surprise, Hana smiled at each of them.

"Hello," she said. "It's nice to meet everyone."

"Okay, now that everyone has met," Sarah said, very business-like, "let's get this—"

"I'm so sorry!" Evan blurted out loudly, interrupting Sarah.

"What?" Sarah asked, confused, though Evan was facing Hana with his head down.

"I'm so sorry I knocked you down on your first day of school and made you drop your papers and made you late, I didn't mean it, honest," he spewed in a single breath.

Hana's confusion quickly gave way to surprise as she

took a step away from Evan.

"You pushed her down on her first day of school?" Sarah said with disgust.

"It was an accident!" Evan protested.

"Dude." Kyle mirrored his sister's disapproval, shaking his head, "Not cool, dude."

Evan ignored everyone and focused on Hana, finally making eye contact and speaking to her directly.

"I'm really sorry," he said. "I was really late and I didn't see you. I would have stopped to help, but if I had, we both would have been late, and..." He winced. "I would have been marked off ten percent from the test." It sounded stupid and selfish when he said it out loud.

"Evan, that's no excuse," Sarah said flatly.

To his surprise, it was Hana who came to his rescue.

"No, it's all right," she said. "I understand."

"What?" Evan and Sarah asked in chorus.

"It's fine, really," Hana said. "I was already late because I had trouble finding the right room, and there was no harm done, honest."

"I'm sorry if I hurt you..."

"Oh no, I'm fine," she said with a smile. "Truly, no harm done."

Relief washed through him. He was surprised that she would forgive him so quickly, but he was glad that she had. "You really weren't hurt?" he asked, doubting that she had escaped unscathed as his shoulder was still tender, the bruise only now fading.

"Honest." She smiled again.

All those books must have cushioned her, Evan reasoned. Or he'd struck her bag at just the wrong angle. Regardless, he was relieved that he hadn't caused her any lasting harm.

"All right then," Sarah said, retaking control of the situation. "Anyone else want to apologize for something stupid they've done?" She looked at Oliver, who had a reputation for being a troublemaker.

"Don't look at me! I haven't done anything... lately," he said with a wide smile.

While Evan chuckled, Sarah shook her head briefly and continued getting the study session organized.

"So, where are we headed?" she asked the group.

"Well," Evan scratched the back of his head. "I originally figured we'd study at Katie's house, but she's sick, so that's out of the question. And the library is going to close in about five minutes, so that won't work either."

Evan briefly considered suggesting the small, two-bedroom apartment he shared with his aunt and sister. He would have been happy to invite everyone over, but the problem was space. With five people plus his sister, it would be cramped.

Deciding to leave it as a last resort, he looked at Sarah. "Where do you live?" he asked.

"Not very far, but we can't study there. We have family visiting, and our house is packed with relatives, complete with several toddlers."

Kyle groaned. "Yeah, it's crazy town."

Evan wondered briefly if Kyle really wanted to study or if he just wanted to get away from their crowded house.

"We could study at my house," Hana said quietly, causing everyone to look in her direction. Clearing her throat and squaring her shoulders, she continued, "It's not very far, and we'd have plenty of space to spread out in the living room. My sister will be there, but she mostly stays in her room, so it won't be a problem."

"All right," Sarah said. "Sounds like it's all settled then."

A moment later, Hana was leading the group off the school grounds, and to Evan's surprise, she turned in the direction he would normally go on his way home.

"I didn't know you had a sister," Sarah said as they walked.

"Oh yes," Hana said. "We're twins."

"Identical or fraternal?" Sarah asked.

"Um, identical, mostly."

"Really? Does she go to Riverview?"

"Uh, no," Hana said with a note of hesitation in her voice.

"Does she go to Lakewood, then?" Sarah asked, referring to the only other high school that was remotely close to this part of town.

"No." Then, after a brief pause, Hana elaborated. "I guess you'd say she's homeschooled."

"Any particular reason?"

"She's not great around strangers," Hana said. "It's just easier for everyone if she stays home."

It occurred to Evan that they were about to bring a house full of strangers over and wondered if his apartment might be a better alternative after all.

"If she's uncomfortable around strangers, we can find somewhere else," he said. "It doesn't have to be at your house."

Hana quickly waved away his suggestion. "It'll be fine," she said. "Like I said, she just stays in her room most of the time, so there won't be a problem."

"If you're sure." Evan hoped she didn't feel pressured.

"I'm sure," she said with a beaming smile.

Chapter Three

The Sister

When they reached a modest two-story home halfway between school and Evan's apartment, Hana announced they had arrived. The house was cute, with a small grassy patch of a lawn, a short white picket fence, and well-maintained bushes and flowers around the perimeter. The house was painted a pristine white with light blue trim and shutters. It looked so picturesque that it reminded Evan of real estate brochures.

The front door opened to a small, tiled entry area with a carpeted living room stretching off to the right and a dining room to the left. Between them a hallway reached deeper into the home, leading to a kitchen and a stairwell leading up. Along the walls were a few paintings depicting a rural countryside with rolling hills and a large cottage near a winding river. They seemed to be a part of a set as they were all in the same place but from different angles and times of day.

The house was clearly lived in, though Hana and her family kept it meticulously clean without a hint of clutter, as though it had been prepared for them specifically. As they walked into the living room, Evan noted it was spacious enough for the five of them. *This is much better than my tiny place.*

"Nice place," Kyle said as they migrated into the living room that had a pair of plush, white couches and a glass-topped redwood coffee table between.

"Thank you. Please, take a seat wherever you'd like." Hana glanced toward the stairs, her smile drooping slightly to a more anxious expression. "I'm going to go tell my sister that we have guests. I'll be right back."

Hana made a brief excursion upstairs while everyone else settled in and spread their materials around the table. By the time she returned a minute later, Sarah was already directing their efforts on how they should proceed, even dictating the seating, placing Evan next to herself with Hana directly across from him, nestled between Oliver and Kyle.

"Are we ready?" Sarah asked without waiting for an answer. "Okay, so, covalent bonds..."

Several hours passed in focused concentration. They had reviewed most of the material for the exam, and even Oliver was taking the session seriously, much to Evan's surprise. He was beginning to feel confident about the test when Oliver's phone rang.

As Oliver talked, Evan stretched and enjoyed the brief respite. They had been going non-stop, and his muscles were tense and sore. He had to give Sarah credit; she was an excellent mentor and had done a masterful job of keeping everyone focused. She was relentless, insisting that they review every little thing, drilling it into them over and over to ensure they fully grasped the concepts before moving on.

"All right, Mom." Oliver hung up. "Sorry, folks, I've got to go. Thanks for the help," he said with a smirk. "This was *almost* fun."

As Oliver packed up, Sarah looked at her watch and blinked in surprise. "Oh, wow, it's late! We were supposed to be home thirty minutes ago."

That officially heralded the end of their study session, and the room became a flurry of movement.

"Thank you so much, Sarah," Evan said as he helped her pack up her books. "I really appreciate all your help. Truly."

"No problem." She surveyed the room, and Evan followed her gaze to the small mountain of trash they were leaving in their wake. The mess mainly consisted of empty soda cans, discarded bags of chips, and wadded-up papers strewn haphazardly across the table and spilling onto the floor.

"Evan, can you stay to help clean up?" Sarah asked as Hana escorted Oliver and Kyle to the door. "I would stay, but we're really late."

"No sweat, I got this."

Moments later, Hana closed her front door, having waved their friends goodbye as Evan moved around the room, corralling the various bits of rubbish.

"Thank you for helping, but I can clean up," Hana said as she returned to the living room. "It's not that bad."

"Nonsense. This is the least I can do since we invaded your house and everything," Evan said with a smile. "Besides, this is nothing. At home, my aunt works late all the time, so it's mostly just my sister and me, and I'm used to cleaning."

"You have a sister too?"

"Yeah, her name is Ellie; she's ten."

"Oh," Hana said, glancing at the clock hanging in the hallway. "If you need to get home, you don't have to stay. I totally understand."

"That's cool, but I'm sure she's fine. Knowing Ellie, she's probably already finished her homework and is watching TV or something."

"Are you sure?"

"Yeah, no problem," Evan said with a smile.

He was about to ask more about her own family when the sound of someone coming down the stairs floated into the living room, almost as if Hana's curiosity about his sister had summoned her own.

Evan watched as a teenage girl came down the stairs, pausing when she got to the bottom and glared. "Who's that?" she asked sharply, pointing at him.

At first, Evan wasn't sure that she was Hana's sister, as they looked totally different from each other. It was hard to believe that they were related, let alone identical twins.

Where Hana had long, silver hair, a pale complexion, and a well-groomed, conservative appearance, her sister had disheveled short black hair that was dyed red at the tips and a warm, olive skin tone. Compared to Hana's more athletic build, her sister had a more curvaceous, plump figure and was completely comfortable showing it off in a thin, pink camisole and form-fitting boy shorts, both edged in black lace. The outfit left little to the imagination. The feature they appeared to share was a strikingly similar pair of mercury-colored, almost luminescent eyes.

"Hello, Mara," Hana said sweetly to the newcomer. "This is Evan. We're in the same English class. Evan, this is my sister, Mara."

Mara looked at Evan through squinted eyes with a look of guarded suspicion.

Hoping to make a good first impression, Evan walked

over and reached out his hand.

"Hi. It's nice to meet you."

Mara briefly looked down at Evan's extended hand, then crossed her arms in front of her, ignoring him completely. She looked back at Hana and continued in the same accusatory tone. "What's he doing here? I thought everyone left ten minutes ago."

"He stayed behind to help clean up," Hana said. "We kind of made a mess earlier." Hana drew attention to the armful of trash to emphasize her point before heading deeper into the house, toward the kitchen.

Recognizing he wasn't likely to make any positive inroads with Hana's sister, Evan returned to cleaning. Mara followed him into the living room, plopping down on the shorter of the two couches, staring at him as he worked.

"How old are you?" she asked a moment later, catching Evan off guard.

"Oh, um, seventeen," Evan said, keeping his tone pleasant and conversational. "How about you?"

Mara ignored his counter-question and fired off another on the heels of his answer. "Do you live around here?"

"Yes, just a couple blocks away, actually. Up on Pine. Have you—"

"What were you studying?"

"Chemistry."

"Do you play any sports?"

"No, but I like—"

"What's your favorite subject?"

"Um." She clearly wasn't about to let him get a word in, and he started to sweat under the barrage. "Math, I guess?"

"Are you a good student?"

"Not terrible, I suppose."

"Do you have a job?"

"Yes, I work over at—"

"Have you lived here long?"

"About ten years," he said, ceasing any attempts at cleaning and deciding to hold his ground against her onslaught.

"Were you born here?"

"No, I was born in Chicago."

"Where did you go to middle school?"

"Seabrook."

"Do you have a girlfriend?"

"Uh.... no."

Only now did Evan see the playful glint in Mara's eye, like a cat playing with a toy. Still not wanting to appear rude, he decided on a strategic retreat and began moving toward the kitchen, intending to deliver the last load of trash himself rather than wait for Hana's return.

"So, Evan, do you suck at chemistry or do you just like my sister?"

"Wha—" The tip of Evan's shoe caught on the edge of the tile floor. As he stumbled, he dropped the trash in his hands, which included two soda cans, still partly full. They crashed loudly on the tile, bouncing and splashing their contents all over the floor.

As he caught himself on a nearby chair, Mara laughed hysterically, grasping at her sides as she rolled back into the couch. So much for a good first impression—for either of them.

Trying his best to ignore her laughter, Evan knelt to clean up as Hana returned, towel in hand.

"I'm sorry about that," Hana said under her breath as

she leaned down to help. "My sister can be a bit rude. She doesn't talk to other people often."

"It's all right," Evan said. "I'm just sorry I spilled soda on your floor."

Mara's laughter faded as the two worked, though she continued watching them with a mischievous grin.

A few minutes later, the floor was clean, and Evan was back in the living room, grabbing his books and notes, trying his best to ignore the twin sister who was still watching him intently.

As he stuffed his books into his backpack, Mara spoke up again. "You never answered my question about chemistry and my sister."

Evan considered ignoring her entirely but took a small breath and answered politely. "I don't normally suck at chemistry," he said. "I'm trying to get into college, so it's important that I keep my grades up. I didn't do well on the practice exam, so I asked for some help."

Evan expected some kind of sarcastic quip or another question, but Mara remained quiet, watching him put away his belongings.

Finally, when Evan had put everything away and shouldered his backpack, she spoke again. "So, did you finish all the studying you needed to get done?"

Evan looked up at her, confused. "What?"

Mara rolled her eyes. "Are you all set for your test, or do you need more help?"

He was better prepared than he had been, but there was still some material they hadn't reviewed, and the test was tomorrow. He'd intended to head home and do a little more cramming, but he always did better studying with others.

He looked at Hana, who was standing in the hallway, watching him pack up, and was torn. Today's study session had been extremely productive, and he would like to review the rest of the material, but he felt awkward asking for more help. She'd already done so much for the group—it seemed selfish to impose, and it was getting late.

"You should stay," Mara said in an amused tone. "You should keep studying. My sister will help you."

"That's all right. I can finish at home," he said, cautious about Mara's motivations.

"If you need more help," Hana spoke up, "you're welcome to stay longer. And if Mara gets too rude, I'll kick her out." She gave Mara a mischievous smile of her own.

The sisters glared at each other, sparks flying, and Evan suspected that a clash between these two could escalate quickly. What had he wandered into?

As the tension in the room rose, he felt he should say something to diffuse the situation. "You won't get in any trouble if I stay longer? Your mom and dad won't get mad if I'm here when they get home?"

The sisters stopped their glaring contest and turned their attention back to him.

Mara chuckled at the question while Hana gave her a brief but scathing look. "No, our parents won't mind," Hana said. "Our mom works nights and won't be home until morning."

"What about your dad?"

"Um..." The sisters shared a glance, and after a beat, Hana went on. "Dad's overseas on a business trip at the moment."

"Oh, Okay." Evan weighed his need to study against

his other responsibilities. He really wanted to stay, but his aunt worked late, and his sister was just a kid. While Ellie did well on her own, he didn't like to leave her alone for too long. "I need to check on my sister, see if she needs me to come home."

"Of course," Hana said with a smile.

Evan stepped away into the entryway and called his home phone.

"Hey there, kiddo," his Aunt Maddie answered.

"Oh, um, hi," Evan stammered, surprised that Aunt Maddie had answered the phone instead of Ellie. Suddenly, he felt nervous about asking to stay longer with Hana's parents away for the night.

"I was just about to call you. Are you over at Oliver's?" she asked.

"Uh, no. I'm at Hana's."

"Hana? Someone new?"

Evan was surprised at her strangely upbeat tone. "Yeah. She transferred to school a few weeks ago. She's in my English class. Anyway, we're studying for my chemistry test tomorrow, and things are going good, so I wanted to see if it was okay for me to stay longer."

"As long as it's okay with her parents, that's fine with me."

"Um, Hana says they're cool with it," he said, uncertain how much truth there was to his statement.

"What time do you think you'll be home?"

"No later than ten, I imagine," Evan said, relieved at his aunt's calm acceptance.

"Wait," she said suddenly, causing his heart to skip a beat. "She's in your English class, and you're studying chemistry?"

"Uh..."

"You know what? Never mind. You kids have fun and just be sure to be home before eleven, all right?"

"Oh, sure. Thanks," he said.

"Love you. Make good choices," she said and hung up abruptly.

Evan stared at his phone for a moment before returning it to his pocket and shaking his head.

"We're good," he announced as he returned to the living room. "I just need to be home by eleven."

"Of course," Hana said with a smile.

The two of them returned to the living room table, where Evan unpacked his books and notes, and they picked up where they had left off. While they worked, Mara stayed on the couch, feet tucked under her, lounging and watching. After a while, she laid her head down, closed her eyes, and was snoring softly within moments.

"Is your sister really asleep?" Evan asked softly across the short table.

Hana looked at Mara and giggled. "Yeah, she's pretty good at that. That's another reason she's homeschooled. She struggles to stay awake in class."

"Is she narcoleptic?"

"Something like that..." she said, turning her attention back to the chemistry textbook.

Evan didn't press the matter, understanding that talking about sensitive medical conditions could be uncomfortable. Instead, he returned to studying, picking up where they'd left off.

It was another hour before they had finished reviewing the last of the material, with Hana giving him an impromptu quiz by throwing random questions at him from the textbook. When she had exhausted her questions, he glanced at the five pages of notes with a satisfied grin, feeling confident he was going to crush the test.

"Thank you so much," he said as he set his notes down on the table. "This was awesome, you're really..." the rest of his statement was interrupted by an embarrassingly loud growl from his stomach. The gurgling continued for several long seconds while he blushed vividly.

"Was that you?" she asked, glancing at his stomach.

Evan chuckled in embarrassment. "Yeah, sorry. It's way past dinner time for me."

"It is kind of late, isn't it?" she noted, looking at the clock on the wall behind them that showed that it was nearly ten o'clock.

"Yeah," Evan sighed. "I should probably head home and get something to eat."

"If you're not in a hurry, I could make us a snack," Hana offered.

"I don't want you to go through any trouble on my account."

"Stay put. I'll be right back." She smiled as she bounced up and headed toward the kitchen.

Evan watched her walk away, happy that she had invited him to stay longer. He wasn't expected home yet and was hoping for a chance to get to know her better.

To pass the time until she returned, he lounged further into the couch before picking up his notes and skimming over them, though his mind was thinking more about Hana than chemistry. It wasn't long before he got the sense of being watched, and a glance showed that, sure enough, Mara had awakened and was watching him intently. Evan smiled at her tentatively, hoping that she wouldn't create another awkward scene with more probing questions. To his relief, she remained quiet, looking at him sleepily with a vaguely bored expression. After another quick smile, Evan returned to his notes.

As he sat waiting, his eyes kept returning to Mara's couch, and as he looked closer, noticing resemblances between her and her sister. While their hair and skin tone were notably different, they shared the same facial structure with matching lips, cheeks, and eyebrow shape. The most striking similarity was their eyes. They each had bright, nearly colorless irises that he couldn't remember ever seeing before. They had the most intriguing quality of echoing the surrounding colors, reflecting whatever hue was nearby. As he watched, he could see blue, green, and red from around the room mirrored in them. Even with their similarities, however, it would be easy to overlook that they were siblings, let alone twins. Where Hana was elegant and demure, Mara had an unmistakable look of mischievousness with her dark hair and playful smirk.

"Like what you see?" she asked flirtatiously.

Evan realized he had been staring and hid behind his notes. A bright red flush bloomed across his face and down the back of his neck. "Sorry," he mumbled.

Mara chuckled.

Evan turned his face toward his notes, trying to think of a polite way to start a conversation when Mara began humming softly under her breath. The quiet, calming tune seemed vaguely familiar, but he couldn't quite place it. He closed his eyes and concentrated on the melody, trying in vain to identify the song.

As Mara continued humming, a wave of fatigue washed through him as though the exertions of the day had caught up with him all at once. He suddenly felt heavy and drained. Without thinking, he leaned across the couch to rest, and within seconds, he was asleep and dreaming.

Chapter Four

The Dream

Evan found himself just outside of school on the route home as the sun slowly set on the horizon. The sky was painted in a vast expanse of blues, purples, and pinks as the last light of the sun filtered through the scattered clouds. The world around him was vibrant and dazzling, awash in brilliant color. Even the warmth of the afternoon sun seemed amplified, yet not uncomfortably hot, reaching through his shirt and warming his skin. It was a gorgeous afternoon, almost exaggerated in its perfection.

He glanced around, briefly wondering how he had gotten there when he saw Hana exiting the school grounds to head home. As she turned and spotted him, she grinned, her eyes sparkling as she skipped to catch up. His lingering disorientation evaporated as she came to a stop in front of him.

"Going home?" she asked cheerfully.

"Uh, yeah."

"Mind if I walk with you?"

Evan's heart skipped a beat as he stared at her. In the afternoon light, her mercurial eyes reflected the blue sky as the sun danced on the edges of her silver hair. He had never seen someone so beautiful in his life.

"Yeah. That'd be great," he heard himself say, though how his brain could form words at that moment was a complete mystery.

She looked away as a light blush spread across her cheeks, making her face look warm and beguiling. The two of them headed toward their neighborhood, and for a short time, they walked in silence before Evan began rambling in nervousness. He told her one of his most amusing stories from his youth. It was one of his classic misadventures with Oliver that always got a laugh. His nervousness eased as he talked and was further emboldened when she would gasp or giggle at the appropriate times. When he finally reached the ending, he looked around and found that they had arrived at her house, the two of them standing on the sidewalk in front of her short, white picket fence. The walk felt shorter than it had before, and he wished it had taken much, much longer.

"Would you like to come in?" Hana asked, looking away from him as she shoved her hands into her pockets. "Mara isn't home today."

"Um, sure," Evan answered after a momentary pause, feeling a rush of excitement as the whole thing felt vaguely forbidden.

He followed her in. As they stood in the entryway, the reality of their privacy sank in. An electric tension grew between them, causing Evan's heart to speed up in nervous anticipation.

"I really like your house," he said, trying to sound casual.

"Thank you. Would you like to see my room?"

Evan's pulse jumped another notch. He hesitated,

excited yet wary about the invitation. Something in the way she asked gave him pause; her voice was low, nearly a whisper. He sensed she was asking about more than a simple tour. He felt she wanted to share something private, something secret.

There was no denying that he was attracted to this strange and mysterious girl standing before him. Transcending her appearance, he sensed an air of strength and power to her that inexorably drew him in, though looking at her now, she seemed pensive and uncertain. Her hands picked at a loose thread on her blouse with head turned away, trying yet failing to hide the crimson blush spreading across her cheeks.

At this moment, all her strength and confidence fell away and in their place was a quiet vulnerability that called to him more powerfully than anything else.

"Sure," he heard himself answer.

The smile she returned to him was blinding in its radiance, lighting up her entire face. Reaching out her hand, she took him and lightly led him up the stairs, stopping at the first door on the left. Hanging from the door was a small chalkboard sign with the name "Hana" written in bright pink.

For a moment they stood there, looking at the closed door before she turned back to him.

"Are you sure?" she asked with her eyes staring into his. He sensed a palpable gravity in her question.

It was as if a bucket of cold water had been thrown on him. The illicit thrill that had filled him during the short walk up the stairs vanished and was replaced by trepidation and caution. In those three short words, Evan doubted everything, wondering what he was getting himself into.

Suddenly, he questioned if the whole picture-perfect house was just a facade, a disguise for some hidden truth, something forbidden and possibly dangerous. Something about that moment made him reconsider Hana, too, wondering if everything he'd learned about her so far wasn't but a single facet of a greater whole, perhaps something he didn't want to know.

As he stood there, "Are you sure," transformed in his mind into something more: "Do you really want to know the truth about me and my world?" she seemed to ask. "There's no going back if you change your mind."

Chills ran up his arms and legs as he looked back at her, unable to explain how he knew what she meant, but certain he was right. He sensed something ominous behind the cheerfully inviting chalkboard sign, though he couldn't imagine what it might be. There were hidden truths inside, secrets and mysteries he wanted to discover. His revelation gave him pause, however, causing him to wonder if he should turn away and let her keep her secrets. He hesitated for another moment before giving in to the siren's song of whatever was concealed beyond the door, and he simply nodded his acceptance.

With a smile that seemed equal parts of relief and apprehension, she released his hand and opened the door, stepping inside and leaving him alone at the threshold.

As she entered, she flicked the light switch. The dim lights did little to illuminate the space, leaving the edges cast in shadows with only the center well lit. Despite the murkiness, he could still make out much of the innards of the room which contained a wooden dresser, desk, and a small bookshelf, all in a matching dark brown veneer. Across the room lay a bed of the same dark brown wood, complete with four tall bedposts that almost reached the ceiling. Light gauzy fabric draped between each of them, giving the bed a secluded aura. His heart jumped again, and Evan worried it was loud enough for her to hear.

A variety of odd decorations adorned the various pieces of furniture. On her dresser sat a small violet-colored glass bottle of perfume alongside a black jewelry box with ornate silver scrollwork wrapping around the top with a bone-shaped keyhole. As he spied the bottle, he inhaled and smelled the faint aroma of Hana's perfume. Next to the jewelry box sat what appeared to be a human skull with a raven perched atop of it, watching him with its black, beady eyes. It seemed amazingly lifelike, and Evan couldn't tell if it was real or not, causing another chill to run down his spine.

On Hana's closet door hung an intricately painted representation of the night's sky with a panorama of the galaxy stretching across it. In the center of the painting was a large, glowing image of the moon, resplendent in its depiction of its battered, ancient past. It seemed almost too big for the image, yet it fit perfectly.

In a far corner of the room, Evan saw a variety of stuffed animals and dolls, their eyes reflecting the dim light at him as their faces and bodies melded into the shadows. He guessed they were simply decorations, but like the raven, their eyes seemed to be watching him intently.

On the floor lay a large red plush carpet, perfectly circular and placed in the center of the room. It reminded Evan of a giant pool of blood, slowly oozing outward. The room was completely silent, except for his rapid breathing and the pounding of his pulse in his eardrums. He wondered if she could hear it too.

"What do you think?" She raised her hand, gesturing to the space around her.

Again, he had that sense that she wasn't just asking about her room with its odd decorations and dim lighting, but about her and her world. Looking around, he couldn't shake the feeling that there was something vaguely threatening about the space and the girl within it.

He stood on the threshold, senses heightened, heart beating fast in his chest. The sense of danger amplified his reservations, while the room and girl inside almost dared him to rise to the challenge. He couldn't decide what intrigued him more—Hana or the bizarre world she stood in the center of—but he knew he desperately wanted to understand both.

"You have a very... intriguing room," he said finally. "It's not quite what I imagined it would look like, honestly."

"And me? What is your honest opinion of me?" she asked.

Evan looked at her carefully as she stood there. Compared to the darkness that filled every corner, she was a singular bright beacon of light. Her long silvery hair and pale skin were at odds with the surrounding dimness, while her eyes reflected the bright red of the carpet. Standing in the center of the oppressive room, she appeared isolated and alone; the heavy atmosphere enveloping her like a cloak.

"I'm not sure, really," he said as he stepped forward, hoping to chase away the darkness from around her. "But I'd like a chance to get to know you better."

She rewarded him with a blushing smile as he approached her. "So, have you ever kissed a girl before, Evan?"

The abrupt change of topic took Evan by surprise, causing him to break into a cold sweat. He swallowed nervously, nodding his head though his last kiss had been in the fourth grade when a classmate had dared him to kiss Katie.

"Oh," she breathed, looking down and away. "I haven't. Kissed a boy, that is."

"Okay." Evan stood frozen in place, his heart racing, uncertainty and excitement warring within him.

She could definitely hear his heart now, right?

"Would you like to kiss me?" she asked demurely.

His interest in her had been steadily growing since they'd arrived at her house and now exploded into a near-insatiable desire to know what it felt like to hold her. He easily imagined their bodies pressing against each other, his arms wrapped around her back while his lips caressed hers. The thought that she longed for the same thing washed away any lingering reservations he may have had. Unable to think about anything else, he nodded enthusiastically, blushing brightly.

"I'm glad." She smiled again, sending another jolt through him. Then she pointed to a spot just below his chin. "You'll have to set that aside, though."

Confused, Evan looked down and saw that he was wearing an unusual silver necklace with a large red crystal that glowed lightly in the dark room. When he lifted it to inspect it, he saw it was filled with a bright red fluid.

"What's this?" he asked, having no idea where he had gotten such a thing or why he'd been wearing it.

"It's not important," she replied in a dismissive whisper. "But if you want to kiss me, you'll need to set it aside."

Something warned him against removing the

necklace—that it was somehow dangerous to abandon it. He was about to ask more about the odd jewelry when he looked up, and the words died on his tongue. The few inches that had separated them a moment before had vanished. Her eyes were bright and inviting, and her sweet, intoxicating aroma greeted him.

His gaze fell to her lips which were soft and inviting. Overwhelmed by her closeness, all clarity of thought evaporated. Without further hesitation, he removed the red-jeweled necklace, intending to set it on the dresser. As he reached out his hand, the raven stretched out its head and carefully snatched it from his grasp, returning to its perch on the skull with the necklace dangling from its beak.

Evan gave little thought to the bird as Hana closed her eyes and leaned in. As the gap diminished, he followed her example and concentrated on the sensation of their lips coming together, sensing her warmth a moment before they touched. As they kissed, Evan felt himself melt into her; the soft caress of her returned kiss overwhelmed him.

He thought it would be a simple, quick kiss, but apparently, Hana had other intentions. As they remained connected, she drew even closer, their bodies touching in a dozen places.

Evan's heart pounded in his chest as he enfolded Hana in his arms and held her tightly. Her lips parted as they kissed, and he felt a jolt of raw passion run through him as if lightning had struck him. His tongue began a tentative exploration of the shape of her lips and mouth, briefly connecting with hers, sending fresh waves of intensity throughout his body.

Though it seemed to stretch on for an eternity, the

kiss ended much sooner than he would have liked. As she pulled away and out of his arms, he reached blindly for her in the expansive darkness, but she was gone. He needed to find her—he needed to continue the kiss.

As he opened his eyes to see where she had fled, he was briefly disoriented to find that instead of standing in the dim surroundings of Hana's room, he was laying on his side on the padded cushion of her couch, Hana's brilliant silver eyes staring back at him mere inches away.

Caught up in the lingering intensity of the dream, he leaned closer to resume the kiss they had started. His mind was still buzzing from the sensation of her lips on his, and he reacted more from instinct than conscious thought. As their lips were about to meet again, a crash behind him snapped him out of his reverie.

Spinning his head around, he saw Hana standing just beyond the couch with her long silver hair. A food tray rang on the tile at her feet as a trio of sandwiches spilled across the floor.

But if Hana was standing behind the couch, who had he been about to kiss? Evan's head spun back around to find that it was Mara lying next to him with a knowing, mischievous smirk on her face.

Evan bolted upright, his mind seizing to a halt. It didn't help that his dream lingered as he struggled to separate reality from fantasy. His mind refused to function properly, filling him with confusion and exploding panic.

He didn't know what was going on, but a singular, overpowering impulse pushed itself through his confusion: flee!

"I've got to go!" he exclaimed as he sprang up off the

couch. Grabbing his backpack, he bolted out of the house and running away without looking back.

Chapter Five

The Kiss

The alarm blared, and Evan reached to silence it at the first beep. Even though he had been up late the night before fretting over the previous day's events, he felt wide awake, his mind alert and racing.

The last look on Hana's face was burned into his consciousness. Her eyes wide with shock, mouth half-open in disbelief, staring at him lying next to Mara, about to kiss her. What had she seen, exactly? What had it looked like from her perspective?

With little enthusiasm, he got himself ready for the day. Showering, dressing, and breakfast passed by in a blur.

"Have a great day!" his sister called as he left the house.

The sentiment haunted him as he headed to school. Was it even possible to have a great day? What could he hope for after such a disaster? He tried to consider his predicament to see if there was any way he could salvage the situation. He was so absorbed in his thoughts that he completely forgot to wait for Oliver and Katie at their usual corner.

He arrived at his first-period classroom and found the

door locked. A glance at his watch told him he was extremely early in his preoccupation; he had arrived nearly an hour before class began. He tried to distract himself by reviewing his textbook, but his mind couldn't focus on the words. Instead, he sat there, contemplating what he should say to Hana until Mr. Hanson appeared, briefcase and lunchbox in hand. He gave Evan a confused look, then unlocked the classroom.

"I appreciate your enthusiasm, Mr. Morgan," he said. "But you are aware that there isn't a test today, right?"

Evan nodded mutely and shuffled to his seat. For a brief, insane moment, he thought about asking Mr. Hanson for advice—surely there was something in literature that related to this situation—but dismissed the idea quickly.

No, it would have to be total avoidance. That was his only option. She may have been willing to excuse him for knocking her down on her first day, but there was no way she was going to forgive him for making a move on her sister.

He considered how he could explain what happened on the off chance that she'd give him an opportunity, and everything he contemplated led to disaster. He'd passed out and woke up in the middle of an erotic dream about her? No way. He nodded off and when he woke up he thought it would be cool to lock lips with her twin narcoleptic sister? Ugh!

With a groan, Evan slammed his forehead onto his desktop with a loud bang. A few seconds later, he let his head fall to the side so he could watch the clock. It was still way too early for Hana to show up, but it was nearly the normal time when he would meet up with Oliver and Katie on their way to school. So, fishing out his phone, he sent a quick text to them to let them know he had gone ahead.

It wasn't long before other students started filing in. Evan tried looking out the window to relax but found he kept straining to watch the door out of the corners of his eyes. His nervous mind cataloged the hair color of every head that entered, watching for the bright silver shine that would announce Hana's arrival and his impending doom.

"Morning!" Oliver said enthusiastically as he sat down.

Evan jumped in alarm. He had been singularly focused on spotting Hana and had entirely overlooked Oliver and Katie's arrival.

Oliver chuckled as he settled into his chair. "Looks like you're still asleep, man. Stayed up too late making out with Miss Blackmore, did you?"

A sudden wave of embarrassment flooded through Evan, and he lashed out without thought. "We just studied," he snapped. "Then I went home."

"Whoa! Take it easy dude. I was just kidding." Oliver raised his arms in surrender and leaned away.

"Sorry," Evan said, further embarrassed by his overreaction.

"So, are you ready for that chemistry test?" Oliver asked as he settled himself.

"Oh no!" Evan had forgotten about the chemistry test entirely! He tried to recall the hours spent in Hana's living room, and not a single scientific principle came to mind. The only thing he could remember was waking up on her couch, lying next to Mara, about to kiss her. Anxiety raced through him at the thought of failing his chemistry test. If he couldn't remember anything when the time came, what would have been the point of the study session and the disaster that followed?

Uncertain if he even remembered to bring his textbook, Evan grabbed his backpack and began rummaging through it, digging until he'd found it. He had the book, but the stack of notes he'd labored over was nowhere to be seen.

"Crap," he mumbled under his breath.

He didn't need to think too long or hard to remember where they were. The end of his time at Hana's house was burned vividly into his memory. The five pages of notes were sitting on the corner of the coffee table as he raced out of the house while Hana and Mara watched in wide-eyed shock.

"What's wrong?" Oliver asked.

Evan considered telling him everything but quickly shook his head. There was always the slim chance that Oliver wouldn't tease him, but the whole thing was still unbelievably embarrassing. Maybe he'd tell the story when he was old and gray, but not today.

"I left my notes at Hana's house," he moaned.

"No problem, dude." Oliver smiled cheerfully. "I bet she'll bring them for you. If I'm right, you can buy me lunch!"

The thought of facing Hana after his panicked flight made Evan feel anything but cheerful. His stomach clenched, and he began to sweat. He tried to think of some way of getting his notes from Hana without having to talk to her, but his mind kept spinning in useless circles. He was quickly working himself up into a frenzy of nervous turmoil when Oliver abruptly interrupted his thoughts.

"There she is now," Oliver said. "Just go ask her."

Evan whipped his head around, and sure enough, there she was. His gaze was riveted to her every move as she crossed the front of the room to her seat. She looked wary, keeping a thin, light smile on her face that didn't reach her eyes. When she made it to her desk and was about to sit down, her head turned in Evan's direction. As she looked at him, her smile disappeared, and a vague look of displeasure followed in its wake.

Unbridled panic gripped him. Looking into her disappointed face, all his fears and nervousness reached an impossible peak as all the confusion and embarrassment from the night before came crashing in. Her unspoken warning of no going back once he'd entered her world at her bedroom door, mixed imagery from his bizarre dream, assaulted his already anxious mind. Suddenly, he felt cornered, trapped. Reasonable thought evaporated, and all he could think of was escape. He had to get out!

A glance around revealed no obvious path to freedom. The direct route required him to walk past her, which meant certain death. She was still looking in his direction, so stealth was impossible. As his fevered mind scanned the room, a new avenue presented itself.

Evan didn't hesitate. Surprising everyone, he stood up abruptly, kicking off a nearby empty seat and hurtling over several rows of desks, missing a seated student by inches and landing hard two rows over. Losing his balance, his momentum carried him into a linebacker from the football team. They collided heavily, throwing the football player to the floor but leaving Evan standing upright, though woozy. Without pausing, he turned and sprinted up the row toward the door. One final acrobatic dodge around two girls entering the class, and he was out. Without a single look over his shoulder, Evan fled. Again.

A couple of quick turns later, he found himself in the boy's bathroom, leaning against a sink, panting heavily. As he caught his breath, he thought about what had just happened and slid further into despair. He couldn't believe what he had just done.

A couple of minutes later, the door opened halfway, and Oliver called out for him. "Hey, Evan, you in here?"

"Yeah, I'm here." It relieved him it was Oliver and not the teacher.

"Dude, what the hell?" Oliver asked with genuine concern. "Are you okay?"

"Yeah, I'm all right," he lied. "I just—I just don't feel well. I thought I was about to throw up."

"Really?" Oliver didn't sound convinced.

"Uh, yeah."

Oliver looked at him carefully with an appraising eye. "Are you feeling better now?" he asked diplomatically. "Got it all out of your system?"

The thought of returning to class brought back all his emotional turmoil. He could taste bile rising in his chest and believed that he might actually vomit.

"Not really."

A couple of seconds passed in silence while Oliver stood there watching Evan slowly breathing in and out, trying not to get sick.

"All right. I'll tell Mr. Hanson that I found you throwing up in here and sent you to the nurse's office."

"Thanks," Evan exhaled in relief.

"I'll grab your stuff and meet you in history?"

"Yeah, sure. I'll see you there."

"You look terrible," Oliver said. "Maybe you *should* go

to the nurse's office."

"That's not a bad idea, actually."

With a nod, Oliver returned to class while Evan headed toward the nurse's office, where he remained until the period ended.

For the rest of the morning, Evan returned to worrying about Hana. What could she possibly think of his outrageous behavior? Did she think he tried to kiss Mara? Did she think he's the type of guy that would make a move on any girl he sees the moment he's introduced to them? Would she ever even consider dating him now? And what could she possibly think about his crazy escape from their English class?

Thoughts of Hana haunted him all morning, carrying him into his fourth-period chemistry class in a daze, unable to concentrate on anything else. When he sat down at his desk, he felt nauseous again.

"You owe me lunch, by the way," Oliver said as he sat down.

"What are you talking about?" Evan stared back, not comprehending.

"Remember? We bet whether or not Hana would bring your notes. Well, she did, and I stuffed them in your chemistry book."

Oliver reached across the desk and opened the cover of Evan's textbook. Tucked just inside was a small stack of papers, neatly arranged and held together with a single blue paper clip.

"See? Lunch is on you, bud," Oliver said as he smirked.

Looking down in disbelief, Evan noted that along with his chemistry notes, there was a small card clipped with his pages. The card contained a simple hand-written note. In a looping, elegant-looking script, she had left him an encouraging message: "Best of Luck. ~ Hana"

In addition to the small card, Evan found she had taken the time to look over his notes, adding small comments and notations throughout. Peppered across the pages, she had highlighted key principles that were likely to show up on the test or were important foundational concepts that aided in the overall understanding of the material. She hadn't marked up his notes before the fiasco with Mara, so she must have taken the time afterward, despite the incident. But why?

He stared down at her numerous additions in total confusion. Why had she taken the time to do this? From the quantity she'd added, it must have taken her at least an hour or more to go through all of it. He was certain she'd be furious with him, but why would she go to such lengths to help him if she was upset? It didn't make sense.

The only thing he could think was that regardless of whatever she might have seen, she apparently didn't completely hate him. He latched onto that singular thought and felt a little hopeful after all. Before he could contemplate for long, however, the class was called to order, and the tests were handed out.

As they handed Evan his test packet from the classmate in front of him, he felt calm as his worries surrounding Hana subsided. Suddenly his mind was clear, and the mountain of facts and formulas he'd crammed into his brain bubbled up to the surface as he began reading the first few test questions.

Forty minutes later, Evan closed his test booklet and set down his pencil, relief washing through him. He was confident in his performance, having answered every question with ease and only having to refer to his notes sparingly. Looking over at Oliver, he noted he was grinning as well.

"How'd it go?" Evan asked.

"Pretty sure I just got a C, maybe even a B," Oliver said smugly. "That should make my mom happy. How'd you do?"

"Pretty good, actually. I guess all that studying paid off."

The bell rang, and the two of them headed to lunch. With the test behind him and the thought that he might still salvage the situation with Hana, Evan was quite optimistic as they headed to their usual spot.

"So, are you going to tell me what happened this morning?" Oliver asked as soon as they were alone. "Why you freaked out like that?"

Evan groaned. "I did something *really* stupid last night after studying. I thought she was going to be super pissed."

"She who?" Oliver asked. "You mean Hana?"

Evan nodded.

"What happened?" Oliver gave him a sly smile. "Did you make a pass at the mysterious twin sister behind Hana's back or something?"

"No!" Evan said as he blushed violently.

"Oh my god, dude!" Oliver exclaimed loudly, causing nearby students to look in their direction. "You totally did, didn't you?"

A mixture of embarrassment and frustration gripped him at how uncomfortably close to the truth Oliver's quip was.

"You know what? Forget it! I'm sorry I told you anything!" Evan fumed, pulling his backpack tighter and walking away, deciding he would rather eat alone.

Oliver's hand shot out and grabbed his arm. "Hey, man, I'm sorry. I was just teasing. I didn't mean to piss you off."

The sincerity of Oliver's voice gave Evan pause. His friend meant well, and there was no way he could have known how close to the truth he was.

"Friends?" Oliver asked after a couple of seconds.

"Yeah, sure," Evan said. "Of course."

"Cool." Oliver looked relieved. "So, you wanna talk about it? 'Cuz you seem really worked up."

Evan considered for a moment and decided to confide in his friend. He wondered if he was overreacting and figured someone else could help provide some clarity if he was. They continued to their usual lunch spot while Evan described the events of the previous night, starting from when Oliver went home at the end of the study session.

He told the entire story, with every bizarre detail until the kiss. When he got to that point, he suddenly didn't want to share. Despite it all occurring in a dream, that moment continued to resonate as a deeply personal experience. Despite knowing he was being irrational, he omitted the kiss with Hana, skipping ahead to groggily waking up on the couch and the near kiss with Mara. He wrapped up the story with the crash as Hana dropped the tray of food and their shocked reaction as he fled the house.

To his credit, Oliver remained quiet throughout the telling, only asking for clarification a few times. When Evan finished, Oliver finally spoke up. "Wow, that's freaky."

"Yeah, you're telling me," Evan said, rubbing the back of his neck. It felt better to tell someone, but he was getting anxious again.

"You just passed out on her couch?" Oliver raised an eyebrow in disbelief.

"Apparently," Evan groaned. "One second I'm reading my notes, and then *bam*, I'm being invited into Hana's bedroom. And just as that's getting good, I'm back on the couch." Evan shook his head in disbelief. Hearing himself describe the sequence of events made it sound even more ridiculous than he remembered. "It's just so bizarre."

Oliver nodded in agreement. "And when you woke up, why was Hana's sister lying so close to you?"

"Dude, I have no idea."

Oliver sat thoughtfully for a moment. "So, you're all worked up because you think Hana caught you making a move on her sister?"

"Exactly."

"Which you weren't actually doing."

"Right."

"Well, that's easy enough to clear up," Oliver shrugged. "Just tell her the truth."

"And just how do you suggest I do that?" Evan groaned. "Tell her I had some quasi-erotic dream about her in her bedroom?"

"Ah, I see your point. That could be bad." Oliver considered briefly. "Why not just leave that part out?" he shrugged.

"And then how do I explain why I tried to kiss her

sister right when I woke up?"

Oliver didn't immediately offer any advice but stroked his chin with his hand in a classic pose of someone in thought as he nodded comically.

Evan sighed. "So, if I can't tell her about the dream, what do I say?"

"Hmmm, this could be tricky," Oliver said, nodding again exaggeratedly, causing Evan to chuckle. "The falling asleep part is easy... you were reading chemistry notes. That would put anyone to sleep. It's the whole sister-kissing thing that's the problem."

The two of them were still considering Evan's dilemma when the bell rang, signaling an end to their lunch period.

"You know what the worst part is?" Evan asked as he slung his backpack over his shoulder while crumpling his empty lunch bag. "I don't actually know if Hana is even mad at me. I mean, she brought the chemistry notes and even sent me a 'good luck' card along with them."

"Who knows?" Oliver teased. "Perhaps she *likes* the idea of you making out with her sister."

"Not helpful!" Evan punched Oliver lightly in the arm as they headed to their next classes, though the thought of Hana approving of his dating Mara wormed its way into his head as yet another thing to worry about.

Chapter Six

Near-Death Experiences

As Evan poured himself a ridiculously large bowl of cereal, he basked in the lazy morning. Sunday had finally arrived, and beyond a few minor household chores, his day was wide open for relaxing and goofing off. Besides having complete freedom for whatever might strike his fancy, the house was empty with his aunt and sister both out for most of the day. He didn't even have to go to work as Vicky, the other part-timer who worked at the bookstore, had called him the day before and had asked to swap Sunday for the following Tuesday as she had some college event she wanted to attend. It was a rare Sunday off, and Evan was thoroughly enjoying it.

He hadn't lifted a finger all morning, even skipping his usual shower and grooming and lounging around the apartment in an old, tattered set of pajamas. When he caught sight of himself in the mirror, he laughed at the majestic height of his bedhead. His light-brown hair was standing straight up, easily adding five inches of height. Just for fun, he messed with it for a couple of minutes to see just how high he could get it and had left it that way, his hazel-green eyes sparkling in amusement.

His subconscious nagged at him briefly that he should

use his time to study English or Math, but there was plenty of time in the day for such things. He still felt elated with his performance on the chemistry test and wasn't ready to dive into more work just yet.

As he ate his breakfast, he found himself thinking about Hana yet again. Evan couldn't shake the feeling that she was uniquely special, and he didn't want to ruin everything before he'd really gotten to know her. He still didn't know what she thought of him and his bizarre behavior, but her brief note suggested that there might still be hope for him. He had to make amends somehow but didn't know how. Oliver had been no help on that front, and Evan couldn't blame him. The whole situation was ridiculous.

His life until the last couple of weeks had seemed perfectly mundane, if not boring, but the second he ran into her—literally—it had become a chaotic, comedic storm. As he thought about what his crazy antics must look like with his stumbling, panicking, and freaking out, he groaned loudly. He tried to think of a way of explaining his bizarre behavior, but he hadn't gotten far, as any time his mind wandered toward the subject of Hana, lingering thoughts of that incredibly vivid dream came bubbling up.

Every detail was locked securely in his memory, down to the feel of her burgundy carpet underfoot and the smell of her as he held her close. He remembered exactly how it felt to touch her: her smooth skin and her cool lips, the sensation of strength and vulnerability, and the instinctual understanding that there were deeper mysteries to uncover. The dream led inevitably to that kiss and the passion of that moment. Even as he sat in his living room, eating a late breakfast in front of the television, he wasn't watching the show. He was thinking about her.

"This is ridiculous!" he said to no one, turning off the TV. "I need to think about this logically."

What did he really know about Hana? He thought about it and came up with a surprisingly short list: crashing into her followed by her death glare, the study session, and the disastrous fiasco afterward constituted every interaction they'd shared. It couldn't have been more than six hours if he added up all of the time they'd spent together outside of class. All he really knew was that she was roughly the same age as him, had striking hair, pretty eyes, and was good at chemistry. Oh, and that she has an evil twin. Then *why* was it that whenever he thought about her, his pulse raced, and he felt giddy?

Without intending to, he had memorized everything about her from the past few weeks, even the stuff most people would consider insignificant. He could describe in detail the way she dressed, the way her hair flowed and swung as she walked, and every smile he'd seen on her, from the smallest smirk to the time she had burst out laughing during the study session. And now, added to his growing collection, was the aroma of her perfume, the smoothness of her skin, and the unbelievable sensation of her lips, even though they had all occurred within his own imagination. *You couldn't fall in love with someone based entirely on a single, suggestive dream, likely brought on by overactive teenage hormones, right?*

Right?

As he shoved the last spoonful of milk and cereal in his face, Evan resolved he wouldn't allow fantasy to override common sense. There was no reason to let his imagination run wild. It made much more sense to take the time to get to know her for who she really was and stop hyper-focusing on his fantasy version of her.

He groaned in disgust when he thought about how he must appear to her. Every time they came together, it had ended with Evan acting ridiculous. From their first encounter of him knocking her down, to running out of her house, to tackling a football player in the middle of class the next day. He couldn't explain it, but something about her turned everything up to eleven, and his instinctive reaction was to be crazier than he had ever been before in his life. She had to think that he was a total mess through and through.

He had to stop acting like an idiot and have a proper conversation with her. He resolved that the next time he saw her, he would stop overreacting and show her the real Evan. The responsible, level-headed teenager he knew himself to be. Easy.

The doorbell rang, interrupting his musings. Setting down his empty bowl, Evan headed toward the door to see who might visit on a Sunday morning.

When he peered through the peephole, his heart nearly jumped out of his chest. Hana stood on the other side, hands folded in front of her, waiting patiently, dressed in a long, pleated denim skirt with a blue and white striped V-neck blouse underneath a long, light gray cardigan.

What was she doing *here*?

Evan spun around, throwing his back to the door and looking around the apartment in a panic—the place was a mess. His lazy morning had left a table full of dinner dishes from the night before, several bags of trash were waiting to be taken out, and piles of clean laundry were strewn across the living room to be folded. A glance at the hallway mirror reminded him of his disheveled state as well, with his awful pajamas and outrageous hair.

If he wanted to make a good impression on her, he couldn't let her see his house in this state. Especially not after seeing how meticulously clean her house was. As he stood there, mind racing, the doorbell rang again, causing him to jump in surprise.

"Just a minute!" he called as he sprinted to the dining room.

He quickly grabbed all the dishes from the table, balancing them precariously in his arms, and headed for the kitchen. His plan of throwing them in the sink proved impossible as it was occupied with Ellie's upcoming Halloween costume which was currently being dyed a muddy gray color.

What the heck?! Halloween is two months away! Why are they doing this now? He railed internally.

With no other options, he threw open the refrigerator and shoved the stack of dirty dishes in unceremoniously, ignoring the unsettling sounds of the refrigerator's contents shifting inside haphazardly.

Next, he grabbed the three bags of trash and shoved them under the kitchen sink, knocking over various cleaning supplies. There was too much crammed into the tiny space, and the doors refused to stay closed, threatening to fly open and pour trash all over the floor. In a moment of inspiration, he grabbed a wooden spoon from the nearby counter and ran it through the handles of the cupboards, pinning them together to keep them closed.

Two down and one to go, he thought as he ran into the living room to address the piles of laundry.

"Evan?" Hana called through the door curiously.

"One second!" he yelled back as he grabbed an armful of pants, shorts, and underwear. Having corralled all the clean clothes, he spun in place, looking for a hiding spot. Finally, he settled on the sliding glass door that led to the small balcony his family rarely used. He threw the door open, tossing the pile of clothes into the farthest corner, slamming it shut, and pulling the curtains closed.

As he ran back to the front door, he took a quick, satisfying glance around the house. It would have to do. As for his personal appearance, there was no time.

With a sigh, he opened the door.

"Good morning!" he smiled cheerfully, running his hand through his frazzled hair, hoping he could tame it without being too obvious.

"Good morning." Hana glanced at his forehead, where Evan could feel the beads of sweat forming from his frantic efforts. "Did I come at a bad time?"

"Not at all," he said as he wiped the sweat away. "Just uh, doing some morning exercises."

"Oh, okay."

"Why don't you come in, and I'll get myself cleaned up?"

"Sure, thank you."

Leaving the door open behind him, Evan jogged down the short hallway while Hana entered, pausing just beyond their kitchen table. Once in his bedroom, Evan grabbed the closest pair of clean clothes and quickly changed.

"So, what brings you here this morning?" he called down the hall as he threw off his pajamas.

"Oh," she said from the living room. "Uh, I wanted to see if you'd like to go to lunch today."

"Lunch?" He hadn't expected her at his doorstep, let

alone that she'd ask him to go eat. To his surprise, he stood up too quickly and banged his head on the open underwear drawer, causing him to hiss in pain and grab his head.

"Ah shi... sure!" he called out, trying to ignore the stabbing pain in his skull. "That sounds cool."

Slamming the dresser drawer closed with an evil glare, he moved on to the bathroom to finish getting ready.

As he grabbed his toothbrush and loaded it with toothpaste, he continued their conversation across the apartment. "So, what's the occasion? Why the sudden lunch invitation?"

"Um, yes." She sounded embarrassed. "I wanted to apologize for the prank Mara played on you the other day and thought that perhaps you'd let me treat you to lunch to make up for it."

"Prank?" He nearly sprayed his mouthful of toothpaste all over the bathroom mirror.

"You know," Hana said. "Lying down next to you when you fell asleep."

"Oh, that!" Evan quickly brushed his hair, wincing from the sting as the brush passed over the bump on his head. "It was no big deal. Besides, I should be the one apologizing to you for being so weird. Especially after you helped me out so much."

"Okay."

When he rejoined her, she hadn't moved from the spot near the kitchen table.

"So, your chemistry test went well?" she asked.

"Quite!" he said, thinking it immediately sounded silly. "So, uh, thanks again. And sorry for acting like an idiot."

"Well, I'm glad, and you're very welcome." Hana smiled warmly. "But I'd still like to make up for it."

"You really don't need to worry about it," Evan said, "but I'd be happy to join you for lunch, regardless."

"I'm not interrupting anything, am I? Showing up unannounced and all?"

"Not at all," he answered with a grin. "I've finished all my weekend chores, so going out for lunch sounds great."

"Oh, good."

"Let me put on my shoes, and I'll be all set."

She nodded, and Evan grabbed his sneakers from the rack near the door. As he went to tie the laces, something occurred to him.

"Hey, can I ask you something?"

"Sure."

"How did you know where I live? Do you have magic powers or something?"

"Um..." Hana's eyes widened in surprise before she blushed and looked away. "I'm not allowed to tell you. They swore me to secrecy on pain of death."

"So, Oliver then."

"Maybe."

"Cryptic." Evan chuckled as he finished tying his shoes. "So, uh, did you have a place in mind? For lunch, I mean?"

"No, not really," Hana said with a shrug. "I don't really know the area very well yet, so I was kind of hoping you'd have some ideas."

"Oh, sure." He smiled. "Do you like pizza?"

Hana returned his smile and nodded. "Sounds good!"

As they left the apartment and Evan was locking up, his cell phone rang in his pocket. The caller ID read

"Thousand Oaks," which was the medical center where his aunt worked. For an instant, he worried that something had happened to her and answered the call immediately. "Hello?" he said anxiously.

"Hey, Evan," his aunt said on the other end, sounding calm. "Are you still at the house?"

"Sort of," he said, wondering why she'd be calling from an office phone and not her cell. "I was just leaving."

"Perfect! Can you do me a *huge* favor?"

"That depends; whatcha need?"

"I forgot my cell phone this morning. Can you swing by and drop it off for me on your way out?"

"Yeah, no problem," he said, relieved it was something trivial. "I was just heading to lunch with a friend, so I'll drop it off on our way. Be there in a few minutes."

"Thank you so much, kiddo! See you soon."

"No sweat."

As Evan hung up the phone, Hana looked at him curiously. "Is there a problem?"

"No, not really. My aunt forgot her phone and wants me to bring it to her. Do you mind if we make a quick stop before lunch? It won't take long; it's not far."

"Of course. That's fine."

A few minutes later, after a brief search through his aunt's room, Evan was closing the front door when a muted crashing sound echoed from somewhere in the kitchen. He briefly considered investigating but figured it would be fine until he got back. With a turn of the key, he locked the apartment, and they were on their way.

"So, your aunt works weekends?" Hana asked as they walked down the stairs from Evan's apartment.

"Sometimes. She's a resident doctor at the Thousand Oaks Nursing Home right around the corner. They've been a little short-staffed lately, so she's had to pick up more shifts than usual."

"She's a doctor?"

"Yeah, an oncologist." Hana's face was blank, so he clarified. "Cancer doctor."

Hana nodded, though she had a confused look on her face. "And she works at a nursing home? As a doctor?"

"Well, sort of," he said. "It's not strictly a nursing home. It's an extension of the medical university. It is kind of an experimental place where cancer patients check in and live while they receive treatment. It's primarily for the elderly or those that need constant attention and can't get it at home. So, they have doctors on the premises twenty-four hours a day, but it's more like assisted living than a hospital. Everyone has their own mini-apartment, and there's a cafeteria, a common room for activities, and scheduled events like tai chi and games and movies and such." Evan shrugged. "It feels a lot more like a nursing home to me, so that's how I describe it to others. But they have nearly everything a hospital does."

"That sounds pretty cool," Hana said. "How long has your aunt worked there?"

"About eight years, I think? She started working there when my Aunt Elaine was first diagnosed with cancer."

"Oh. Does your Aunt Elaine live at Thousand Oaks too?"

"Not anymore. She died about two years ago. But she lived there for a while before she passed. That's why we live so close, so we could see her easily."

"I, I'm sorry." Hana looked abashed. "I didn't mean to

pry.”

“Oh, don’t worry about it,” he said with a smile he hoped was reassuring. “She was sick for a very long time, and it was years ago. It’s not a sensitive subject for me anymore. I mean, I still miss her sometimes, but she was in a lot of pain at the end, and I’m glad she’s not suffering anymore.”

Evan wasn’t surprised when Hana asked no more questions. Talking about the passing of his aunt often killed conversations or made for awkward scenes. He changed the subject to something less depressing.

“So, do you like bowling?” he asked.

Hana looked at him quizzically before shaking her head. “I don’t know. I’ve never been bowling.”

“Really? You’ve never been bowling?”

“It isn’t a popular sport where I come from,” she shrugged.

“Really? Where are you from? I just assumed that bowling was a thing across the country.”

“Well, it probably is, but this is my first time living in this country, actually.”

“Wait, what?”

“You didn’t know?”

“Well, no. I just assumed you were from another city or something. I mean, you don’t have an accent or anything!”

“Yeah, my dad was very insistent that we learn how to speak fluently before he agreed to let us move. We watched a *lot* of movies.”

“Wow.” Evan paused, trying to digest this new revelation. “So, where are you from? Originally?”

“Greece.”

“Really? That’s cool. I wouldn’t have ever guessed,

though. You don't look Greek."

"Really?" she said with a sly smile. "And what do Greek girls look like?"

"Speaking of looks, you said that you and Mara are identical twins, right?" he said evasively.

Hana's smile faltered a little. "Yes, we are."

"But you look nothing alike. Well, except for your eye color."

Hana looked away as they walked, and Evan guessed that he'd blundered into sensitive territory.

"We used to look exactly alike," she said, "When we were little, I had the same dark hair and pretty skin as her. But that changed a few years ago."

"Did you get sick?" Evan offered, knowing better than most the physical transformations people could undergo when they were battling something serious.

"Yeah," she said as her voice trailed off. "Something like that."

They had just turned the last corner before the nursing home came into view, and Evan was glad for the easy change of topic.

"Here we are!" he announced.

"Oh, you weren't kidding when you said it was close."

"Told ya," he said with a smirk as they walked into the facility and headed toward the guest reception.

"All visitors have to sign in," he said as he wrote his information into the visitor registry before handing the clipboard to Hana.

"Good morning, Evan," said a receptionist as Hana filled in her details.

"Hey, George."

"Here to see your aunt?"

"Yeah, she forgot some of her stuff, so I'm just

dropping it off." He held up the cell phone to emphasize his errand.

"She's scheduled to do rounds right now, but she should be done soon." George gestured through the secured doors. "Why don't you go wait in the lounge, and I'll let her know you're here."

"Cool, thanks."

The attendant buzzed them through and into the hallway that led to the large, brightly lit room. Chairs and couches filled the open space with small tables scattered throughout. Several residents and a few visitors sat around the large room, most of them engaged in some form of quiet activity like reading, playing cards, or chatting.

"This is the lounge," Evan said. "It's basically a big communal social area where residents and guests hang out, play games, watch television, or whatever."

"Okay." Hana looked around with an uneasy air. Evan guessed that this was probably her first time in a medical facility like this.

"Let's sit over there." Evan pointed to a pair of comfortable-looking chairs near the lounge's entrance. They hadn't gone more than a few steps when one resident stopped in front of them.

"Are you here for me?" asked the elderly woman. "I had a feeling I'd be seeing you soon."

"Good morning, Mrs. Richardson," Evan smiled reassuringly, having experienced bouts of confusion from residents in the past. "How are you today?"

It took a second, but the old woman finally recognized him. "Oh, hello, Evan. It's nice to see you again."

"It's nice to see you too. How are you feeling today?" Evan motioned Mrs. Richardson to the chairs he had intended to share with Hana.

"Oh, I guess I'm fine," she said pleasantly. "Who is your friend?"

"Oh, right! Mrs. Richardson, this is a friend from school, Hana Blackmore. Hana, this is Mrs. Richardson."

"It's a pleasure to meet you," Hana said quietly as she remained standing several feet away, her hands at her side.

"So, what brings you two here today?" the old woman asked as she eased herself into the plush chair.

"Oh, nothing important," Evan said. "My aunt forgot some stuff at home. We're just stopping by to drop it off."

"Is that so?" Mrs. Richardson glanced back at Hana before smiling at Evan. "Well, that's nice. So how are you doing these days? How's school?"

"Actually, everything is going good."

"*Well*, dear." Mrs. Richardson shook her head. "Everything is going *well*."

"Uh, yes, right, things are going well," he smiled sheepishly.

As Evan related his recent success with his chemistry test to Mrs. Richardson, he noted she appeared distracted as he talked, searching through her pockets and digging into her small bag of needlepoint supplies.

"Is there a problem?" Evan asked after a bit of fruitless searching.

"Oh dear," Mrs. Richardson said in a disappointed tone. "I seem to have forgotten my glasses. Evan dear, would you be so kind as to go fetch them for me, please? I must have left them in my room."

"Um..." Evan looked between Hana and the old woman, reluctant to abandon his friend.

"It's okay," the kindly old woman smiled, "Your friend can stay here and keep me company until you get back."

He looked at Hana. "This will only take a second, okay?"

"That's fine," she smiled, "I'll just wait here."

Still feeling awkward about leaving Hana behind, Evan jogged off toward the dormitories and the room belonging to Mrs. Richardson. He had forgotten that her room was nearly on the opposite side of the facility, and it took longer than he would have liked.

As he approached, he could hear someone moving around inside, likely one of the facility staff cleaning the room while Mrs. Richardson was out.

"Hello?" Evan knocked twice before opening the door. "I'm just looking for Mrs. Richardson's glasses..."

To his surprise, the room was empty. He was certain he'd heard someone moving inside, but a quick check in both the bathroom and the closet proved he was the only one present. It must have been his imagination.

Evan wanted to find the glasses quickly, still feeling unsettled that he had left Hana to tend to the old woman, though he knew her to be kind and easy to get along with. He started with the various obvious surfaces around the room: the little table, the dresser, her nightstand, anywhere she'd likely have set them down. They weren't here. With no glasses in sight, he began a more thorough search.

The room was bright and cheery, with several handmade needlepoint pictures hanging on the walls and a small vase with a single sunflower sitting on the windowsill. With the day's sun pouring in, Evan would have thought the room would feel comforting and homey, but as he moved about the space, looking for the elusive glasses, he couldn't shake the feeling of isolation and loneliness that lingered.

She had adorned the top of her dresser with several small-framed pictures, and while he continued his search, one image caught his attention. It was an old, faded black-and-white photo with a handsome young man in a military uniform and a lovely woman at his side, young and vibrant. The picture was dated April 1957 in Amboise, France. The couple was standing in front of a chapel with a decorative ribbon binding their hands together.

As Evan held the picture, smiling back at the happy couple captured within, an icy breeze passed behind him, causing the hairs on the back of his neck to stand up. An unmistakable sensation that he was no longer alone in the room caused him to spin, though no one was there.

Evan scanned the room, feeling as if something had changed, though he couldn't put a finger on what. It was as if the room had shrunk in size, suddenly feeling tight and constricting where it had been spacious moments earlier. The atmosphere had changed too, with the air feeling thick and heavy, almost as if it were being pressurized. Even the light from the lamp and window seemed dimmer somehow, the walls and floor reflecting a subtle grayness instead of the normal bright white.

Goosebumps erupted up and down the lengths of his arms and legs while he tried his best to shake off his melodramatic fantasies. Nothing had changed in the room; he was just letting his imagination run away with him. Despite his own assurance that there was nothing to fear in the small room, Evan returned the picture to its resting spot and made one last quick pass before giving up and heading back to the lounge, his unease quickly evaporating as he stepped into the hallway.

When he returned, he found Hana sitting in a chair alongside Mrs. Richardson, the two of them talking animatedly.

As he got within earshot, it surprised Evan to hear the old woman telling a story in what sounded like French while Hana listened intently, laughing when Mrs. Richardson finished.

"Sorry," Evan said as he walked up to the pair of them, standing next to Hana's chair. "I couldn't find them,"

"Oh dear," Mrs. Richardson said, "Would I be too much of a bother if I asked you to go check again? I think I left them in my top dresser drawer. The one near the window."

The thought of returning to the room evoked a new set of chills down his back. He really didn't want to return to that strangely ominous place, though he surmised that without her glasses, she wouldn't be able to work on her needlepoint. He hesitated a moment longer, considering his options. "I don't—"

"It's okay." Hana reached out and took his hand lightly. "We're not in a hurry, are we? I'm happy to wait as long as it takes. Besides, I'm really enjoying Annette's stories."

For a moment, Evan stood there, stunned. Hana's light touch set off a flurry of tingles from the back of his hand up to his elbow and beyond.

"Annette?" he asked as the sensation of Hana's light touch distracted him from the conversation.

"That's my first name, dear," the old woman said with a patient smile.

"Right, sorry." Evan blushed. "Are you certain your glasses are in there?" he asked, almost dreading the idea of returning to the creepy place. "I mean, I looked all over, and I didn't find them."

"Perhaps..." the elderly woman mumbled as she pulled her bag to her lap and began carefully removing the contents. As more and more items emerged from its depths, Evan's hope that she would find her glasses dwindled. Finally, she pulled the last bundle of thread out of her sack and turned it upside down for good measure. "Did you check the dresser?" she asked, looking back at him with another smile.

"Sorry. I must have missed them," Evan relented, "I'll be right back."

"Thank you so much," Mrs. Richardson said as Hana helped her return everything back into the bag.

Evan jogged back across the complex, surprising a couple of guests as he passed. This time, when he arrived outside the room, he paused and pressed his ear to the door, listening carefully. The room was silent, though he still knocked twice before opening the door. The room was once again warm and inviting, and he chuckled at himself for his overactive imagination.

He entered a second time, heading directly to the dresser and thoroughly searching the drawer. The glasses weren't there. Not wanting to make a third trip, he performed a much more thorough search, looking in every hiding spot that a pair of glasses could fit.

Evan worked as quickly as he could. While he didn't have the same uncomfortable sense from earlier, he didn't want to linger. Finally, after several long minutes of searching, he found the pair of glasses in a flowery case buried under a stack of clothes, deep within the closet.

"Why would she have put these here?" he asked the empty room.

Having completed his errand, he sped back, running where possible. It had taken him much longer than he had expected, nearly fifteen minutes.

When he returned to the lounge, Hana was arranging a blanket across the older woman as she lay back in her chair, her eyes closed, apparently having fallen asleep.

"Found them," Evan said, loudly enough that Hana raised a finger to her lips.

Hana pointed to an area out of earshot, and the two of them stepped away. "She said she was tired and wanted to rest."

"Yeah, that happens a lot here." Evan stepped forward and placed the glasses on top of the small bag of needlework, returning a moment later. "Sorry that took so long."

"That's okay," Hana said, "I enjoyed talking with her."

"Speaking of that, was she speaking French earlier?"

"Yes, she grew up in France and moved to the U.S. when she married an American soldier," Hana said. "She was telling me a funny story from her time in school."

"And you can speak fluent French too?" he asked rhetorically, impressed and more than a little intimidated.

"Uh, yes. My parents insisted we learn several languages when we were younger," Hana said, as if the accomplishment were something to be ashamed of. He supposed she was just naturally modest.

Finally, his aunt arrived, waving at him from down the hall. "Thank you so much, kiddo!" she said. "I'm so sorry to have kept you waiting."

"No problem," Evan said with a smile. "Aunt Maddie, this is my friend from school, Hana Blackmore. Hana, this is my aunt, Madeline Walker."

"It's a pleasure to meet you." Aunt Maddie extended her hand in greeting.

"Likewise," Hana said, taking the offered hand.

As they shook hands, his aunt looked back at Evan. "Oh, she's just lovely. I can see why you wanted to stay late the other night."

"Yeah, okay," Evan said, blushing wildly. "Here's your phone," he added, thrusting the device into her hands. "We're leaving now."

"You're a lifesaver! Thank you, kiddo." She ruffled his hair playfully.

Before his aunt could embarrass him further, Evan grabbed Hana's hand and began pulling her toward the exit.

"It was nice meeting you," Hana said as Evan dragged her away.

"Have fun, you two!" His aunt called after them, waving.

"She seems like a very nice person," Hana said once they were outside and Evan had let go of her hand.

"Oh yeah, she's great," he said, "Normally."

"Why do you live with her and not your parents? Do they travel for work too?"

Evan had been expecting this particular question and was a little surprised at how long it had taken her to ask. *Better to get it out in the open.*

"They died in a car accident when I was seven, back in Chicago," he said.

"Oh," Hana said mournfully, "I'm so sorry."

"It's fine," Evan chuckled. "Don't worry about it. It was a long time ago, and I'm fine talking about it now. Don't feel bad for asking, either. Everyone does, eventually."

"Are you sure?"

"Totally. Ask anything you want, honest," he said with a smile while holding up his hand as if giving an oath.

"So, you're living with her because your parents... passed away?"

"Yeah," Evan said. "After the accident, there were a couple of options for me and Ellie. I was pretty messed up and needed a lot of medical attention after it all happened. Aunt Maddie had just finished her residency, so Grandpa Morgan asked if she and her partner, Elaine, would take us in, at least temporarily. Well, temporary turned into permanent, and here we are."

"Was Ellie in the accident, too?"

"No, just me. They told me later that we had already dropped her off at daycare, but I don't remember that part."

Hana reached up and twirled her single braid in her hand. "If you don't mind me asking, what happened? The accident, I mean."

Most people who got to know him or his family inevitably would ask the same question, and it rarely went well. He hesitated to tell the complete story as it was a gruesome one, and it often caused others to feel uncomfortable or squeamish.

"Are you sure you want to hear it? It's not pretty."

"If you're okay sharing," Hana said. "I don't want to pry, though."

"No, it's fine."

Evan considered for a moment how to begin and finally just started talking.

"It's funny, actually. I remember little about that day, like where Ellie was, or where we were going or anything like that, but I remember the sky.

"My dad was driving with my mom in the front seat next to him. I was in the back, behind my mom. I think it was still morning, and as we drove, I was staring out the window, my head leaning right up against it so I could see as much sky as possible.

"It was a perfect blue color, like the ocean or a painting. There were white fluffy clouds passing overhead, and I watched them move across the sky as we drove. Then something happened.

"There was a loud crashing sound, and I first thought it was some kind of explosion. The car swerved wildly, and my face slammed into the window, breaking the glass and cutting me pretty bad."

Evan judged Hana's response. The rest of the story got worse from here, and he'd learned long ago to judge peoples' reactions at this point to see if they really wanted to hear the rest. It heartened him to see her watching him carefully, eyes mournful for his tale but not shying away from the brutality, at least for now.

"I don't really know what happened after that," he said. "There was a lot of noise, and I think I remember my dad fighting with the car, but there was nothing he could do—the car was completely out of control. I couldn't see what was going on from the back, though.

"One thing I do remember was my mom looking over at my dad at the last second and saying, 'I love you.' That was the last thing she ever said, right before the car ran into a giant metal beam.

"When we hit, I was thrown from the car, though I don't know if my seatbelt had come undone before the collision or if it just failed. I have no memory of the actual impact, but I remember lying on the street and looking back at the wreckage. The car seemed so far away, though the accident report later said I was only about fifteen feet from where we hit.

"The car was trashed. The report guessed that we were going around fifty miles an hour and suspected that the brakes, steering, and accelerator were damaged in whatever happened to the car. We hit an I-beam for an elevated train straight on, with the front of the car wrapping around it, slicing down the middle and crushing it to the front seats. Glass and metal shards were everywhere, and at that moment, I knew my parents were dead.

"I don't remember being in any pain, so I guess I was in shock?" he said. "Or my mind won't let me remember. You know, like a defense mechanism? At least that's what one doctor told me once.

"Anyway, the street was lined with shops on both sides, and there were a bunch of pedestrians walking around who saw the whole thing. That's just about the last thing I remember: lying on the road, watching a growing pool of blood spread out from my waist, looking at a bunch of strangers and wondering why they were so upset.

"Of all the people on the street that day, there was one girl that stood out in particular. I think she was close to my age, with rich brown hair, light-brown skin, and dark eyes. I remember her because she was dressed all in white. At first, I thought she was an angel, about to take me to heaven, but then I saw she was holding hands with her father. The two of them couldn't have been more different. She was wearing a pretty white dress while he was super tall, dressed entirely in black. Where she was warm and bright, he was dark and cold.

"It wasn't just how they were dressed either, but their expressions were completely opposite as well. He was calm, unruffled, indifferent. He watched the entire scene, emotionless. The little girl, on the other hand, was shocked and horrified, her free hand clasped over her mouth while tears rolled down her cheeks." Evan shook his head, "I remember I wanted to tell the little girl that it was going to be okay, that she didn't need to cry. I guess I've always been a softie.

"The most bizarre thing about the girl and her father, though, is that they are the only people I can really remember. I know other people were there, but I couldn't describe a single one to you. The girl and her dad? Like it was yesterday.

"In the end, I guess I was pretty lucky because one business we crashed in front of was a doctor's office. They ran out when they heard the crash and stabilized me until the ambulance arrived.

"The next thing I remember was waking up in the hospital where Grandma Morgan was sitting in my room, knitting a red scarf. She was so happy when I woke up that she started crying. I still have the scarf too.

"It took about eight months before I could walk on my own again. By then, we were living with Aunt Maddie and Aunt Elaine. When I was all healed up, they asked if we'd like to live with them. A couple of months after that, they adopted us."

Evan looked up at the crystal blue sky without a cloud in sight as he finished his story. He had told his tale so many times over the years that it often felt more like a scene out of a movie than reality. But this time was different. With Hana listening, smiling, nodding, or gasping as he went along, he was transported back to ten years ago.

The relief in his grandmother's eyes, his bitterness during his convalescence in the hospital, and anger at Ellie's easy acclimation of living with their aunts in the very early days after the accident all bubbled to the surface. He was glad when they approached a busy intersection with a small group of pedestrians waiting to cross. It was easy to use the others around him as an excuse to remain quiet as he steadied himself.

After a glance at Hana, Evan guessed she was still absorbing his story as well, looking beyond the people and into traffic, appearing lost in thought.

Chapter Seven

Just Desserts

When the light changed and they could cross, Hana remained withdrawn and quiet. It wasn't until after they had walked another block that Evan interrupted her musings.

"You okay?" he asked carefully.

"Yeah, I'm all right," she said. "I've just never heard anything like that before. I guess I'm still processing."

"It's okay," Evan said. "It's pretty gruesome. I once made a teacher nearly throw up when I told that story in front of my class in the fourth grade."

"Oh, my goodness, you didn't!" Hana laughed.

"Yeah, it was awesome. Mrs. Taylor got super pale and had to run out of class when I lifted my shirt and showed off the scar." To emphasize his story, Evan lifted his shirt slightly, exposing a long, silvery crescent-shaped scar on the right side of his stomach.

"Does it still hurt?" She moved her fingers slightly, as if she was going to touch him, but pulled back.

"Oh no, that was ages ago," Evan said as he pulled his shirt back down. "Everything has long since healed. Sometimes, my wrist gets sore, but only when I play too many video games."

"That's good." Hana smiled. "And your parents' death?" she asked cautiously. "Does that still... bother you?"

Evan looked at the sky and weighed his answer. "Not really, not anymore. I was angry for a really long time, though. I think until my Aunt Elaine got sick, then I got mad because of that."

"That's understandable." Hana nodded. "And now? Are you still mad?"

"No, I've come to terms with all of it," Evan said.

"You've mentioned your aunt Elaine a few times. Who was she?"

"Ah..." Evan sighed, stealing himself for a more sensitive subject. "She was Aunt Maddie's partner. They were together long before Ellie and I went to live with them. She's the only mother that Ellie has ever known and kind of a second mom to me too. Then again, so is Aunt Maddie. Ellie has always called them mom and mom, but for me, it gets confusing fast. I just refer to them as Aunt Maddie and Aunt Elaine."

Hana nodded in understanding. "And your Aunt Elaine got sick?" she asked cautiously.

"Yes. They diagnosed her with leukemia seven years ago. She fought hard, and for a time we thought she was going to beat it, but then everything went south. She passed away about two years ago."

"And you got mad?"

"That's an understatement." Evan shook his head, remembering how bitter he had been and the rage that went with it. "I feel really guilty about it now, though. When she needed me the most, I was too angry to be there for her and avoided everyone for a long time. Then about four years ago, she made me come into her room, and we had a long talk.

"By then, she knew she was terminal, though I didn't learn about that until much later. She was still fighting, but the doctors told her they were losing the battle.

"She sat me down and we talked a lot about life and death," Evan said. "I got angry a few times and said a few really awful things, but she was incredibly patient. Each time I'd get angry and start yelling, she'd let me vent, then calm me down, and we'd keep talking."

He looked down at his hands. "She taught me that death is a part of life. You can't have one without the other. Every living thing will end, eventually. What matters is how we live the life we are given, not how early or tragic our end may be.

"She said that I was lucky, that having experienced such pain and loss, and having overcome it, I could really appreciate all the little things," Evan said. "You never forget the people who you've loved and lost, but you can't let your feelings of loss for the dead overshadow your appreciation for those that are still in your life. 'Let yourself mourn, but remember to let yourself love,' were her exact words."

"Wow," Hana said.

"Yeah. I had just turned thirteen, so I'm not sure I really appreciated what she was telling me then. But I've never forgotten it, and I'll never forget her," he sighed. "I really miss her."

Hana's face was flushed with emotion, but she spoke quietly and calmly. "She sounds like a wonderful person."

"She was," he said. "I think losing her was harder in a lot of ways than my parents. Especially for Ellie."

They were passing Miller's Hardware, which was less

than two blocks from the bowling alley, and Evan realized that he'd been monopolizing the conversation. He wanted to know more about her, so he changed the topic.

"But enough about me," he said as they passed by the window of the hardware store, which was covered in Halloween decorations for sale. "Are you liking Riverview? Is it anything like where you came from?"

"Yes, I'm liking it here, but it's nothing like where I came from," she said, looking around as the cityscape stretched out before them.

"Oh?"

"This is my first time living in a big city. I grew up way out in the country, at the base of a mountain right on top of a big river," Hana said. "There was a little town not too far away, but it was ancient and sparsely populated. Riverview is very different. There are so many people here it's a little intimidating."

"So, I'm guessing that Riverview High must be a little overwhelming, then?" Evan said.

"Sometimes," she said. "I think there are more students at Riverview than in that entire town back home."

Evan tried to imagine what a culture shock it must be to move from the country to a city the size of Riverview and could appreciate why Mara didn't like crowds. The irony, however, was that he hardly considered Riverview to be a big city at all. His earliest memories were of Chicago, where they lived on the twelfth floor of a high-rise apartment complex. Compared to where he and Ellie were born, Riverview was small.

As he tried to picture Riverview from Hana's perspective, they rounded the last corner and were finally within sight of the bowling alley. The enormous building dominated an entire corner of the shopping district, with rows upon rows of parking spaces stretching from its entrance to the street, most of them filled with parked cars. Along one side rose a giant, blinking fish swishing its tail and knocking down a trio of bowling pins with the name "The Fish Bowl" in bright coral and pink above the animated neon.

The place was a favorite destination for kids and family on the weekends, and Evan wasn't surprised to find several groups of people lingering around the parking lot and entrance. As they approached, it struck Evan that he was about to bring Hana into one of the more crowded and noisy places he knew of in all of Riverview.

"Um..." He paused briefly about halfway through the parking lot. "Are you okay with crowds? This place gets pretty busy and loud. So, if you'd like to go somewhere quieter, we can totally do that."

"I'm fine," Hana assured him, her eyes sparkling. "This place looks fun."

"Well, all right then." Evan smiled, looking forward to sharing one of his favorite places around town. "Welcome to the Fish Bowl. Fun for the entire family! We used to come here all the time, and they have the best pizza around, trust me."

"Sounds great," Hana said as he held the door open for her.

The familiar sounds of the bowling alley rose to greet them. Blaring music competed with the cacophony of balls rolling down the lanes and crashing into the wooden pins, while a packed crowd laughed and hollered as they played.

Hana smiled broadly, looking around and scanning every corner from the arcade with its video games and billiard tables, to the main reception and the bowling lanes. Evan followed quietly behind as she stepped closer to the lanes, where a group of bowlers in matching purple jerseys cheered each other on as they practiced. Her eyes sparkled as she followed every new noise that came to them as she took the place in.

As she looked around, he saw her take a deep breath in as the unique aroma of the bowling alley oozed around them. He hadn't noticed it in years, but breathing in himself, he could smell the oddly nostalgic bouquet of fried food, oiled wood, musty carpet, disinfectant spray, and an underlying faint foot odor that mixed to form the distinct perfume that screamed, "bowling alley." He had the wandering thought if anyone in their right mind would ever try to recreate and bottle up the aroma. He chuckled at himself as he pulled lightly on the sleeve of her blouse, drawing her away from all the distractions.

He guided her past the lanes to the back of the building, where the restaurant and bar were tucked away. Being farther away from the action, the restaurant was much quieter, allowing for easier conversation and fewer interruptions. As they slid into an unoccupied booth, Hana continued to watch the nearest lane of bowlers as they hurled their balls into the waiting pins.

"Looks fun, huh?" Evan asked.

"It does!" Hana turned to him, eyes bright. "Is it difficult?"

"No, not really," Evan said. "Well, if you don't care about your score, anyway. There are professionals who take it real serious, but I just goof off and enjoy myself. I considered playing competitively when we came here often, but that was a few years ago." He flexed his bowling arm. "When we're done with lunch, would you like to play a game or two?"

Hana spared a glance at the nearest group of bowlers before returning to Evan. "I, I don't know how," she said timidly.

"Don't worry, I'll teach you." Evan smiled encouragingly. "And like I said, it's not that hard. You just roll the ball down the lane and try to knock over as many pins as you can."

"Okay then. That sounds like fun," she said.

When a server arrived a moment later, Evan greeted him by name.

"Hey, Jimmy," he said.

"Hey, Evan," Jimmy said. "I haven't seen you in here lately."

"Yeah, I've been busy. Can I get a root beer and two slices of pepperoni?"

"Sure." Jimmy made a quick note and turned to Hana. "And for you?"

"Um, that sounds good. I'll have the same."

With a nod, the server walked back toward the kitchen.

"So, if Riverview High is bigger than your hometown, what was your old school like?"

"It was tiny," Hana said. "There were only about two dozen students in the whole place. Classes weren't as structured as Riverview either. We only had three teachers who taught us a variety of subjects. There was a lot of self-paced learning as well."

"Which do you like better? There or here?"

"Hmm, that's tough." She looked off in the distance while she considered. "Some lessons were fun back home, but it was kind of lonely."

"Lonely? I'd have figured that you'd know all the other students if there were so few."

"I guess." Hana shrugged. "I mean, I knew each of them by name, but I couldn't really call most of them friends. The one school taught kids of all ages, so there were only a couple of teenagers. I only had two friends growing up, mostly. One of them moved away a few years ago, and the other left at the end of summer when her dad had to leave for work. After that, the only friend I had was Mara, and to be honest, she didn't really attend school much then, either."

"That does sound lonely," Evan said.

"To be honest," Hana said hesitantly, "I'm actually a little jealous of you and all of your friends."

"Me? Why?"

"You have so many of them."

"Believe me, I don't have that many friends," Evan said while shaking his head.

"How can you say that?" she asked disbelievingly. "You have Oliver, Katie, Sarah, Kyle, George, Jimmy, Mrs. Richardson, and then there's your sister and aunt."

Evan chuckled. "I wouldn't call all of those people friends, exactly," Evan chuckled. "Oliver and Katie, sure, but the others are really just acquaintances."

"You know that hurts, Evan!" Jimmy inserted himself jokingly, having just returned with a tray of food and drinks. "I mean, I was at your fifteenth birthday and everything."

"That's because we had it here! And you worked that day!" Evan said as Hana smirked in amusement.

"Really? But I thought we were besties!" Jimmy joked before returning to his station behind the counter.

"Seriously though," Evan said as he slid a plate of pizza and a soda to Hana's side of the table. "I wouldn't consider myself very popular. If you want to see real popularity, I should introduce you to the school's 'golden boy'. Everyone knows him, and he has dozens of friends."

"Including you?" Hana asked.

"Me? No," Evan laughed. "I mean, I share the same P.E. class with the guy, but we're not close. I'm perfectly content with only having a few close friends," and with a wink he added, "though having a couple more wouldn't hurt."

Hana looked away and blushed, trying to hide her reaction behind her soda as she took a long drink.

"You just seemed to get along so easily with everyone; I just thought they were all your friends," she said a moment later.

"I'm friendly with all of them, sure," Evan shrugged, "but I don't really know most of them well enough to call them my friends. Heck, the study session the other day was probably only the fourth or fifth time I've spoken to Sarah and only the second time I've been in the same room as Kyle."

Hana furrowed her brow. "You don't count Sarah as one of your friends?"

Evan considered for a moment before answering. "Yeah, I guess I would call her a friend now. But before last week, I wouldn't have put her in that category."

Hana nodded. "So, how many times do you need to talk to someone to consider them friends?"

"That's..." Evan smiled awkwardly. "It's not about how many times you talk to someone, but more about what you talk about or how well you get along. I mean, take you for instance—this is what, our third conversation, and I already consider you a friend.”

“You do?” Hana asked, her eyes widening as she took another sip of her soda.

“Sure. As long as you don’t mind.”

“I don’t mind.” She smiled warmly.

The conversation quieted as they focused on their lunch. Hana ate slowly and methodically as Evan scarfed down his first piece. It was evident that Hana had little experience with pizza as she seemed to struggle with managing the floppy piece of food.

“Is this your first pizza?” he asked after watching her work through her slice carefully.

“No, I’ve had it before,” Hana said, setting her piece down to take another quick sip of soda. “Once or twice.”

“You’ve only had pizza once before? How is that possible?”

“There weren’t any places that made it near home. But I’ve had it on vacations.”

It seemed odd how little familiarity she had with the food, though he had to admit he knew nothing about life in super-rural Greece. “So, are you happy you moved here?”

“Yes I am, actually,” Hana said with sparkling eyes. “I wasn’t sure what to expect, but I like it here, even if it gets a little overwhelming sometimes.”

“So, what made your family decide to move, anyway?”

“My mom suggested it.” She fidgeted with her plate, slowly turning it in a circle. “Because of me, actually.”

“Really?” Evan took a sip of his soda. “Why?”

“She knew that my friends had moved away and that I was lonely. She also thought it would be good for Mara and me to experience America. It helped that she has a couple of old friends living in Riverview, and they encouraged us to come here. We still have the house back home, so if it doesn't work out, we can always go back."

"That's cool. What does your mom do?"

"She works nights as a supervisor for a security company. It's essentially the same work she did back home."

"And your dad? Is he back from his trip yet?" Evan asked, recalling the odd look the sisters shared when their father had come up before.

"He's an executive for a large multinational company," she said. "He travels all over the world. We don't see him very often, though he stops in when he can."

"That sounds rough." Evan sympathized, sensing that Hana missed her father.

"It can be," she said. "I'd like to see him more, but he's super important at his company, so I understand. Sometimes he flies one or all of us out to wherever he is, and we visit him there. Mom more often than Mara or me."

"Can I ask you something else? Not about your family," he began tentatively, setting down his piece of pizza for a moment.

"Sure," she said as she wiped the grease off her hands before reaching for her second slice.

"On your second day, when you walked into class, were you mad at me? You know, for knocking you down?"

"No," she said with furrowed brows. "Did you think it upset me?"

"Well, yeah," Evan said. "When you walked into class

that Tuesday, you glared at me. I just figured you were pissed that I'd run you over."

"Oh, no, I had no idea who'd bumped into me," Hana said, shaking her head. "Are you sure I was glaring at *you*?"

"That's what it felt like." Evan shrugged. "And you don't have to be nice. It was much worse than just a 'bump.'"

"The only thing I can remember that might have upset me was that I forgot my pencil case. I discovered that right as I walked into class, so maybe I looked unhappy because of that? Katie lent me a spare, but regardless, I'm sorry if I made you think I was mad at you."

"Don't worry about it." Evan smiled and picked his pizza up again. "Besides, you have every right to be mad. Knocking you down was a total jerk move, and I'm sorry. Again."

"It's fine. Besides, we're friends now, right?"

"Right."

They returned to their lunch, and when she was finished, Hana kept glancing back toward the kitchen.

"Still hungry?" Evan asked.

Hana blushed and nodded. "A little."

"Ever had a pizza cookie?"

"Um, no." Hana looked cautious. "Is that like a piece of pizza with cookies crumbled on top?"

"Ew, no," Evan laughed loudly, waving his hand in the air to get Jimmy's attention.

A moment later, the server arrived.

"One Chocolate Regret, please. With vanilla ice cream."

"Coming right up," Jimmy said, returning to the kitchen.

"Um, Chocolate Regret?" Hana asked suspiciously.

"Don't worry; you'll love it. Trust me," he said with a wink.

"Okay," Hana said.

"So, what do you like to do for fun?" he asked while they waited. "Do you like video games?"

"We don't have any video games at home," she said sheepishly.

"What? Seriously?" Evan gasped. "How is that even possible?"

"My parents think that they're a waste of time and that we should spend our free time bettering ourselves. Besides, I'm not sure that most of the people in our little town have even heard of video games."

"That's unbelievable!" Evan said as he took another sip.

"Yeah," Hana said, biting her lip. "In a lot of ways, Mara and I were pretty sheltered back home."

"So, what did you do for fun then? Tip cows or something? You do know what cows are, right?"

Hana stared at him blankly, cocking her head slightly to one side and squinting, "Cows?" she blinked.

The soda slipped from Evan's grasp, landing loudly on the table as Hana laughed.

"Yes, I know what a cow is," she said while smirking at Evan's stunned reaction. "And as for fun, I like to play music."

"Oh, that's cool," he said, quickly wiping up the soda he spilled. "What instrument do you play?"

"I can play the clarinet, guitar, and cello, though my favorite is the piano."

"Wait, you can play *four* instruments?"

"Yes?" she said with a shrug. "There wasn't much else

to do growing up."

"Riverview must be like a totally different world for you."

"In many ways, yeah."

Jimmy returned with an eight-inch deep-dish pizza pan with a giant chocolate chip cookie baked into it. Sitting atop the massive cookie were three large scoops of vanilla ice cream, topped with chocolate sauce and chocolate sprinkles.

"One Chocolate Regret," Jimmy announced proudly. "Enjoy."

Evan eagerly grabbed one of the two spoons. "Dig in!" he said as he began scooping himself a spoonful of baked cookies and ice cream as Hana followed his lead a moment later.

"Mmmm..." she said, closing her eyes and smiling in delight as she ate.

"Told you..." Evan chuckled before going in for another spoonful.

When the cookie and the ice cream were gone, Evan leaned back, feeling extremely full. As he relaxed, a loud clatter of bowling pins colliding with each other echoed from the bowling alley, followed by a chorus of cheers, drawing Hana's attention back to the action.

"Ready to learn how to bowl?" Evan asked.

"Yes, please." Hana sat up eagerly. "I just need to wash my hands first."

"Of course. The bathrooms are back that way." Evan gestured in the general direction of the entrance, knowing that the bathrooms were easy to find.

"Be right back..." she said.

While Evan waited for her return, his eyes wandered over to the wall of televisions, usually reserved for whatever current sporting events were going on, though today, the game had been interrupted by a breaking news report. Some official was having a press conference about rising tensions in South America, where sporadic fighting had broken out as a minor skirmish was quickly escalating. The headline read that the fighting was threatening to turn into an all-out war in the region and that American troops were standing by in case things got worse. Evan vaguely wondered if his history teacher would bring up the conflict in the coming weeks, groaning at the likelihood of another long report.

A few moments later, Hana returned to the table. "Okay, all set," she said cheerily.

"Cool, let's go get our shoes."

"Shoes?" Hana looked confusedly down at the ones she was wearing.

"I'll explain," Evan chuckled as he led her to the counter for lane and shoe rentals.

Several minutes later, they arrived at their assigned lane with shoes on and balls picked out. Before they started, Evan explained the rules and how the scoring worked. He went first so he could show Hana the process firsthand. When it was finally time for Hana's first throw, she took the ball with trepidation, sliding each finger into its hole carefully.

"Any advice?" she asked.

"Just walk up and roll the ball down the lane hard," Evan said. "You want to hit the tip of the triangle or just off to one side of the first pin. Just be careful not to step into the lane—it's super slippery."

Hana stood behind the white starting line and held her ball up to her chest, just as Evan had shown a moment earlier. With a deep breath, she stepped forward and hurled the ball forward. Evan watched in shock as the ball flew with surprising speed several feet above the lane. It sailed through the air, finally landing halfway down, bouncing past the midway point before rolling toward the pins. Unfortunately, her aim had been off, and the ball slowly fell to one side, falling into the gutter several feet shy of the pins.

"Was that right?" she asked, disappointed.

"Sort of," Evan said, trying to be encouraging. "You had the right motion, but you want to roll it, not throw it. It's more important to aim than use a lot of force."

"Oh," she said. "Okay."

"Besides, we have a lot of bowling ahead of us, and you don't want to hurt yourself."

"Right. I think I understand." She smiled.

Hana's next throw was much better, with the ball rolling down the center of the lane, only veering off at the end to clip a few pins.

As the four pins cracked and fell, Hana jumped in excitement. "I hit some!"

"Nice!" Evan said while applauding.

As the game progressed, Hana steadily improved with each toss, and when she got her first strike in the eighth frame, the two of them celebrated loudly enough that they drew curious glances from the people in a nearby lane.

Evan admired her as the game progressed—her every movement fluid and graceful. When she had first selected her ball, he had worried that she would find it too heavy as she had skipped the lighter ones and had picked one of the heaviest the alley had. With every throw, the weight seemed trivial as she hurled it again and again with ease. He had assumed that the power of her first throw had been a fluke, but it quickly became clear that she was much stronger than she looked.

Near the end of the first game, as she wound up for another toss, he glimpsed her right leg as she stepped into her throw. For a moment, her skirt flared up, and he thought he saw something along the side of her leg, starting just above her shoe.

On her next throw, he paid closer attention to her ankle and became convinced something was there. It appeared that she had a tattoo running up the side of her leg, though it surprised him she would, considering her age. Perhaps it was more common in other countries for teenagers to have tattoos than in America? It was hard to tell what it might be, as he could only glimpse the bottom of something long and thin. He considered asking her about it but was ashamed to admit to just how closely he had been watching her every move.

Evan was pleased with his performance for the first game, especially considering he hadn't played in a long time. He didn't quite break one hundred but had gotten respectably close with a ninety-one. It impressed him how quickly Hana seemed to pick up the game, barely able to hit the pins in her first few frames but coming on strong near the end, though she still trailed by over twenty points when it was all over.

For the second game, they changed positions, and Hana bowled first. Before approaching the lane, however, she fished out a small hair band from her pocket and took a moment to gather her long silver hair into a ponytail, looking over at Evan with a playful challenge in her eye.

"Oh, getting serious, are we?" he asked teasingly.

"I think I have the hang of this now," she said, just as

mischievously, "so get ready for a proper battle."

Evan laughed in return as she confidently walked up to the lane, ball in hand. After a brief pause to center herself, she rocked forward and went into her throw. Evan couldn't help but appreciate her form as she took her first step, one leg moving forward while the other stretched out behind her, the upper half of her body leaning into her throwing motion.

The ball slid from her hand at the top of the lane with unmistakable grace and rolled smoothly toward the ten pins at the far end. With a satisfying crash, the ball connected with the center of the triangle of pins, throwing them back and into each other.

Evan sensed he was up for a real fight as all ten pins fell on her very first throw, and she returned with a gleaming smile, almost strutting back to her seat.

While Evan didn't match her strike, he spared, and from then on, the battle was on. The score flip-flopped between them for the rest of the game, with each of them pulling off a strike or a spare when they needed it most. By the end of the ninth frame, Hana had a slight lead, and as she walked to her seat after getting her final spare, she held her head high.

"Last frame," she said with a sparkle in her eye. "Looks like you're going to lose this time."

Evan looked at the score and worried. Their scores had been close at the end of the seventh frame, but his luck had apparently run out, and now he was trailing. It would require a strike or a spare if he hoped to catch up to her, and while winning wasn't necessary, he enjoyed the challenge and this new side of Hana.

"You're pretty smug for only your second time playing, don't you think?"

"What do you mean?" She gave him a wry smile. "You're just mad that you've played for years, and I'm about to beat you on only my second try."

"Not really. I haven't played in more than a year..."

"Okay, if you're going to make excuses..."

"Well, I *did* intentionally throw the fourth and fifth frames just to make you feel better," he said with a smirk.

"You did not!"

"Yes, I did!" he said overly dramatically.

"All right then." Hana crossed her arms. "If you're so great, then show me."

"Okay then."

With a fearless look of his own, Evan grabbed his ball and positioned himself in front of the lane. With care, he aimed, took a deep breath, and began his throwing motion.

The ball sprang from his fingertips in one easy swing and flew down the lane. He watched with bated breath as it rolled end over end, curving ever so slightly in the last few feet, colliding perfectly with the first two pins, crashing into them at just the right angle to cascade into the rest.

"Yes!" He jumped for joy as all ten pins fell with a crash.

"Very nice." Hana applauded his performance as he returned and waited for his ball.

"Not feeling so confident now, are you?" he asked, teasing her again.

"Don't get too full of yourself. I'm still ahead."

"The game's not over yet," he said, still glowing from his strike.

Once the ball returned, he picked it up and readied

himself for his next shot. It was the tenth frame, and because he had dropped all ten pins on his first throw, he would have two more throws to pull off an upset.

He was proud of the last strike, and he tried to remember exactly what he had done and where he had started from, hoping to recreate the lucky shot. He shifted slightly from side to side before finally settling on a spot.

"Are you going to bowl or dance?" Hana asked.

"Watch this," Evan announced as he stepped into motion and threw the ball down the lane.

It was a beautiful shot, rolling fast and straight, heading right where his last ball had connected. Then with a few feet to go, the ball curved, and instead of colliding at the perfect spot, it connected a few inches off the mark. Evan watched in disappointment as what began as a promising flurry of flying pins only dropped half of the bunch, leaving five standing when it was all done.

"Well done," Hana said encouragingly.

Evan glanced at the score. He was still behind and needed to knock over at least three pins to win. This was just a friendly match, but suddenly, proving himself to Hana was vital, and he desperately wanted to win.

When the ball returned, Evan grabbed it, found his place, and took a deep breath to settle himself for his last throw. This time, Evan put all his strength into it, hoping to send the remaining pins flying into each other in glorious victory. As he stepped into his motion, he swung the ball around as hard as possible, heaving it down the lane. As the ball flew from his fingers, the added momentum of his swing threw off his balance, pulling him farther forward than he had expected, causing his right foot to land beyond the white foul line and onto the waxed surface of the lane.

As soon as he stepped onto the slick surface, his foot shot forward, dragging him further down the aisle. Once his second foot set down on the slippery surface, he was done for. He spun with no control as he desperately tried to remain upright before falling, landing hard, face first, nearly an entire body's length into the lane.

He lay still for a moment, stunned from the acrobatic fall, until he heard his ball connect with the pins at the far end. The extra effort had caused his ball to miss the mark entirely, glancing off the far-left pin, taking it and another behind it down with a crash, leaving the other three untouched.

"Oh my gosh, Evan!" Hana ran up to the edge of the lane behind him, stopping just short of the slippery lane. "Are you all right?"

"Yeah, I'm pretty sure nothing's broken." Not wanting to fall a second time, he carefully crawled back up the lane until he was safely back on the bowling platform.

"What happened?" she asked, reaching out a hand to help him to his feet.

"Honestly? I threw it too hard and lost my balance. Totally my fault. I guess that's what I get for trying to show off," he said with a grimace as he stood.

"Well, I'm glad you're okay."

"Thanks."

As they walked back to the seats, Hana noted the score on the digital display. "Would you like to re-do your last shot? You probably would have done better if you hadn't fallen."

Evan ached all over from the fall, having landed hard on his knee, scraping it badly under his jeans. He figured it was his reward for being overly competitive and trying too hard to win.

"No, I'm fine," he said. "I fell *after* I let go of the ball, so it's a fair score. And my fault." He sat down, wincing slightly as the fabric of his pants dragged across his wound.

"Are you sure you're okay?" Hana asked, her eyes darting to his knee and back up to his face in apparent concern.

"I'm fine," Evan said with an encouraging smile. "Good game, by the way."

"I still think you should have repeated your last frame," Hana said as they walked home.

"No, you won fair and square," Evan said as he handed her a soda he'd bought on their way out of the bowling alley, opening his can a moment later. "Even if I hadn't fallen, the score would have been the same. I fell after I let go, honest."

Hana's eyes narrowed as she pursed her lips, obviously skeptical. While he was being honest about the throw, he didn't want to admit that his knee hurt badly enough after the fall that even if he had tried again, he wouldn't have done any better. Besides, it was his fault for trying so hard to beat her rather than just having a good time.

"So, did you have fun?" he asked, hoping to divert the conversation as he gulped the fizzy drink.

"Well, it's not cow-tipping, but yeah, it was very fun."

Evan laughed loudly, spewing soda several feet in front of him as it ejected through his mouth and nose, burning on the way out. Hana laughed alongside him, eyes sparkling with mischief.

As they walked, they took a leisurely pace partly because of Evan's knee, though Hana didn't appear to be in a hurry either. Evan was considering inviting her back to his house to introduce her to the world of video games when an alarm rang from Hana's watch.

"Oh! I'm sorry, but I have to go," she said as she silenced it, wringing her wrist and glancing up and down the street.

"Oh. Did you need to be back home by a certain time?" Evan checked his watch and saw that it was much later than he had realized.

"I forgot I had an appointment; I'm sorry."

"No worries. Go do what you need to do," Evan said with a smile. "I'll see you tomorrow?"

"Of course! Thanks again for the bowling and pizza. I had a great time."

"Me too."

A moment later, Hana turned around, headed back the way they had come, turning at the nearest corner before disappearing. It disappointed Evan that their time was over, but he was still glowing from their afternoon together.

Evan's bright mood carried him as he walked until a cool breeze passed over him, chilling him through his light jacket. He felt as if someone had walked right past him, but there was no one there when he turned around. The sidewalk was empty, with not a soul in sight.

It was then that he noticed just how unusually quiet it had become. There wasn't a bird chirping or a bug buzzing within earshot. He could only hear the tap from his footsteps as he walked. He picked up the pace, feeling strangely isolated.

A second cool breeze passed by, causing him to pull his jacket closed and wrap his arms around himself to stay warm. It wasn't the usual late-afternoon wind, but a strong, frigid blast of air, like it was about to snow, despite only being late September.

As he continued, an uneasiness settled on him, and he had the distinct sensation that he was being followed, despite being the only person on the entire street. He just couldn't shake the feeling and glanced back several times as he walked. He was nearly home, with only one more turn and a few blocks to go. Hoping to put the creepy street behind him, he picked up his pace while ignoring the pull of his jeans on his scraped knee.

His mood brightened again as he approached the end of the quiet street, toward the next corner where he could see the passing cars and a few pedestrians. A few more houses and an alleyway were all that separated the strangely deserted road and the back of a small strip mall. He was nearly there.

As he passed the last house and neared the corner, another frigid blast of air assaulted him from behind with a surprisingly powerful gust, throwing his hood over his head and causing him to stumble. The wind blew into the alley, throwing up a plume of dust and causing a small stack of cardboard boxes to fall over as it went, though it appeared to dissipate just beyond a large, metal dumpster a few feet from the street.

Evan paused at the alley's entrance, looking into the shadowy depths as the late afternoon sun was mostly obscured from the height of the stores. It was difficult to see very far into it, and while the alley appeared empty, Evan felt another presence, as if something was lurking within its depths.

"Hello?" he called out, his curiosity getting the better of him.

The alley remained still and silent, almost as if it was holding its breath. Cautiously, Evan took a step toward the entrance, staring intently where the gust had seemed to vanish. For a moment, it reminded him of his recent visit to Mrs. Richardson's room, despite the two locations having nothing in common.

"Anyone there?" he called again, taking another tentative step. Leaning to the side, he could nearly see around the corner. As he stood and stared, a puff of wind flowed out of the alley as if exhaling a held breath, bringing with it a foul odor of refuse and rotting trash.

With the late afternoon sun, the threshold of the alley was a stark contrast of warm, inviting light ending abruptly as the shadow from the wall at the alley's entrance painted a solid line of darkness across the concrete and asphalt. The toe of Evan's foot was less than an inch from the very edge of the shadowy line, and looking down, a chill ran down his spine. The alley seemed unnaturally dark and threatening.

Suddenly Evan realized what the alley and Mrs. Richardson's room had in common. It was the light. It was just as bright as everywhere else, but it felt like the sun struggled to find its way into the alley. The shadows seemed exaggerated, stretching further with the darkest recesses having an impenetrable, inky blackness. There was a dumpster less than twenty feet into the alley, but he struggled to see the far side of it, as if the light itself had retreated despite the early hour.

Crouching down, he selected a small rock and tossed it at the large metal dumpster. As the pebble bounced off the metal side with a muted clatter, Evan was startled when something bolted across the narrow alley behind a tall stack of discarded tires and damaged pallets.

Whatever the thing was, it was much larger than he had expected, easily standing the height of a man but much broader. It moved in a flash, sliding across the alley amazingly fast, with Evan barely catching sight of it as it changed hiding spots. As his eyes remained glued to the stack of tires, he tried to make sense of what he'd seen. In that brief instant, Evan could have sworn that he had seen through most of its body as if the wind itself had taken form.

Everything inside of him warned that whatever it was, it was dangerous. Listening to his instincts, Evan took several large steps backward, stopping several feet into the roadway, bathed in the afternoon warmth. If it was a person hiding in the alley, they didn't want to be disturbed, and if it wasn't a person, he didn't want to find out what else it could be.

Without further hesitation, he turned and walked away, a sense of relief washing over him as he turned the corner at the strip mall as the everyday sounds of traffic and pedestrians greeted him.

Evan's thoughts lingered on the strange alley only as long as it took him to pass two stores before he happily returned to thinking about Hana. The sun was setting, and a cool evening breeze wafted through the city. It was a perfect evening. For once, he was glad that the weekend was ending because the following day, he'd get to see her again. They'd been apart for only a few minutes, but he already missed talking with her, looking at her... Even considering his embarrassing loss, their afternoon had gone go well, and he felt energized and eager.

He arrived at his apartment and opened the door, his head still in the clouds as he hung up his jacket and kicked off his shoes. When he turned around, Ellie was standing on the far side of their small dining room, hands balled into fists on her hips and a broken wooden spoon clenched in her grasp.

"So, you've finally come back, have you?" she growled with a fire burning in her hazel-green eyes. He guessed she hadn't been home long, as her honey-blonde hair was still pulled back into the ponytail she used for her tennis practice.

"Hey, Ellie," Evan said cheerfully. "What's up?"

"Do you mind explaining this?" She held up the broken wooden spoon, waving it in front of her.

Evan couldn't fathom what significance there could be in a broken wooden cooking spoon and stared at it for a moment. Finally, he gave up and shrugged.

"All right, then explain why our laundry is in a pile on the patio." She pointed an accusatory finger behind her, where Evan could see socks, underwear, and one pant leg just beyond the half-open glass door.

Evan swallowed, his mind racing for an excuse but knowing there was none. He had forgotten entirely about the chores he had abandoned that morning and the piles of dishes, trash, and clothes he'd stashed around the apartment. He suddenly understood the relevance of the wooden spoon and cringed.

"Ah crap, I'm sorry, squirt," he said. "Something came up, and I had to stash everything in a hurry."

"What could *possibly* have happened for you to shove all of our dirty dishes in the fridge? You knocked over the milk and made a huge mess!" She snarled, waving the broken spoon in the air.

Evan's eyes widened in surprise. He vaguely remembered a crashing sound from the kitchen as he left with Hana hours before and winced at realizing what had caused it.

"Now I have to rewash all the clothes again because they got filthy from being outside," she said. "So, you can take out the trash, wash the dishes, fold laundry, and anything else I can think of!"

Evan knew he had royally screwed up and didn't even consider arguing. He simply nodded his head in meek acceptance and started cleaning.

That night, their aunt got home several hours later than usual, long after Ellie had gone to bed. As she walked through the front door, Evan was sitting at their small dining room table, reviewing his math homework.

"Welcome home," Evan said as she hung up her jacket.

"Oh, hey, kiddo. I didn't expect you to still be awake this late."

"Just reviewing some homework." He tapped his open notebook with his eraser to emphasize his productivity. "We left you some dinner in the fridge."

Aunt Maddie breathed a sigh as she set her belongings down and walked into the kitchen.

"Oh my! You cleaned the whole fridge! Thank you!"

she said as she pulled out her plastic-covered plate of food.

"Yeah, Ellie thought it would be nice," Evan said, too guilty to accept any accolades for the cleaning.

Unexpectedly, his aunt's arms wrapped around him in a fierce hug. "You kids are so sweet. I'm so lucky to have you." A small hitch caught in her voice on the last few syllables.

"Are you okay? Is everything all right?" Evan asked.

His aunt sniffed back a quiet sob. "Yeah, I'm fine." She grabbed her plate and sat down across from him at the small table. "I just had a rough day."

"Want to talk about it?"

"I lost a patient today," she said as she shoved her broccoli around the plate. "It wasn't entirely unexpected, but it's still so hard when it happens."

"Oh, I'm so sorry. What happened?"

"She was one of my cancer patients," Aunt Maddie said. "She'd been fighting for a long time, and I thought she was responding well to the treatment, though now I wonder if she wasn't in a lot more pain than she was admitting. An orderly found her this afternoon in the lounge. They thought she was just sleeping, but she had passed away, quietly."

Chills ran down Evan's spine at the mention of the lounge as a sense of foreboding filled him.

"Uh," Evan swallowed. "Can I ask who it was?"

"Do you remember Mrs. Richardson? She always wore those bright yellow slippers."

Evan opened his mouth to answer, but no words came, so he nodded numbly.

"I'm sorry, kiddo," Aunt Maddie sniffed. "I'm not hungry. Would you mind putting this back for me? I'm just going to bed.”

Evan agreed, saddened by the news. As he wrapped the plastic wrap back over his aunt's dinner, he wondered if he had been the last person to speak to Mrs. Richardson alive.

Chapter Eight

Ghost Stories

Despite the unsettling news about Mrs. Richardson's passing, Evan awoke in high spirits the next morning. When he met up with his friends on the way to school, it was clear that he hadn't been the only one to have a wonderful weekend.

"Not you too," Katie said sourly as Evan arrived, joining her and Oliver at their usual corner.

"Not me too, what?" Evan asked.

"Nothing," she sighed. "Can we go already?"

"What's her problem?" Evan asked as they headed toward school. "Rough morning?"

"I don't know." Oliver shrugged. "I feel great!"

Katie pulled her backpack farther up and ignored the two boys as they walked.

"Hey, what's wrong?" Evan asked as he reached out and lightly pulled on her shoulder.

Katie sighed heavily before falling in alongside the two of them. "Nothing's wrong. I just had a crappy weekend is all."

"I'm sorry to hear that. But at least you're over your fever, right?"

"Barely," she said. "I was still sick last night when I

went to sleep, but I'm better now, so mom let me go to school even though she wanted me to stay home another day."

"And you went to school instead?" Oliver asked, astonished.

"Of course I did!" Katie said, scandalized. "I've missed two days already *and* a test!"

Oliver shook his head in disbelief.

Evan knew how seriously Katie took her education, often becoming despondent if she under-performed below her own expectations. Being forced to miss a couple of days would likely have made her anxious all weekend.

"Speaking of tests," she asked in a happier tone, "how did you two do?"

"Ha!" Oliver chortled. "My mom was so happy with my grade that I didn't have to do any chores all weekend. I played video games non-stop. It was glorious!"

Katie sighed and turned to Evan. "And you? Did you do well enough to keep your grade up?"

"I aced it," he said with a beaming smile. "Sarah and Hana really helped a lot."

"Hey! I was there too!" Oliver said with an exaggerated pout.

"And that should tell you just how good they were," Evan said. "I got a near-perfect score even *with* Oliver in the study group."

"That *is* impressive," Katie said, eyes wide in mock shock.

"That's just mean," Oliver pouted playfully.

When they arrived at their English class, Hana was already seated at her desk, textbook, notebook, and pencil ready. Evan smiled and waved at her as he walked to his desk, a giddy thrill running through him as she waved back with a smile of her own.

"What was that?" Oliver asked in a loud whisper as they sat down.

"What was what? I was just saying hi."

"Yeah, sure." Oliver looked at him suspiciously. "Friday you're freaking out about Hana all day, and today you're all smiles and waves. And you want me to believe that nothing happened?"

Evan groaned quietly. "If you must know, Hana and I had pizza and went bowling on Sunday. She wanted to chat and had never been bowling before, so I thought it would be fun."

"Wait, wait, wait." Oliver looked aghast. "You went out with Hana? On a *date*?"

Oliver's quiet outburst caught Katie's attention, who turned her head in their direction, keenly interested while Hana's head also turned as if trying to catch Evan's response.

"No! It wasn't a date. Not really," Evan whispered, waving his hand to encourage Oliver to keep quiet. "She's new in town and just wants to make friends, okay? It wasn't anything serious."

Evan watched as Hana's head went back to facing forward as Katie leaned over and whispered something to her. As Hana shook her head at whatever Katie asked, he wondered what she thought about their afternoon together. Did she think it was a date? The possibility sent a spark of pleasure through him, surprising himself at how much he liked the idea.

"Yeah, sure," Oliver said unconvincingly.

"Why are you even surprised? You're the one who gave her my address."

"I don't know what you're talking about," Oliver said turning away, sparing a glance back at Evan from the corner of his eye. "You're welcome, by the way," he added.

Evan chuckled as the bell rang and the teacher called the class to order. After a few minutes of gathering recent assignments and discussing various pieces of school news, he began the day's lesson.

"For the next several weeks, we will explore classical western literature, and I thought it would be fun to begin with ancient Greece," Mr. Hanson said. "I want you to review your textbooks, pages 126 to 159, and pick one of the Greek legends to write a report on. This will be due at the end of the week, but let's keep it short—only 500 words."

The class briefly became a flurry of activity as the students pulled out their textbooks and turned to the pages the teacher had noted. Mr. Hanson gave the class a few minutes to skim the book, and the room was quiet until a light snicker floated from Hana's desk.

"Do you find something amusing, Miss Blackmore?" Mr. Hanson asked.

"Uh, no, sir," she said, immediately chastened. "Sorry."

"Well, if this class thinks my lessons are a joke," Mr. Hanson said, "then let's make it 1,000 words, and you can all turn it in on Wednesday."

The students groaned in unison.

"What was that?" Mr. Hanson asked the class. "You want it to be 2,000 words?"

The room quieted instantly, though Evan could still feel an undercurrent of anger flowing through the student body.

The rest of the class proceeded without incident, but when the bell rang, announcing the end of the period, there were a plethora of quiet grumbles and curses, many of them aimed more toward Hana than the teacher.

"Stupid ghost girl," Evan overheard someone say as they passed.

Evan wanted to assure Hana that Mr. Hanson was often punitive like this, having lashed out at nearly everyone at least once, even Katie. Unfortunately, he didn't get the chance: by the time he put his books away, Hana had already left her desk, leaving him with only a glimpse of her long silver hair disappearing through the door in a flash.

"I don't blame her," Oliver said after noting Hana's rapid departure. "It's not her fault that Mr. Hanson's a jerk, but the class was out for blood. It was a good call to escape while she could."

"I just hope she knows that it's not her fault, that's all."

"Why not text her?"

"I would if I had her number," Evan said with a shrug as they headed toward their history class.

"Well, sir, it's your lucky day! For the low, low price of one week's lunch, you too can have your very own copy of Miss Blackmore's cell phone number!"

"And when did you get her number?" Evan asked.

"She gave it to me after you ran out of English last Friday," Oliver said. "Wait, do you mean she gave me her number before you? Ha! Guess we know who she really likes then, huh?"

"Oh yeah!" Evan rolled his eyes, suddenly jealous of his best friend. "I'm sure she's just dying to ask you out. Seriously though—why did she give *you* her number?"

Oliver chuckled. "She wanted me to let her know if you were okay after you 'got sick,'" he emphasized with air quotes.

In the end, Evan got a copy of Hana's number for one half of his Twinkie and the promise to come over to play video games soon, which was a regular event for the two friends.

Evan left school that day, anxious for the evening ahead of him. Unfair or not, he now had a 1,000-word essay to write. He hoped the bookstore would be especially quiet tonight so he could focus on his assignment.

He waited just beyond the school gate while Katie finished closing the library after study hall. As he flipped through the brief list of Greek gods mentioned in his literature book, he looked up and across the street. His attention was drawn to the far side of the four-lane road where a young girl stood, unmoving, watching the few remaining students as they left the school grounds. She seemed younger than a high school student, with long, straight dark hair reaching past her waist. She wore an elaborate outfit with a ruffled checkered red skirt and white top, complete with sleeves in alternating black and white stripes. Under her skirt, she wore black tights with blood-red buckled shoes. Over one shoulder was slung a modest-sized drawstring bag with red hearts decorating the lower half. She didn't look older than thirteen, tops, but her posture and mannerisms suggested more maturity.

While her appearance alone was striking, it was the intensity with which she watched the exiting students that captured his attention. She scanned in Evan's direction, and for an instant, their eyes met as though she felt him watching.

Her presence was unsettling, and the potency of her gaze caused goosebumps to rise on his arms and neck. An eerie sensation spread through Evan as if he were a rabbit locking eyes with a hungry wolf. At that moment, he was afraid to move, secretly hoping that whatever she was looking for wasn't him. Then her eyes continued their search, and he was released from her spell as her gaze moved on to another student as they left the school grounds to head home.

"Ready to go?" Katie asked from behind, causing Evan to jump and spin in alarm. "Jeez, are you okay?" she asked.

"Yeah, I'm fine," he said as he began to point across the street. "Check out that girl—" but when he turned his head, she'd vanished.

He searched up and down the street with no trace of her in sight; she had disappeared in the blink of an eye.

"Who?" Katie asked, looking around in the direction he pointed and examining the entrance of the school.

"She was right there!"

"Who was?"

"I don't know," Evan said. "Some girl dressed like something out of a Tim Burton movie. She was standing right over there, near the crosswalk sign. But now she's gone."

"So, what about her?" Katie asked with a slight frown.

"I don't know, she just..." He couldn't translate the unease he'd felt when their eyes met. "She was weird and creepy."

"That's not a nice thing to say," Katie said.

"But she was!"

"Yeah, sure. Fine," Katie said as she rolled her eyes. "Can we go home now?"

"Uh, yeah, okay." As they walked, he continued to scan up and down the street for the vanished girl to no avail.

An hour later, on his way to the Silver Linings bookstore, Evan was already thinking about his English essay. The shop was often slow on the weekdays, and it regularly provided an excellent time to read, study, or do homework. He hoped that tonight would be one of those nights.

As he walked, his phone chirped, announcing a new text message. It surprised him it was from his aunt and not one of his friends. Aunt Maddie rarely messaged him, often calling instead.

Aunt M: Off to work?

Evan: yep

Evan: I'll be home at the usual time

Aunt M: Do me a favor? Be extra careful tonight,

ok?

Evan read the message three times before responding. His Aunt Maddie wasn't the worrying type, and he couldn't remember the last time he got a message telling him to be careful before.

Evan: Why? Is something going on?

He waited patiently, guessing that his aunt's explanation was lengthy. He secretly wished that he wasn't relegated to an old, archaic phone and would have preferred a newer model that would indicate whether she was still typing or not. Finally, her next message came through:

> Aunt M: The news is reporting that some vandals are running around the area. They damaged a local cemetery last night and even partially dug up a couple of graves.
>
> Aunt M: They even attacked someone. I know that there is that graveyard not too far from your work...
>
> Aunt M: So just keep an eye out and avoid any strange people, all right?
>
> Evan: Sure thing.

It wasn't like her to text him about something she saw on the news, and it was probably just a bunch of kids being kids. Fortunately, the last walk signal changed, and he arrived at the Two Fountains shopping center. It was one of the larger strip malls in the area and boasted a variety of stores and small business offices. Near the organic grocery store, tucked in between a dentist's office and a family insurance agency, was the Silver Linings bookstore, where Evan had worked part-time for nearly two years.

The shop carried an eclectic collection of spiritual and religious materials and a wide variety of items that focused on helping to improve one's mind, body, and spirit. It contained everything from philosophy texts to self-help books to yoga and meditation manuals, fortune-telling, aromatherapy, and more.

Evan unlocked the shop and walked in, smelling the familiar aroma of sandalwood, jasmine, and vanilla from the variety of incense and scented candles that lived near the front of the shop. The aisles were narrow and maze-like, with shelves, cases, and racks haphazardly filled with a wide assortment of items roughly grouped with similar products. The only person who understood the madness of the shop's layout was the owner, Mr. Abernathy. To Evan, the disorganization of the store and its contents added to its distinct, quaint charm, even if he found much of the stuff for sale frivolous.

Only three small sections were organized recognizably: the front counter, which Evan kept tidy, Mr. Abernathy's fortune-telling corner, and the single floor-to-ceiling shelf of books jam-packed with everything from religious studies to astrology, fortune-telling, and mythology literature.

Of the three, the fortune-telling section was the store's biggest attraction, complete with a table covered in purple velvet, a pair of hand-carved wooden chairs, and a glass beaded lamp hanging overhead. Next to it was an array of divination paraphernalia, including crystal balls, Ouija boards, tarot decks, rune stones, and guides for palm reading.

Normally the shop would have already been opened for the day, but as the owner was still on his cross-country vacation, it took Evan a couple of minutes to get ready for guests and switch on the "Open" sign. He had already taken down the poster in the window that advertised fortune-telling services, which was strictly reserved for Mr. Abernathy. Over the years, he had grown a respectable base of loyal customers who made up most of the regular visitors to the shop. With Mr. Abernathy absent, Evan had received precious few patrons in the past two weeks.

Without the kindly owner around to engage in his usual friendly banter, Evan quickly grew bored and started on his English assignment, heading toward the back of the shop to find some relevant source materials.

It took several minutes to browse through the singular bookshelf as it was way over-capacity, with books and magazines squeezed into every conceivable space. Finally, he found what he had been hoping for: a thin, soft-covered book titled *A Primer to The Gods of Olympus & Ancient Greek Mythology* by Muirus Gardner. He flipped through a few pages and decided it would be an ideal starting point with each notable Greek God having a single page dedicated to them, giving him an abbreviated description of each. He returned to his post at the front counter and began flipping through the book for a likely candidate for his report.

As he had expected, it was a slow day, with only three guests arriving in the first two hours of being open, though he answered a slew of calls from patrons asking about Mr. Abernathy's return. With all the free time, Evan got the lion's share of his report written, deciding to write about Hera and researching the lore surrounding her by using Mr. Abernathy's aging computer. As closing time approached, Evan returned the mythology book he'd borrowed when the chime from the front door announced a late-arriving guest.

"I'll be right there!" Evan called from the back of the store.

He crammed the book thoughtlessly onto the shelf and headed back to the front counter, though when he got there, there wasn't anyone else in the shop.

"Hello?" he called out as he glanced around the various displays and shelves, searching for whoever had walked in, but the place was empty.

A quick check outside showed an empty parking lot with only a few people walking around. He swung the door open and closed to test if the wind could have opened it, but as he already knew, it was far too heavy for that. He made one more thorough check of the shop, walking up and down each aisle, ensuring that he was the only one there. *Did I just imagine the bell ringing?*

With a shrug, Evan returned to the front counter and began reviewing the first draft of his essay, though he found it difficult to concentrate. Something had changed, and the charming shop with its strange assortment of baubles and trinkets suddenly felt unsettling and threatening. He had never been uncomfortable in the store before, even when working alone or at night, but this was different. It was as if the darkness from outside had seeped into the place, stalking him, waiting for the right time to strike.

Evan's nervousness grew as the minutes passed, looking up often at every little thing that caught his attention. When the lights of a passing car flashed through the store, the reflection of a dozen points of light from the various glass objects caused him to jump, certain that a pair of bright red eyes had reflected at him from a far corner of the store.

He just couldn't shake the feeling that he was being watched, and when the heater kicked on, ruffling a nearby rack of scarves, he gasped, convinced for an instant that someone had been standing there.

As his pulse returned to normal, he tried to dismiss his overactive imaginings with a chuckle but decided it was close enough to closing time that he began wrapping up.

As he was finishing, he made one last check of the place, calling out, "I'm locking up and turning on the alarm now! If someone's hiding in here, you better come out now, or the police will be called." As he expected, the place was dead quiet.

Shortly afterward, he'd secured the register and had turned off the "Open" sign. With the security alarm turned on, he closed and bolted the door, checking twice that it was securely locked. Now that he was outside the bizarre little shop, he immediately felt better, though he still took the city bus and its bright, inviting lights rather than walking home in the dark.

When Wednesday morning rolled around and it was time to turn in his essay, Evan felt reasonably sure that his score would be adequate, though he knew it wasn't his best work. Considering the required length and the short turnaround time, he would have to accept whatever grade he got.

He watched as the other students turned in their papers and noted he wasn't the only one concerned about the quality of their work. When Oliver stepped up to the basket for completed assignments, he turned in a hastily scribbled one-page paper that was sure to elicit Mr. Hanson's scorn.

However, when Thursday morning arrived, it wasn't Oliver's paper that the teacher critiqued the hardest.

With a slap that drew the attention of the entire class, Mr. Hanson dropped five pages of neatly written script onto Hana's desk. "Please explain yourself, Miss Blackmore," he added.

"Explain what, sir?" she asked, confused.

"Did you really think you could get away with turning in this garbage and that I would actually give you credit?" Mr. Hanson said as he glared at her. "Even Mr. Branch picked an *actual* literary figure from Greek lore for his essay—if you could call it that."

"But sir—"

"And, you neglected to cite your sources, even if they were from a comic book." Mr. Hanson's face contorted into a sneer. "I expect another paper from you tomorrow morning, and it better be about an *actual* Greek literary figure."

Evan could hear the murmur of chuckles around him as the teacher began distributing the rest of the graded papers. "Serves her right," someone whispered nearby.

Evan tuned that out. He sympathized completely with Hana and felt an almost physical pain watching her as she reviewed the numerous red-marked comments plastered all over her pages. Even if Mr. Hanson hated

Hana's paper, there was no reason to go that far.

"Brutal," Oliver said under his breath, echoing Evan's feelings. "Here, look at this."

Oliver's paper was devoid of any commentary or critique, even though the paper was utterly inadequate. A red 63 was marked at the top as the only sign that the teacher had even bothered to read it.

At lunch, Evan vented to Oliver. "That was totally uncalled for," he said. "If Mr. Hanson was going to humiliate someone, he should have picked you."

"Fair," Oliver said, shoving half of a sandwich in his mouth, continuing to speak through a mouth full of food. "Mr. Hanson has always been a jackass, though."

"That's no excuse. She turned in five pages at least; It was clearly well over 1,000 words, and she always takes her work seriously. It couldn't have been worse than yours."

Oliver chewed contemplatively. "I wonder what she wrote to upset him so much. Perhaps she invented some Greek god who punishes old men with premature balding and toxic bad breath when they pick on teenage girls or something."

Evan laughed at the image of Mr. Hanson's hair falling out in large clumps while a toxic green cloud emanated from his mouth every time he opened it.

"So, have you heard about the Graveyard Smasher?" Oliver asked, changing the subject unexpectedly.

"The what?"

"The Graveyard Smasher. That's what they're calling him, anyway. How have you not heard about this?" Oliver asked, his eyes wide and mouth agape as Evan stared back at him blankly. "It's all over the news."

"Well, Aunt Maddie mentioned something about some

vandals the other night, but she said nothing about a 'Graveyard Smasher.'" He used air quotes to emphasize the mysterious title. "I thought it was a bunch of kids or something."

"The police don't think it's just a bunch of vandals anymore," Oliver said. "They think someone is running around, intentionally targeting graveyards, smashing them up, and trying to dig up bodies. The Smasher even assaulted a groundskeeper yesterday in broad daylight."

"Seriously?"

"Seriously. Look at these pictures." Oliver handed Evan his phone, which was opened to a local news article on the recent vandalism and the assault.

Evan was surprised at the amount of damage and understood why the police no longer thought it was simply a bunch of kids. The video showed clips of tombstones broken in half, coffins partially pulled out of the ground, and a section of wrought-iron fence bent and knocked over.

Oliver continued his story while Evan looked at the various images in the article. "Yeah, someone jumped the groundskeeper from behind yesterday. He didn't see his attacker, though he remembered seeing a young teenage girl walking away. Can you imagine? A full-grown man getting pummeled by some middle-schooler?"

Evan shook his head while scrolling through the photos. "There is no way a single person could have done all this."

"That's what the news says, too," Oliver said. "The police still want to question her, and, apparently, they can't find her. It's like she vanished after the place got trashed."

"That's crazy," Evan said as he skimmed the article,

reading much of what Oliver had already described.

The story recounted the young woman the police were hoping to question, causing the hairs on the back of his neck to stand up on end. The description in the article precisely matched the girl Evan had seen Monday after school, complete with a checkered skirt and a backpack with heart-shaped patterns across it.

"Dude, I've seen this girl!" Evan exclaimed.

"Seriously? You know who she is?"

"No, not really. I mean, I don't know her name or anything, but I saw her the other day. She was hanging around school Monday afternoon, just across the street."

"Are you sure?" Oliver asked. "I mean, what are the odds of you seeing this girl on the same day as someone trashed the graveyard?"

Evan quickly scrolled back up and stared in disbelief as he looked at the date of the attack. Oliver was right; it had happened Monday afternoon, not long after he'd left the school grounds. Who was this strange girl, and what was her connection to the Graveyard Smasher? Was it all just a big coincidence? It seemed unlikely.

As Evan reread the news article, searching for any clues to tie the mystery together, Katie appeared from around the corner, waving at them as she arrived.

"Hey, Katie," Evan said, welcoming her.

"Sup..." Oliver mumbled as he drank his soda.

"Hey, guys." Katie looked around. "Have either of you seen Hana?"

Evan frowned. "Not since English."

"Why? What's up?" Oliver chimed in.

"I wanted to check on her," Katie said. "Mr. Hanson was pretty brutal this morning, and someone passed a nasty note to her right before class let out. She seemed pretty upset when the bell rang."

"Sorry," Evan said. "She's never had lunch with us. I just assumed that she sat with you and Sarah in front of the library."

"No, not since her first week," Katie said. "I figured she was with you guys since you seemed so close."

"See?" Oliver said while elbowing Evan in the ribs. "Told you everyone could see that there's something between you two."

"We're just friends," Evan said exasperatedly. "We went bowling and had pizza. That's it."

"So, you *did* go on a date with Hana," Katie said, her eyes wide in surprise.

"It wasn't a date!" Evan exclaimed as he threw up his hands. "She came over last weekend to talk about school, and I introduced her to the Fish Bowl. She said she'd never been bowling, so we played a couple of games. No big deal." Evan looked back at Oliver sternly. "And *not* a date!"

"Yeah, right, *not* a date," Oliver said. "That's why you've had a big, goofy smile on your face all week and wave to her every day."

"You know what? How about I help you look for her?" Evan said to Katie as he got to his feet, tossing Oliver's phone back to him. "It's better than hanging out with this idiot."

"Sure! That'd be great," Katie answered with a smile.

"See you later," Oliver chuckled as the two of them headed back towards the center of the school.

"Later..." Evan called back with a wave.

"So, not a date?" Katie asked playfully once they were well beyond earshot.

"No!" he said firmly.

"Okay," she relented with a chuckle. "If you say so."

Evan desperately wanted to change the subject. "Where should we start?"

"I guess the cafeteria?"

With a nod, they headed in that direction.

"Can I ask you a question?" Katie asked in a much more serious tone.

"Sure," Evan said with a nod.

"Did anything happen between Sarah and Hana during the study session?"

"I don't think so." Evan frowned. "Why?"

"I don't know." Katie shrugged. "When I mentioned to Sarah that I was worried about Hana, I got the impression that they didn't get along. Everything was fine when Hana first arrived, so I wondered if something happened at the study session."

"Not that I remember." Evan considered it again, then shook his head. "Other than making an ass out of myself after everyone left, everything else went fine."

"Oh, no! What did you do?"

He didn't want to explain the whole crazy story, so he abbreviated it drastically. "I fell asleep on her couch at one point and spilled some soda on her floor."

"Jeez, Evan, what would make you do such a thing?"

"I don't know, hormones?"

"That's not how that works." Katie scowled at him in disapproval. "Sounds like you were just being an idiot."

"Hence why I tried to make up for it with pizza and bowling."

"Aha! Now the not-a-date thing is starting to make sense."

"Definitely not a date," Evan said. "So, you think there's a problem between Sarah and Hana?"

"I didn't use to think so, but now I'm not so sure," Katie said. "When Hana first got here, we all had lunch together at our usual table. Then Sarah gradually stopped showing up. It seemed like Sarah had other places to be whenever Hana was there. I remember mentioning it to Hana once, how it seemed weird that Sarah wasn't around. And now that I think about it, it was right after that when Hana stopped coming. Then Sarah started showing up again."

"Did you ask Sarah about it?"

"Honestly? I thought nothing of it until now. No one said anything. I just thought they got busy, and it all just sort of happened." Katie sighed. "But now I feel bad."

"It could be just a coincidence," Evan said.

"Maybe," Katie said unconvincingly.

Once they were inside the cafeteria, Evan scanned the large room and spotted Hana reading a newspaper in a far corner. Tapping Katie on the shoulder, he pointed to their destination and worked his way through the mass of other students. The place was packed with teenagers filling every available space, eating, laughing, and playing games, except for Hana's corner.

As Evan picked his way through the crowd, he noted how much her table stood out from the others, as hers was the only one with only a single person. Sitting by herself, her corner looked isolated and lonely, with no one else lingering anywhere nearby. In addition to being empty, it seemed that everyone was avoiding walking past her.

"Is she reading a newspaper?" he asked as he snaked a path to her table.

"Obviously," Katie said.

"Yeah, but who reads a newspaper these days?"

"Oh, I don't know, people who want to know what's going on around them?" Katie shook her head.

"But where did she even get one?" he asked, pausing briefly for a large procession of students as they passed by.

"The store? A newsstand? The school library?" Katie ticked off possibilities on one hand.

"Wait, our library has newspapers?" Evan turned his head in surprise as they continued.

"You... What..." Katie stammered. "How do you not know that we have newspapers in the library? You're there every day for study hall!"

"Guess I just never noticed." He shrugged while chuckling at her shocked expression.

"You're unbelievable," Katie mumbled as they arrived at the table.

"Hey, Hana. Whatcha doin?" Evan asked as she still hadn't noticed their arrival, her head down in concentration as she appeared to be taking notes from a newspaper article.

"Oh! Hi guys," she said with a start, snapping her notebook shut. "What brings you two here?"

"We wanted to check up on you," Katie said as she sat down at the table. "You looked upset after English."

As Evan sat down, he glanced at the newspaper and noted that it was opened to an extensive two-page article about the Graveyard Smasher. Was he the only person in Riverview who hadn't heard about this?

"Oh, I'm fine." Hana smiled wanly as she folded the newspaper carefully and set it aside. "Just disappointed in myself for upsetting Mr. Hanson."

"Don't feel bad about that," Evan chuckled. "He hates everyone, even Katie."

"He does not," Katie said.

"Okay, maybe not Katie," Evan said grudgingly.

"He's strict, but fair," Katie insisted.

"Fair?" Evan asked, astonished. "He gave Oliver a sixty-three on that disgrace of a paper he turned in. I know for a fact that Oliver didn't cite any sources and wrote 400 words at best. I can almost guarantee you he wrote his paper late last night. And he gave Hana a two, even though she wrote five pages and I'm sure wrote a much better essay."

"How did you know I only got a two?" Hana asked.

"I could see it over your shoulder when you were looking at it. I saw all of his red notes too, but I couldn't read them," he admitted while feeling self-conscious about spying on her.

"Why did you get such a low score? Did he say?" Katie asked, inserting herself.

"He chastised me for picking a fictional person. He said that since I didn't write about any of the actual Greek Gods, I didn't deserve any credit. The two points were for getting my name correct."

"Fictional? It's Greek mythology! It's all fictional," Evan said, eliciting a smile from Hana.

"So, who did you write about?" Katie asked curiously.

"I wrote about the twin librarians of Casena: Vivlio and Mathisi," Hana said. "One of them is blind but gifted with poetry and wordsmithing, while the other is deaf but gifted with memory and the ability to always know the truth of any statement."

"Wait, if the guy is deaf, how can he hear if something is a lie or not?" Evan asked.

"When they were young, their mother petitioned the gods, and Hephaestus crafted a pair of rings for the two of them," Hana said. "As long as they are close, they can see or hear what the other does and know each other's thoughts. While it helps them overcome their disabilities, it comes at a cost, and their story is pretty interesting."

"Cool," Katie said. "I've never heard of them."

"They're fairly obscure, and that's why I thought Mr. Hanson would appreciate a report on them," Hana said. "I guess he must have assumed that I made it all up."

"But you're from Greece!" Evan said. "You would know Greek lore better than anyone."

"Wait, you're from Greece?" Katie asked as her head whipped around from Evan to stare at Hana.

Evan chuckled at Katie's reaction and how similar it was to his own when he'd learned the same thing. Katie's curiosity was piqued, and Hana spent the rest of their lunch hour relaying the same story she'd shared with Evan about her recent move to the States.

As Katie and Evan walked home after school that day, Katie came to a sudden stop. "Hey, Evan, what are you doing this weekend?"

Evan considered briefly. "Mr. Abernathy is back in town and didn't schedule me for Saturday as a reward for taking care of the shop when he was out. So, I was going to take Ellie to the mall for a new backpack and some sneakers. Then on Sunday, I work eleven to three and have plans afterward to play video games with Oliver at his place."

"Perfect!" Katie beamed.

"What's perfect?" Evan blinked, wondering for a moment if Katie was interested in joining them in their online adventures.

"On Saturday, how about I invite Sarah and Hana to join us?" Katie asked. "If they spend time together, I'm sure they'll become friends. I bet they're both just shy."

"Join *us*?" Evan asked. "When did I get wrapped up in this?"

With large, pleading eyes, Katie looked up at Evan in her most persuasive, doe-eyed expression. "Please, Evan?" she asked. "I didn't even notice they weren't friends. I need your help. Besides, Ellie is super cute, and everyone likes her. She can help break the ice."

Evan knew he was being manipulated and groaned. Even though he had no idea how he could help Sarah and Hana become friends, he had never denied either Ellie or Katie when they gave him that look. With a large, overly dramatic sigh of defeat, he reluctantly agreed.

"Oh, all right, you win," he said. "We'll go with you. Besides, I guess I owe you some ice cream."

"Thanks, Evan. You're the best!" Katie stood up on her tiptoes and delivered a quick kiss on his cheek.

Chapter Nine

Maturity

"Come on, squirt!" Evan called from the front door. "We're going to miss the bus!"

"I'm coming!" Ellie ran down the hall, slipping her arms into her jacket as she went.

A quick look at his watch told Evan they would need to run the entire way if they were going to make it in time. "No choice, Ellie!" He stooped down. "Hop on."

Ellie looked at him reluctantly, and it reminded Evan just how much she'd grown in the past year. He knew she didn't like being treated like a child, but they were out of time. With a sigh, she climbed onto his back.

After a quick adjustment, Evan was off again, carrying her out to the street as fast as possible. As he ran, he noted that ten-year-old Ellie was much heavier than the last time he gave her a piggyback ride. She was growing up fast, and he wondered if this was the last piggyback ride he'd ever give her.

They rounded the last corner, and the bus was already at their stop, doors open with the last passenger climbing in. Evan was getting tired but pushed himself on the last leg to arrive just as the bus driver was about to close the door. Evan sat Ellie down as they boarded with a sheepish grin toward the driver, who was rolling her eyes at their delay.

The bus ride took long enough for Evan to cool off and Ellie to lightly doze. They made it to the Bainbridge Mall in less than an hour, arriving last as everyone else was already standing together near the entrance.

As they exited the bus, Ellie ran to the others as she cried out in glee. "Katie Kat!"

"Jellybean!" Katie called out as Ellie threw herself into her open arms.

The two of them spun around, giggling and laughing as Evan watched and smiled. He was always amused at how easily Ellie brought out the childish side of Katie, who was often the more reserved member of his friends.

"Hey, everyone." He smiled, happy to see them all in good spirits. "Hana, this is Ellie, my kid sister," he added when the two girls had stopped spinning.

"Hello," Hana smiled, though Evan noticed that she didn't move closer while keeping her hands behind her.

"Hi!" Ellie beamed back at her. "It's nice to meet you."

For a moment, Evan thought Hana looked tense, with a slight furrowing of her brow, but it evaporated with Ellie's warm response.

"So, what would everyone think about visiting Pirate's Bay after lunch?" Sarah asked. "When I told my dad where we were going, he gave me five passes, good for a round of mini-golf, some tokens, and a couple of rides."

"That's awesome!" Katie said. "Thanks, Sarah!"

"Yeah, thanks!" Evan agreed.

"Let's go now!" Ellie said, jumping up and down.

"I don't think they're open yet," Sarah said. "I was

thinking we'd go later."

"Right after lunch?" Ellie kept bouncing on her toes.

"Sure," Sarah chuckled.

"How did your dad get free passes?" Evan asked.

"Apparently, several people didn't show up to some kind of team-building event his work set up," Sarah said. "They expire soon, so he told me I should take as many as I wanted."

"That was super nice!" Katie gushed. "Thank you."

"It's no big deal." Sarah flushed at the praise.

Evan noted Hana seemed indifferent about all of it. She looked from face to face, staying quiet and to the side, keeping her hands behind her back.

"Not excited about going to Pirate's Bay?" Evan asked as they headed into the mall, when he could ask her in relative privacy.

"Um, well, I'm not sure. What is it?"

"Oh, it's a mini-golf and arcade park," he said. "It also has a couple of rides, like bumper boats and a go-kart track."

"That sounds fun!" Hana smiled, her indifference replaced with the same infectious eagerness everyone else had.

As they headed into the mall, their first stop was the big department store, where Ellie and Evan focused on what they'd come for. It didn't take long to find a backpack, but shoes presented more of a challenge.

"Why does everything have to be pink?" Ellie asked, annoyed as they entered their third shoe store.

"Isn't that what little girls like?" Evan teased.

Ellie and Katie grunted in unison while Katie glared at him with furrowed brows.

Finally, at the very last shoe store in the mall, Ellie

found a pair of tennis shoes in her size with a stylish blue and black design. Alongside them was a pair of cute silver heels that caught her eye. As Evan watched Ellie put the stylish heels on, Katie approached.

"Growing up fast, huh?" Katie noted quietly while watching Ellie examine herself in a mirror, spinning from side to side.

"Yeah," Evan said wistfully as he watched his kid sister take yet another step to maturity right in front of him. "Pretty soon, she'll be taller than you, you know."

Katie growled and punched him in the arm, walking over and admiring the shiny shoes.

"Those look fantastic on you, Jellybean," she said as she gave Evan a playfully evil smirk. "You should totally make Evan get them for you."

Evan sighed when Ellie turned her big eyes on him. "Can I, Evan? Pleeeeaaasseeeee...."

"Sure, why not?" He answered with a smile. It wasn't often that his little sister asked for anything frivolous, and Evan was happy to indulge her.

Ellie squealed happily. "You're the best!" she said, throwing her arms around Evan in a tight hug.

As the cashier rang up the shoes a few minutes later, Evan looked at his watch, noting that it was still early.

"Looks like we still have plenty of time," he said to the group when they all gathered outside the shoe store. "Any suggestions on where we should go next?"

"How about the bookstore?" Sarah suggested.

"Perfect!" Katie nodded vigorously.

A few minutes later, they arrived at the bookstore. Hana, Katie, and Ellie plunged headlong into the depths of the store while Evan hung back, shadowing Sarah as she browsed the displays at the front. He was hoping for an opportunity to speak to her privately without causing a scene. He approached while she browsed the best-sellers shelf, but she spun around before he got to her.

"Why are you stalking me?"

"I, uh, um, wasn't stalking you," he said, glancing around quickly to make sure no one else could hear them.

"Yes, you were," Sarah said. "You've been following me since we entered the store."

Evan paused, blushing that she'd caught him so easily. He briefly considered lying but decided to approach the problem directly.

"Okay, yes, you're right," he said. "I *was* stalking you, but not in a creepy way. I was just hoping to ask you something and didn't want the others around."

Sarah smiled a knowing smile and shook her head slightly. "Evan, I know what you want to ask me," she began, "and I think it's very sweet, but my answer is no."

Evan had no idea what she was talking about and was momentarily stunned to silence by the strange turn of events.

"Please don't misunderstand me," she said with an earnest expression. "I think you're a very nice guy, and under different circumstances, I would probably say 'yes,' but..."

As she talked, Evan finally pieced together what she was trying to say. *She thinks I'm asking her on a date!* He couldn't help but feel a little hurt by the immediate rejection but had to stop the conversation before things got out of hand.

"...there is no way I could do that to—"

"Woah, woah! Hold on a second. I think you have the wrong idea," he said, waving his arms in front of him.

"What?" Sarah said, taking a half step backward, though she quickly recovered, narrowing her eyes. "You weren't just about to ask me out?"

"No! Not even—" Then he saw her cool expression, and his face flushed. "I mean, um, you're very pretty, and I don't—"

Sarah raised her hand abruptly in front of Evan's face.

"Stop. Just, stop," she said before taking a deep, settling breath. "Let's start over. What did you want to talk to me about?"

He had originally intended to begin with some small talk before getting to the point but decided to keep everything crystal clear and stick with the direct approach.

"Do you hate Hana?" he asked bluntly.

Sarah's eyes widened as she took a half-step backward. Whatever she had expected him to talk to her about, this line of questioning hadn't been it. Evan watched and could easily see her initial surprise turn to contemplation as she considered the question. Finally, after a full minute, she let out an enormous sigh.

"No, not really," she said.

"Not really? But there is *something* you don't like about her?"

"I don't know. Maybe?" Sarah shrugged, avoiding eye contact and turning back to the row of books, pulling one off the shelf randomly and flipping it open.

"Why?" Evan pressed. "Is it because she's friends with Katie?"

"No, that's not it," she said dismissively. "She just..."

Evan waited for her to finish her statement.

After a moment, she snapped the book closed,

slamming it back into its spot while sighing. "I don't know, okay?"

"Is it because of her hair? Or the way she dresses?"

"No, none of that nonsense," she said with a frown. "Do you really think I'm that shallow?"

"I'm sorry," Evan said, "and no, I don't think you're shallow. Not at all. But I've never known you to be so resistant to anyone. Heck, you even put up with Oliver, and he's an idiot." He shrugged. "So, I don't understand why you don't like Hana."

Sarah let her eyes drift across another row of books while she considered her response.

"I guess," she began hesitantly, "I don't know how to put it. But there's something just, odd about her—unsettling." Annoyance painted her face. "Why do you care if I like Hana or not? Does it really matter?"

"Look, it doesn't bother me, but it bothers Katie," he said. "She wants to be friends with both of you, but that's going to be impossible if you hate Hana."

"I never said I hate her," Sarah said defensively.

"Sorry, you're right; you never said that you hate her," Evan said. "But you don't like her. And Katie thinks Hana sits all alone at lunch because when she's around, you're not."

"She stopped coming because of me?"

"Hana didn't say so, but Katie noticed you were avoiding her," he said. "She also noticed that you came back when Hana stopped hanging around."

"Crap. Now I feel like a monster," Sarah sighed.

Evan considered his next words carefully. He knew he couldn't force a friendship between them, but he had promised Katie that he would do what he could to help.

"Look, no one thinks you're a monster, okay? But why

not give Hana another chance?" Evan said. "You seemed to get along just fine last week during the study session."

Sarah considered for a few seconds before closing her eyes and sighing.

"Yeah, you're right," she said cautiously. "And she wasn't creepy when we were studying. When she first showed up, I felt, I don't know, threatened or something."

"Threatened?" Evan asked.

"It doesn't matter." Sarah shook her head. "I'll give her another chance. Okay?"

"Thanks, Sarah."

"Sure," she said dismissively. "But next time you want to talk, don't get all stalker scary, all right? Just come up and say what's on your mind."

"Okay. I promise."

Having completed his mission, Evan nodded to Sarah and walked away as she returned to browsing the shelf of books. All the talk about Hana had made him wonder what section of the bookstore interested her, so he headed off to find where she had gotten to.

When he finally found her, she was crouched down in the Paranormal Studies section with rows of books filled with various topics such as famous hauntings, demonic possessions, bizarre missing person cases, and tales of alien abductions. For someone who outwardly appeared to be serious, it surprised Evan to find her here of all places.

As he approached, she was flipping through a book about ghosts, wholly entranced. In addition to the book she was reading, several were stacked neatly on the floor next to her.

"So, here's where you've been hiding," he said

casually as he approached.

"Oh, hi, Evan. Were you guys looking for me?" she said as she stood and looked around.

"Uh, no, not really," he said as he smiled, suddenly aware that they were the only two people in the aisle, out of the eyesight of everyone else. "So, uh, you like ghost stories?" He grasped for something to say, feeling silly for the obviousness of his statement.

"Yeah, actually," she said modestly as she looked at the cover of the book she held. "It's actually a hobby of mine about ghosts. Mara likes to tease me over it."

"Oh, don't listen to her," Evan said, waving the comment away. "There's nothing wrong with liking weird stuff. Heck, come by the bookstore I work at. If you like ghosts and spirits and stuff, you'll really like it there."

"I'd love to," Hana said, her grimace replaced by a broad smile.

Evan didn't know what else to say, so he stood awkwardly for a moment before the memory of his bizarre dream crept into his thoughts. The two of them standing alone in the aisle reminded him of being in the front hall of her house, electricity running between them. The series of events that followed raced through his brain, and he was suddenly nervous, feeling the blood rising to his cheeks. Not wanting to explain why he would suddenly start blushing for no reason, he stood on his tiptoes to peer over the shelves to see what the others were doing and found them making their way to the checkout.

"Uh, looks like the others are ready to go," he said, nodding toward the front counter.

"Oh, should we join them?" she asked with an almost

reluctant tone in her voice.

Instantly, his mind returned to the moment in his dream where she had asked if he wanted to visit her room. With a quick shake of his head to clear his wayward thoughts, he chastised himself for his overactive imagination.

Hana's eyebrows pulled together as she tilted her head. "Is everything okay?"

"Oh, yeah, sorry," he said as he brought himself back to reality. "Did you want to get that?" he asked, trying to keep his wayward thoughts grounded.

"I think so, yes," she said.

As the two of them emerged from the aisle, Ellie caught sight of them and waved them over.

"Look what Katie's getting for me," Ellie said proudly as they arrived. She held up a book that featured an image of a young high school girl on the cover, her hair being swept in the wind along with a flurry of cherry blossoms.

"Cherry Blossom High?" Evan read the title aloud, noting that it was the first in a series.

"It's fantastic," Katie said while gushing over Ellie's shoulder. "They just released the translated versions of issues 140 through 145," she said, glancing down at the small stack of books in her hands.

"I didn't know you liked that kind of thing," Evan said, reaching for the top book in Katie's stack and flipping through it.

"Is there something wrong with romance?" Katie challenged.

"Oh, no," Evan said while quickly returning the book with the others. "I, uh, just didn't know, is all. It's cool. What do you think, Hana?" Evan amended, hoping to divert the conversation away from himself.

Hana, however, wasn't paying attention, her gaze locked on the cover of a nearby rack of tabloids. Evan glanced over and saw what had caught her attention.

"The Graveyard Smasher is angering the dead! Exclusive pictures inside!" It proclaimed in bright yellow letters. "Psychic experts tell all!"

"Hey, you were reading about the Graveyard Smasher the other day, weren't you?" Evan noted.

"What?" Hana asked in a surprised tone, her head whipping back to him and the others.

"At lunch... You were taking notes for some kind of school report or something?" he said.

"Oh, right, yes. A school report," she said as she nodded.

"I bet this would be fun to add to your essay," Evan said jokingly as he reached over and grabbed the tabloid.

He opened it up and scanned the purported evidence of a grainy, enhanced image from one of the destroyed graveyards. In one corner, they had circled a hazy white smudge, claiming it was photographic evidence of a distraught spirit angered by the vandalism.

"What do you think?" Evan asked, deducing that if she liked ghosts, this would be a fun addition to whatever assignment she had.

"Um, okay. Sure." She smiled hesitantly, taking the magazine and glancing through it.

"Next, please." The checkout attendant called and motioned to Katie, who added Ellie's book to her stack and fished out her wallet.

Even with the time spent in the bookstore, it was still early for lunch, so the five of them visited a handful of other shops and storefronts. While walking down one corridor, Katie noted a sign in a window advertising "60%-70% off all swimwear."

"Ooh, swimsuits are on sale!" Katie exclaimed in delight. "Let's go see what they have!"

Evan groaned. "Why are you looking at swimsuits? Summer is over. You're not going to go swimming again until next year."

"Exactly. That's why they're on sale. They're going to be super cheap!" Katie was glowing. "C'mon, Ellie, let's see if they have anything in your size."

Ellie beamed at Katie, and while holding hands, they plunged into the store, heading directly toward the racks of discounted swimwear. The rest of them followed, amused at Katie and Ellie's childishness. He guessed it was a surrogate sister kind of thing—even though Katie was an only child; she had always been like a big sister to Ellie.

Evan reluctantly tagged along, growing a little anxious. Ellie had reached that age when she no longer wanted the cute, childish clothing and frequently asked for more adult styles. Evan still struggled with the idea of his little sister growing up and was determined not to get dragged into this fiasco. The only thing that could be worse than watching his little sister parade a bunch of revealing swimwear in front of him is if they forced him to go underwear shopping. Luckily, his aunt always made those trips with her.

"You don't like swimsuits?" Hana asked as they

approached the swimwear section.

"I like swimsuits just fine," Evan said. "I just don't want to see my little sister in something revealing, that's all."

"So, what do you consider to be revealing?" she asked. "Something like this?" She picked a blue and white bikini from a nearby rack, holding it up to her as if she were wearing it.

At her invitation, Evan took an admiring look at Hana's figure, easily imagining how she would look in it. As he pictured her in the swimsuit, he blushed wildly, finally turning his head away in embarrassment.

"Yeah, something like that," he mumbled.

While looking away, Evan spotted something that made his stomach drop. Walking into the store at that exact moment were Oliver and his cousin Mike, laughing loudly as they walked past the various displays near the entrance.

Evan's mood swung rapidly from amusement to annoyance. He quickly scanned for the others and found himself alone with Hana—the other three having disappeared, likely into the nearby fitting rooms.

Evan could easily imagine Oliver's reaction if he saw him with Hana in the girl's swimsuit section and the teasing that would ensue. That would be bad enough on its own, but with Mike accompanying, there was sure to be a scene.

"Quick!" He grabbed Hana's hand and pulled her toward the changing booths, keeping his head down. "This way!"

They moved through the racks of swimsuits and into the fitting rooms, Evan pulling Hana into the nearest changing booth before drawing the fabric curtain closed.

"What are we doing? What's going on?"

"Shh," he said while putting a finger to his lips. "It's Oliver and Mike. They're right outside," he whispered.

When it appeared that Hana would remain quiet, he turned around and pulled a small section of the curtain aside to peek. The two boys stopped at the swimsuits and were holding various articles up to each other, laughing obnoxiously. "Is there something wrong?" Hana asked quietly.

"Uh, no, not really." Evan only now realized how close he and Hana were, his thoughts returning to the memory of his strange dream and their intimate embrace. "I, uh, just don't want them to see us right now."

"Oh," she whispered, a hint of confusion in her voice. "Who's Mike?"

"He's Oliver's cousin and a complete jackass," Evan said. "Whenever Oliver's uncle comes to visit, the two of them hang out together."

"And you don't like him?"

"That's an understatement. The last time he visited, we all hung out together. Mike really pissed me off, and we nearly got into a fight."

"Oh, dear." Hana frowned. "What happened?"

"He said some shit, and I lost my cool."

"Okay," Hana said with a nod. "And we're hiding because you don't want to get into another fight?"

"Yeah. And I don't want them to see me with you."

"Why not?" Hana sounded a little hurt. "Is there something wrong with being seen with me?"

"No! Not at all!" He glanced back at her before looking away, his heart pounding in his chest over the words about to pour out of his mouth. "It's because I have a huge crush on you, and Oliver's noticed. I don't want him to tease me about it is all. I guess I'm just a coward."

Evan held his breath and watched the two boys as they continued their juvenile tour of the lady's swimwear. He couldn't believe that he had just blurted that out, quickly becoming nervous about how she would react to his impromptu confession. It kept him rooted in place with his back turned to her, staring out but barely registering what was happening outside the little room.

Suffocating silence filled the small changing booth. Hana remained perfectly still, not making a sound. He could sense her behind him but was too nervous to turn around. After a few minutes, the two boys moved on, and the coast was clear.

As their laughter faded away, Evan knew he had to face her. With a deep breath to steady himself, he steeled his courage and stood up, slowly turning, keeping his eyes closed until the very last moment.

"So," he said. "Um, looks like..."

As Evan opened his eyes, it stunned him how close Hana was, their faces practically touching. Before his mind could register what was going on, she leaned in, closed her eyes, and kissed him.

Eyes wide with shock, Evan was utterly overwhelmed. Hana's face filled his vision, and his sharp intake of breath filled his lungs with her lightly perfumed scent.

As she kissed him, she leaned in, pinning him to the wall, and nothing could have prepared him for the incredible reaction that filled his body. Every nerve lit up on fire as warmth spread to every corner, immediately followed by goosebumps and tingles. It was like an electric shock, freezing him in place, and he couldn't move until she released him.

It lasted for only a moment, then she was gone, fleeing past the curtain before Evan fully registered what was happening. He remained motionless for several more seconds before his knees gave out, and he slowly slid down the booth wall.

Evan sat on the floor; his heart raced wildly while a whirlwind of emotions surged through him. The lingering sensation of fire slowly faded as he sat there, breathing in and out rapidly.

The kiss left him dizzy. He couldn't think straight other than the singular thought that it had been too brief, even as it had seemed to go on and on.

Through all his emotional turmoil, he clearly understood one thing: he was utterly, madly in love with Hana Blackmore.

A few minutes passed, and Evan returned to earth when he heard Sarah's voice calling out. "Evan? Are you in there?"

Collecting himself with another large breath, he got to his feet and exited the changing booth. As he returned to the lady's swimwear section, Sarah was standing near the entrance of the dressing rooms, noting his emergence with a raised eyebrow.

"What were you doing in there?" she asked him, scanning up and down and noting that he was neither returning something that didn't fit nor holding any merchandise.

Evan spared a glance at Hana, who was lingering nearby, hands picking at random items as she watched his exchange with Sarah from the corner of her eye.

So, it was a secret. Okay—he could work with that.

"Hiding from Oliver and Mike," he said, which was kind of true.

"What?" Sarah asked, glancing around the store for the other boys before looking back at Evan with a quizzical expression on her face.

"Evan, look at this!" Ellie called to him from a few rows over, holding up a new bathing suit. "Can I get it?"

Evan was grateful for the timely distraction and stepped over to Ellie, leaving Sarah standing there with a confused expression.

The suit was a two-piece bright orange and red affair. The bottoms had a white ruffle running around the waist, with a wide top and broad shoulder straps that would tie into a large bow in the back. He had to admit that it was cute and nowhere near as revealing as a classic bikini. His little sister wasn't so little anymore, whether or not he wanted her to grow up.

He briefly considered objecting but noticed Katie watching him carefully. He knew she'd struggled the last couple of years with her lack of height, which got her treated as less mature than she was. He didn't want to be one of those people who judge others based on superficial reasons, which included continually picturing his younger sister as a child.

With that in mind, he opted to be the more mature person and accept that she was quickly growing up.

"Sure thing, Jellybean," he said with a beaming smile.

"Thank you!" She threw her arms around him in an enormous hug.

The rest of the shopping trip and lunch at the soda shop flew by in a blur of laughter, goofiness, and—at least for Evan—curiosity over what Hana was thinking the whole time. Since the encounter in the changing booth, she'd hardly spoken to him, though he kept catching her watching him out of the corner of her eyes and blushing every time their eyes met.

They finally arrived at the amusement park, and after turning in their special passes, got their wristbands and stash of tokens. After a brief planning session, they decided their first event would be a round of mini-golf.

"How about we break up into teams?" Sarah suggested as Evan picked up his ball and club. "My family does it all the time. It's fun to see who gets the better score."

"I want to be on Katie Kat's team!" Ellie bounced up and down in unbridled excitement.

"I pick Hana," Sarah said, surprising everyone.

"I guess that leaves Evan on my team," Katie said in feigned disappointment.

"Gee, thanks," Evan said with a smirk. "I'll have you know I'm actually pretty good at mini-golf. You two are in trouble now."

"We'll see." Hana's quick retort earned a conspiring smile from Sarah.

It didn't surprise Evan that Sarah had a competitive streak, considering how seriously she took her schoolwork. He wondered just how good she might be if her family visited often, but he didn't get nervous until he overheard a discussion between her and Hana.

"Ever played golf before?" Sarah asked.

"No, sorry," Hana answered meekly.

"Don't worry about it," Sarah said. "I have a plan. Just follow my lead, and we'll cream them."

"All right," Hana said with an enthusiastic smile.

Why did Evan have a bad feeling about all this?

The beginning of the game proceeded without

incident, but Sarah's master plan revealed itself when they were about halfway through the course. Until that point, the score between the two teams had been close, though Evan's team had a narrow lead. It helped that the scoring method averaged the strokes by the number of golfers on each team, and Ellie was nearly as good as Evan and Katie.

He had watched Hana struggle with the game early, though she improved quickly, just as she had with the bowling. Sarah's voice carried over from the next fairway as he set up for his shot on the thirteenth hole.

"So, Hana, are there any boys you like at school?" she asked, just as Evan began his swing.

Evan's head spun around toward their voices, hitting the ball well off the mark. With a powerful bounce, his ball struck a small concrete wall and ricocheted high into the air. Evan watched in dismay as it took two giant bounces and plopped into a nearby pond.

Any hope of hearing Hana's answer was drowned in the laughter of a nearby group of kids who howled at his disastrous shot. By the time Evan had returned with a new ball, Sarah and Hana were well ahead of them.

Evan tried to keep his cool and get his head back in the game, but the damage was done. He had trouble thinking of anything other than Sarah's question and how he hadn't heard Hana's answer.

After that, every time Evan lined up for a shot, Sarah and Hana just happened to be in the vicinity, often with Sarah watching him with a knowing look. It became clear that Sarah had deduced his growing interest with Hana and was using his easily flustered nature to keep him off his game.

Evan concentrated on the last few holes with renewed

determination, though it didn't help much. With growing dismay, he watched as his abysmal performance gave Sarah's team a solid lead.

A pair of lucky shots from Ellie and Katie closed the gap at the seventeenth hole, creating an opportunity for an upset. Sarah and Hana had finished, and a quick look at the scorecard gave Evan hope. His team could still win if they did well on the last hole. Unfortunately, the last hole was tricky.

At the beginning of the fairway, the ball had to travel down a narrow, smooth aisle while avoiding a concrete obstacle course made to look like ocean waves. At the end of the aisle was a ramp designed to launch the ball over a small pond of water and into the final challenge.

At the far end was a statue of Blackbeard himself standing next to his cannon, the Widowmaker, as it pointed directly at the golfer. Flowing from the end of the cannon was a near-constant cloud of fog as if the weapon were still steaming from its last firing. Occasionally, the statue would call out "Fire the Widowmaker!" and the cannon would belch out an enormous cloud of steam, ejecting your ball back at you if you timed your shot wrong.

The goal was to get the ball up the ramp, across the water, and into the cannon's barrel. If you aimed well and timed it right, you could get your ball down the barrel, and it would "backfire," causing a large cloud of fog to eject from the back of the barrel, eclipsing the statue of Blackbeard, and another recording of him angrily screaming as his big gun blew up in his face would trigger.

This was the most interactive of all the holes on the course and was a fan favorite. Evan watched nervously as Ellie lined up her shot. Sarah and Katie helped coach her on how to time it to avoid the cloud of steam, but it was up to her to hit it straight and with the right amount of power to get the ball down the barrel.

She hit it with a loud *clack*, the ball sailing smoothly down the lane, past the obstacles, up the ramp, and neatly into the dark barrel of the giant black cannon. As the ball disappeared into the black hole, Blackbeard screamed as a giant cloud of fog enveloped him. Ellie jumped up and down in delight as she got her third hole-in-one for the day.

Katie repeated the success a few moments later, and Evan felt even more confident. His team celebrated while Sarah and Hana watched, stone-faced and waiting. One last glance at the scorecard confirmed Evan's suspicions: if he also got a hole-in-one, their team would win. Even if he took two tries to get the shot, they would at least tie. He'd have to miss twice to lose, which was highly unlikely.

As Evan lined up his shot, he tried to clear his mind. He looked down the fairway and watched the steam oozing out of the barrel. He needed to wait to take his shot after the next big burst of steam emerged.

"Um, I need to go to the bathroom..." Ellie announced right as Evan was about to take his shot, causing him to halt mid-swing.

He took a half-step away from the ball when Katie came to the rescue. "Come on, Jellybean," she said. "I'll take you, and we can return our stuff while we're at it."

"Okay, thanks," Ellie said before turning back to Evan. "You got this."

As they walked away, Evan settled himself back on the ball, waiting again for the next big puff of steam while Sarah and Hana watched on.

As the barrel released its big blast of fog, Sarah chose that moment to ask Hana another question louder than necessary, ensuring Evan would overhear.

"So," she asked Hana, "have you ever kissed a boy?"

As Evan swung, he lost his grip, his club clipping a nearby barrier and flying out of his hands toward a nearby couple, forcing them to duck.

Sarah burst out laughing while Evan blushed furiously.

"You play dirty, Sarah Jones," he shot in her direction as he passed her on his way to get his club.

"Whatever do you mean?" she asked in an overly innocent tone. "Are you particularly interested in the kissing habits of our Hana?"

Evan retrieved his club, apologizing profusely to the couple, and returned to take his shot. He was determined to make it this time as Sarah and Hana watched on.

"A tie would be fine," he told himself as he lined up for his shot. "Just tie the game."

This time, as the giant puff of steam exploded from the cannon, it wasn't Sarah who said anything, but Hana. As Evan pulled back and readied his swing, she answered Sarah's earlier question. "Well," she said as Evan swung, sounding embarrassed and mischievous, "only once."

Even as his arms moved, Evan felt himself drawn back to that moment in the changing booth. And now, realizing it was Hana's first kiss, his heart raced, and it swept him up in the emotional whirlwind of that moment.

The surge of adrenaline caused Evan to swing far harder than he had intended, connecting with the ball with a loud *crack*. Instead of rolling down the fairway, it flew directly toward Blackbeard's laughing face, easily six feet above the ground. It bounced off his nose with another loud *clack* and flew high into the air.

To Evan, his disgrace seemed to last an eternity as the ball hovered in the air before returning to earth, landing back on the course and striking one of the concrete waves that bracketed the fairway. He counted at least twelve bounces as the ball ricocheted back and forth in the narrow lane toward the water hazard. He watched, increasingly embarrassed, until—with a quiet plop—the ball fell into the water, ending their game.

Standing there, club in hand, having watched the most fantastic display of failure in his life, the absurdity of his performance struck him. He laughed uncontrollably, quickly infecting the others.

He might have lost the match, but he couldn't have gone out more spectacularly if he had tried.

"How could you have missed three times?" Ellie chastised Evan as they turned in their clubs. "I'm ten years old, and I got it. Just like everyone else..."

"Sorry, squirt, guess I was distracted," Evan explained, glaring at Sarah playfully and causing her to snicker.

Evan got his revenge when they visited the Siren's Grotto bumper boats later that afternoon.

As their turn for the ride arrived, Katie and Ellie stood together, waiting for the bored ride attendant to direct them on which boat to take. He took one look at them and frowned.

"Sorry, kids," he said, "but children need to be accompanied by an adult."

"I'll have you know that I'm seventeen years old!" Katie yelled, suddenly irate as she reached into her purse and pulled out a laminated ID card. "See? Right here on my *driver's* license! *Seventeen*!"

Everyone turned toward the yelling while Evan pulled Katie back from the cowering attendant.

"Jeez, calm down!" he said, surprised by the uncharacteristic intensity in her eyes.

The attendant quickly apologized. "I'm sorry... I didn't know." He held open the gate. "Please enjoy your ride."

"Thank you!" Katie's suddenly cheery voice showed no trace of her rage from a second earlier.

"That was overly intense," Evan said as they walked around the edge of the large pool, heading for their assigned boats.

"Easy for you to say!" Katie said before sighing. "You're right. I'm sorry. I'm just so tired of that crap."

Evan could sympathize with how frustrating it must be for her. Back at school, she was regularly mistaken for a freshman. To his knowledge, only a few boys had shown any interest in dating her—mostly freshmen who thought she was cute at first, then learned she was a junior and intimidatingly academic. He genuinely wanted her to find happiness and was confident that eventually, someone would appreciate how exceptional she was and not judge her by her size and appearance. Then he remembered his teasing of her size earlier and regretted it. He would need to make sure he apologized later and catch himself from any more short jokes in the future.

"So, when did you get your driver's license?" he asked

with genuine interest, hoping to change the topic and surprised that she hadn't told him when she'd gotten it.

"Over the summer," she said enthusiastically. "Are you jealous?"

"A little, yeah. Why didn't you say anything?"

"I wanted to surprise you and Oliver by driving us all to school when school started, but I chickened out."

They arrived at the pool's edge and looked out over a fleet of bumper boats modeled like miniature pirate ships.

When they were instructed, the five of them climbed in and buckled their safety belts. The pool was around fifty feet across, with fifteen tiny boats moored along its edge. Each boat had an independent gas-powered engine, and once released, the people inside had complete control over the steering and speed. To keep everyone safe, each boat was nestled inside a series of rubber inner tubes, allowing them to crash into each other without causing harm. In addition, each boat had a water cannon mounted on the front that squirted a stream of water several feet in front of them, allowing them to attack each other.

When the bell rang, most of the boats headed toward the pool's center though Evan went straight for Sarah, aiming his water cannon with deadly precision.

Laughing aloud, he delighted in her look of shock as the cold water splashed on her shoulder and streaked across her face and torso. Her surprise from the cold water caused her to lose control temporarily, and Evan completed the task of ensuring that both her front and back were soaking wet.

Sarah tried to turn in his direction to counterattack but struggled with the controls and missed him by a mile. It didn't take long for the others to come to her defense, though, and within a few seconds, Evan was attacked by both Ellie and Hana, who rammed him from both sides.

After that, it was a free-for-all, and Evan attacked anyone and everyone who dared come within range, satisfied that his revenge was complete. After her initial struggles, Sarah got the hang of it and returned fire at every opportunity. Ten minutes later, the five of them exited the pool, soaking wet and laughing loudly.

Chapter Ten

Old Friends

The group left the amusement park much later than they had intended, having stayed well past sundown. Evan couldn't remember the last time he had so much fun and regretted that it had to end.

Sarah was the first of the little group to separate when her bus arrived before the others. Her goodbye was brief, and Evan was pleased to see that she insisted on a hug from Hana after embracing Katie and Ellie.

A short while later, the bus for the rest of them arrived—only half full, so they had plenty of seats to choose from.

"Thank you so much for inviting me, Katie," Hana said as the bus turned toward their neighborhood. "I had a lot of fun."

"You're welcome!" Katie beamed. "It was nice to see you and Sarah getting along so well."

"She's very nice," Hana said as she shot Evan a sidelong look. "And very good at games."

"Yeah, she's pretty cool," Evan said.

"Thank you." Katie smiled broadly, her dimples deepening.

When the bus arrived at Katie's stop, she gave Ellie a

fierce hug and waved to the others. A moment later, it was pulling away as Ellie leaned into Evan's shoulder and fell asleep, her exhaustion finally catching up with her.

When they finally arrived at their stop, Evan picked up Ellie and struggled to juggle their shopping bags.

"Would you like some help?" Hana asked, noticing his predicament.

"That would be awesome. Thanks!"

As they walked home, they relived their favorite parts of the day, and by the time they hit the park between their respective homes, they were laughing loudly. Evan hadn't felt this relaxed in a long time, and he thought about asking Hana what she was up to tomorrow. *Maybe she'd like to hang out—maybe just the two of us...*

An unseen voice called out from the shadows, cutting through their laughter.

"Well, hello there, Thanatos. Having a pleasant evening stroll, are we?"

Hana was startled, the remnants of her laughter dying on the wind as she came to an abrupt stop. She looked confused, though Evan sensed an underlying tension as well. The voice had a pleasant, youthful, feminine quality, but the inflection was unmistakably sinister as Evan looked around, trying to place where it was coming from.

While Evan struggled to find the speaker, Hana stared fixedly toward the center of the park, where a meandering concrete pathway flowed between several benches and a nearby swing set as a warm smile spread across her face. Evan followed her gaze and finally spied the newcomer.

The mysterious person was sitting atop a park lamp,

only her silhouette visible. The only part of her he could see was her right foot as it dangled over the edge, wrapped in a bright red shoe fastened by a strap at her ankle and a small silver buckle.

Evan squinted to get a better look at her and struggled with the blinding light of the lamp. Now that he knew where she was, he wondered how she'd gotten up there as it was easily ten feet off the ground with no structures or trees nearby.

"It's been a long time," the strange girl continued in a sickly-sweet tone, "Did you miss me?"

"Who's that?" Evan whispered to Hana.

"Good evening, Deidre," Hana said, clearly recognizing the owner of the voice.

"An old friend," Hana said quietly while she continued to watch the girl on the lamppost. "It has been a while. I didn't expect you to come visit."

"I didn't expect you to suddenly disappear," Deidre hissed back. "I'm sorry." Hana looked abashed. "Would you like to go to my house and catch up?"

"Hmmm." The other girl considered briefly before shaking her head, her annoyance evaporating. "No. I like it here better. We can be alone, and I don't think I'm quite ready to share you yet. Besides, I think I feel like playing."

While he couldn't see her clearly with the silhouetted light, he knew she was looking directly at him as she mentioned wanting to "play." Evan couldn't explain why, but he was immediately wary of the girl on the lamppost.

Her voice was soft and inviting, but as she directed her words toward him, a chill ran down his spine, causing him to shiver. Hana glanced at him from the side of her eye as her calm demeanor faded.

"You should probably take your sister and go home," Hana said. "Right now."

"But—"

Hana handed Evan the bags from their shopping trip

and gave him a sober look. "Please, Evan. Take Ellie and go home. We'll talk later."

"Awwww." Deidre playfully swung her foot back and forth. "Are you sending your little pets home? Don't you think they should stay? It'll be more fun that way."

Hana stepped away from Evan and approached the odd girl on the lamppost.

"Maybe another time," she said with a strained smile. "Like you said, this isn't the time for sharing, right?"

"Oh, very well," the girl sighed heavily.

Evan spared another glance in the lamp's direction. Something about the girl filled him with a sense of dread, causing the hairs on the back of his neck to stand up on end, but the command in Hana's voice had been unmistakable, and he felt compelled to do as she'd asked.

Slowly, Evan began moving away from the bizarre scene. He didn't want to leave Hana alone, but Ellie's safety was paramount. Whatever this was, Hana seemed to have it under control, and he trusted her judgment. The girl on the lamppost seemed to have lost interest in him, continuing her conversation with Hana, though Evan was too far away to hear them clearly. He chose a route that would take him behind some nearby bushes but allowed him to move without losing sight of the lamppost or the girl on top of it.

Once within the relative safety of the bushes, Evan wrapped Ellie up in his jacket and set her on the ground behind a large tree along with their bags. This part of the park was in complete darkness, and he didn't think the two girls could see this far. The desire to ensure Hana's safety—coupled with insane curiosity—drove Evan to sneak back to the line of bushes, moving as quietly as he could until he could once again see the two girls talking.

While he remained well hidden, the distance made it impossible to hear what they were saying, though he knew their conversation continued because Hana kept responding. A few minutes passed with Hana looking up above the lamp, talking as the other girl swung her foot back and forth. Then the discussion seemed to pause as the mysterious girl pulled her foot up and stood atop the lamp. Evan expected she was going to get herself down by sliding down the pole and was astonished when she simply stepped off, plunging toward the concrete below.

With impossible grace, she landed easily, completely unfazed by the ten-foot drop. To Evan's further surprise, Hana didn't react in the slightest to her falling ten feet without a care. With the newcomer now bathed in the lamp's light, Evan finally got a good look at her and had to slap a hand over his mouth to muffle his gasp of shock.

He recognized her.

She was unquestionably the same girl he had seen standing outside their school and from the news article about the "Graveyard Smasher." Somehow, this odd, mysterious girl who the police suspected of tearing up entire cemeteries was standing a few feet in front of Hana, talking like old friends.

Evan remained still, watching their conversation and wondering who she was and under what circumstances Hana knew her. He guessed she was one of Hana's friends from Greece, though he couldn't imagine the strange girl living in the countryside. As he continued to spy on them, he couldn't shake the sensation that there was something unsettling, even threatening about her. He thought about calling the police but hesitated, choosing to watch their interaction further.

As they talked, something Hana said must have struck the younger girl as funny. In a smooth, effortless movement, she threw her head back and spun around on one foot while laughing loudly. Her amusement seemed to ease some tension in Hana, and she looked a little more relaxed.

Evan had the exact opposite reaction to Deidre's laugh. He caught the edges of the sound, and it sent a wave of shivers through him. The girl's laugh was tinged with a hysterical edge that unsettled him even from this distance. As she spun, Evan noticed she was holding something in her left land he couldn't see previously: some kind of stuffed animal.

At first, he assumed it was a teddy bear or something, but the shape was obviously wrong. It had an elongated, thin body with arms that reached nearly its feet and a short, stubby tail. It had a bear-like snout with a permanently stitched evil grin for a mouth and two miss-matched black beads for eyes. It was disturbing to look at—some monstrous mockery of a child's toy.

On her third spin, the light from the lamp reflected off the strange toy's eyes, and for an instant, they gleamed with a bright red glow. At that moment, Evan's eyes locked with the small toy, and he knew he'd been spotted.

In some horrible way, that thing was alive!

Deidre stopped instantly, and her head whipped around to look directly at Evan. A fresh wave of fear struck him as he realized she knew he was there, despite the distance and darkness.

Hana followed Deidre's gaze, and her eyes widened when she saw Evan. He couldn't imagine how they could see him hiding in the dark bushes, but all three of them were staring directly at him: Hana, Deidre, and the disfigured bear.

For a moment, everything froze, then chaos erupted.

The stuffed thing jumped out of Deidre's hands and ran directly toward Evan's hiding spot. As the thing ran, it grew, doubling in the space of a few feet and continuing its rapid engorgement.

Evan froze in shock. He couldn't process the impossible scenario playing out in front of him. The strange toy continued to grow as it barreled toward him, distorting as it went, growing larger and more grotesque with each step. It made a half-growling, half-choking sound as it ran, repulsing Evan and causing him to fall backward.

This couldn't be real. Could it?

The creature kept coming. With a horrifying tearing sound, the stitching of its mouth ripped apart to show two rows of razor-sharp teeth, and a huge, green tongue rolled out of its mouth, spraying spittle with every bound. Its growl became a maniacal roar.

Beyond the approaching creature, Hana yelled something to Deidre, who was racked by another round of hysterical laughter. With her head cocked to one side, she looked at Evan through a waterfall of dark hair, her eyes glinting in macabre delight at his impending evisceration.

Evan couldn't move. Panic rooted him in place between the bushes. He knew he needed to run before the distorted horror reached him, but disbelief assaulted him that any of this could be real. The absurd impossibility of it all warred with every instinct in his body.

Hana's scream from across the small park finally

sparked him to action. "Evan!"

The sound of her distress broke him out of his daze, and he found he could move once again.

As he picked himself off the ground, another horrendous ripping sound came from the approaching monster as a set of blade-like claws erupted from each of the now massive arms. As it charged toward him, those claws scraped across the concrete path, sending sparks flying as it carved deep gouges into the stone. The terrifying sound resonated within Evan's bones, and he felt as much as heard the agony of the lacerated concrete.

Waves of terror coursed through him, and the modicum of courage he had gathered quickly fled, leaving him petrified once again. He had to get away, grab Ellie, and get as far away from here as possible, but his terror robbed him of any chance at running. His entire body felt so weak and powerless that all he could do was remain standing.

Evan clearly heard Deirdre's childish voice as it closed. "Deimos," she said coolly, "*kill.*"

Evan tore his gaze away from his oncoming demise and looked desperately at Hana. Their eyes met for a moment, and her expression changed from concerned apprehension to one of steely determination. Then she began moving.

Hana reached down and grabbed the edge of her skirt, pulling it up and exposing her left leg to her hip. Down the entire length of her left leg stretched a long, dark tattoo. It went from just above her ankle up to the top of her thigh. The image was that of an intricate black and silver scythe.

Even from this distance, Evan could see the incredible

artistry of the image. It was exquisite in every detail, with a long black shaft down its length and a grip near its center. The shaft itself had a slight S curve to it and looked sleek and smooth as it stretched to her ankle. Near her hip was a vicious-looking silver blade that wrapped around her side, coming to a point someplace beyond view. The blade was a bright silver that gleamed in the dim light of the park lamp. Evan could easily imagine someone cutting themselves if they dared to touch it.

Reaching down and across with her right hand, Hana moved as if she intended to grab it. As her hand neared, the entire length of the sinister-looking weapon glowed briefly and in the next moment was comfortably in her grip, leaving the length of her leg bare.

Deidre's laughter ended abruptly as Hana leaped into the air, jumping twenty feet straight up. While ascending, she swung the weapon up in a long, curving arc. As the scythe sliced the air, the blade's edge glowed brightly, leaving behind a silver sickle of light in its wake. When her swing reached its apex, the crescent of light flew off the blade and moved forward at incredible speed.

The monstrosity was nearly upon Evan, slowing its forward momentum as it raised its arm, ready to strike. With an evil grin spreading across its face, it let out an eager growl of anticipation as the gleaming bladed paw fell.

The glowing crescent of light struck the creature's back and cleaved it in half. As the sickle of light passed through the beast and beyond, Evan was enveloped in a white cloud of padded viscera. Fluff and stuffing rained down around him as the creature exploded open and fell into two pieces around him.

Hana landed lightly on the ground. "Leave him alone," she said, pointing her scythe at Deidre.

"So, you *do* want to play." A sinister smile spread across Deidre's face as she turned her attention back to Hana.

Hana took a cautionary step backward as Deidre reached around to her bag, pulling it to her chest and thrusting her arm deep within. Laughing maniacally, Deidre pulled forth an armful of terrible, miniature stuffed animals, each unique unto itself, all of them nightmarish. Each was a grotesque mutation of what might once have been an adorable stuffed animal; their horrific deformities and threatening assortment of claws, teeth, and spines distorted any resemblance it had to a cute and cuddly toy.

With abandon, Deidre tossed the creatures to the ground, where they exploded in size and horror, reaching back into her bag for more. Her creations ranged from a few feet tall to well over six feet, and as they landed, they plunged toward Hana, snarling, flying, or oozing their way across the small park.

As each monster attacked, Hana responded calmly, with unnatural grace and speed, her scythe slashing in silver arcs. Evan watched in astonishment as she worked her way through the small army of terrors, jumping, spinning, and maneuvering through the pack with ease. Each time she moved, she swung her scythe through a monster, causing it to explode in a small cloud of stuffing and stitches. Within moments, the park was littered with the remnants of their nightmarish bodies.

Deidre appeared to have an unending supply of the monsters in her little backpack as she bounced, laughed, and cartwheeled around the edge of the small concrete square. Every time Hana cut a distorted creature down, Deidre threw more into the fray.

Motion close to him drew Evan's attention away from the spectacle of the two girls battling. At first, he couldn't tell what had caught his eye, but as he looked closer, what he saw filled him with terror and disbelief.

The remains of the defeated monster lay at his feet, its two halves sliced cleanly with mounds of stuffing and fluff scattered about on the ground. As he watched, he spied a single length of black thread stealthily and methodically weaving its way in and out of the edges of the monster's disconnected leg. As it went, it carefully drew the new stitches tight, pulling the piece of leg up to the torso, reconnecting the severed limb.

He tried to call Hana's name, but his mouth wouldn't work. Evan could only watch, frozen in disbelief. Once the limb rejoined the body, the thread moved on to another damaged section, and the deflated leg began growing as if the missing stuffing was regenerating itself now that it was whole once again.

"Ha—" He tried saying her name again but could only produce a squeak. A profound terror he had never known robbed him of his voice.

As though whatever force was at work to repair the monstrosity realized he had noticed, the thread sped up, working faster to repair the monster. As Evan watched in shock, he saw a second thread join the first, arriving from the direction of the creepy little girl as she threw another handful of monsters at Hana.

Now that he knew what to look for, Evan noticed that each time Deidre reached into her bag for more monsters, she was also drawing forth threaded needles.

As she threw the next batch, Evan noticed that the needles and thread weren't headed in his direction but to an area Hana had just vacated as she worked her way through another wave of attackers.

Evan worried that the small army was likely putting themselves back together, just like the monster at his feet, but a fresh surge of terror racked him as he saw something much worse. Instead of simply repairing themselves, the dismembered monsters were sewing themselves to each other, forming an abomination of dozens of horrors rolled into one.

Hana hadn't noticed. She was busy dealing with the steady stream of the beasts that Deidre threw upon the battleground. It was clear to Evan that this had been Deidre's plan from the beginning: distract Hana while a new and more terrible horror formed behind her to catch her unaware.

He had to do something. He had to protect Hana.

His paralysis suddenly lifted, and Evan leaped into motion, sprinting toward the center of the battlefield.

As he began moving, a blast of air from behind him propelled him forward, accompanied by the sound of ripping fabric and something like bones scraping together. He felt nothing at first, but on his next step, his back flared in an explosion of pain. The beast hadn't finished putting itself together yet but had swiped at him as he ran past.

He could feel the warmth spreading across his back and down his sides as the gash bled profusely. Exerting all his will, he forced himself to push through the pain. The behemoth behind Hana was half-formed, and she was about to be blindsided.

As he ran, his lungs were on fire, the taste of blood

filling his mouth as his breaths came in great gasps, drying him out and stealing his voice. He knew he couldn't call out the warning he had initially intended, but he was moving, and the two girls weren't that far away. He knew he could reach them if he kept going. He pushed himself to reach Hana in time, even as his vision blurred, and he lost feeling in his extremities.

As Evan closed the distance, the abomination finished forming itself on the far side of the battlefield. He was nearly there, with only a small wooden bench between himself and the two girls.

Deidre saw Evan's approach first and gave him a mocking smile. "Oh look, Thanatos—here comes your hero!"

Hana looked back at him, her eyes wide with terror.

Evan launched himself over the bench with all of his remaining strength. As he flew over, his leg trailed too far behind, and his foot caught on the top of the seatback. He collided with the bench with a terrible crash. Pain erupted everywhere as his momentum plunged him off the bench and onto the concrete below. With a single roll, he came to a stop on the cool pathway.

"Oh," Deidre giggled at Evan's crumpled form. "I guess not."

All thought left him as he lay motionless, pain blaring everywhere. A trickle of blood ran down his face as his other wounds oozed beneath him. A small puddle appeared at his waist where the blood from the gouges in his back seeped under him.

Evan looked down at the spreading pool of blood and vaguely remembered a similar scene years ago but couldn't hold on to the thought for long.

"Sooooo heroic," Deidre snickered.

Hana stared at Evan's crumpled form. He could feel himself slipping into unconsciousness, but not before doing what he had to do. With the last of his strength, Evan raised one hand and pointed beyond her, where the monster was closing in.

As Hana turned and looked, the thing rose to its full height, nearly twenty feet tall. It was a mass of arms, legs, and teeth. Spines and scales spread haphazardly over its amorphous body, and a hundred button eyes erupted across its massive form.

Hana bellowed a terrifying scream of agony and rage. The sound cleared Evan's vision for a moment, and all he could see was her. A cold, ominous breeze began churning beneath her with her scythe in hand, billowing out her skirt and sending her silver hair swirling. The whirlwind began gathering nearby fluff, and within seconds, Hana stood in the eye of a vortex of wind and debris. Her eyes were wide with rage as she screamed at the towering behemoth.

Even as it reached toward her, she moved in a flurry of motion, tearing through the air in front of her dozens of times, so fast that all Evan saw was a blur of silver and black. Each slice was resplendent in silver light as they struck the monstrous horror again and again. The creature didn't have time to pull back before it erupted in a cloud of fabric, buttons, and stuffing. There wasn't a piece remaining larger than a finger's length.

As the debris rained down, Hana stood for a second, breathing, then turned toward him. "Evan!"

She carelessly discarded the scythe as she knelt, and the magical weapon vanished before touching the ground.

Reaching down tenderly, Hana cupped Evan's head in

her hands and gently turned him to face her. Tears flowed down her cheeks and fell upon Evan's upturned face.

"Why didn't you just go home?" she asked, her voice weak and beseeching.

Behind her, Deidre stood motionless, watching, assessing. "How very amusing," she said before turning away, melding into the darkness of the park. The grotesquely enormous bear followed, shrinking as it ran to catch up.

As Deidre disappeared, Evan looked back at Hana one last time before losing consciousness, his vision filling with a cool, silver glow.

Chapter Eleven

Revelations

Evan awoke groggy and fuzzy-headed, the remnants of something scary and worrisome slinking away as his surroundings came into focus. He was in his bed with sunlight pouring in from half-open blinds. A glance at the clock told him he had slept in late, and the morning was well underway.

He tried to remember how he had arrived in his room and couldn't recall coming home the night before. As he tried to remember, all he could come up with was a hazy image of Hana jumping around and fighting demonic stuffed animals. The only thing he could recall was his collision with the bench, which ended with his blood pouring out onto the concrete.

Evan sat up with a start, hands reaching for his back. His skin was smooth and dry, with no blood, no wounds, nothing. Remembering how he'd hit his head after crashing into the bench, he searched his forehead and found that it was completely intact, without a scratch or bruise anywhere on it. He was perfectly fine.

"Was it all just a dream?" he asked the empty room.

Looking around, he spotted the new shoes and backpack they'd brought home from the mall next to

Ellie's bed on her half of the room. As he continued to scan, his eyes fell upon her new bathing suit, and in a rush, the memory of hiding with Hana in the small changing booth came crashing back. He vividly recalled his confession and the unforgettable kiss that followed.

Evan breathed a sigh of relief. At least *that* part had been real.

Suddenly, his strange dream about a battle in the park seemed ridiculous, and he quickly dismissed it as a product of too much excitement from their adventures at the mall. With a spring in his step, Evan got ready for the day ahead.

When he joined the rest of the family a short while later, Ellie was in the living room watching television and eating cereal while his aunt sat at their small dining table, reading a newspaper and sipping her morning coffee.

"Well, look who finally rose from the dead," his aunt teased. "Did you sleep well?"

"Yes, I did, thank you," Evan said as he loaded a slice of bread into the toaster.

"I was just about to come wake you up," Ellie said between spoonfuls, eyes still glued to her TV show. "Don't you have to work today?"

"Yeah. I can't believe I slept in so late."

Aunt Maddie nodded. "I'm not surprised. You looked exhausted when you got home last night."

As he waited for his toast, he tried to recall the end of the previous day. He clearly remembered the bus stop and walking home with Hana while carrying Ellie, but after that, it blurred into that bizarre dream, with no memory of leaving the park, getting to their apartment, or climbing into bed.

"You were here when we got home?" he asked.

"Of course. I stayed awake until I was sure you two were home safe," Maddie said. "You got back much later than I expected. I was beginning to worry."

"Really?" Evan asked, troubled that he couldn't remember getting home. "Um, did I look okay? I mean, were my clothes all right?"

"I guess?" His aunt tilted her head to the side and looked at him with a blank expression. "I'm not sure I know what you mean."

Evan didn't know how to ask if he had come home with shredded, blood-soaked clothing or if there had been a massive gash across his forehead—at least not without raising a bunch of new, awkward questions.

"Sorry, never mind," he said, knowing that if he had arrived home bloodied, his aunt wouldn't be so relaxed this morning.

It seemed impossible that he had nearly died at the hands of a giant demonic stuffed bear. The fact that his taxed mind had projected images of the "Graveyard Smasher" girl into his dream just proved how absurd the whole thing was. It still surprised him how stubbornly the hazy dream lingered instead of fading away like nearly all of his others.

His toast popped up, hot and ready. Evan returned to making his breakfast by slathering it with copious amounts of grape jelly.

"So, should I read anything into the fact that Hana escorted you home last night?" his aunt asked unexpectedly.

The jelly knife slipped out of Evan's hands and bounced on the counter, ringing loudly across the small kitchen. Both Maddie and Ellie looked at him quizzically.

"Uh, no," he tried to sound nonchalant. "She was just helping me carry stuff because Ellie fell asleep."

"Well, that was nice of her," Maddie remarked with a note of amusement.

As his aunt returned to reading her paper, Evan sat down across from her and began eating his toast. His thoughts quickly returned to Hana and the events from the day before. Just the thought of her made his heart skip and a smile spread across his face. He wanted to share the burgeoning details of his relationship with his aunt, but until things were more official, he decided it was best to keep it private. Luckily, his aunt had no idea anything was going on between them.

"So, are you two dating?" Maddie asked casually from behind her paper.

Evan spat out his mouthful of jellied toast, spewing it across the small table and into the back of her newspaper.

"What..." he sputtered. "What do you mean?"

Aunt Maddie lowered her paper and looked at him quizzically, bursting into laughter a second later.

"You're dating Hana?" Ellie asked from the other room.

Evan's head swung back and forth between Ellie and Aunt Maddie, his mind struggling to come up with an adequate answer. He was saved by the alarm on his phone, reminding him it was time to leave for work.

"Gotta go!" He jumped up from the kitchen table, grateful for the timely excuse to retreat from their interrogation despite having plenty of time before he needed to arrive at the bookstore.

"Like dating, dating?" Ellie asked insistently. "Evan!"

He ignored her, determined to escape.

"Don't forget to take your scarf," Aunt Maddie called as Evan threw on his shoes and jacket. "It's going to be chilly tonight, and you don't want to catch a cold."

"Bye!" he said as he headed out, grabbing his scarf on his way.

It was a lovely morning, and Evan skipped the bus and walked to work. As he went, he considered how to answer his aunt's question. He wasn't exactly certain what his relationship with Hana was at that moment. He had told her how he felt, albeit indirectly, and he could only interpret her kiss as an acceptance of those feelings, but it wasn't like they'd talked about it. He turned it over in his mind as he walked, still reveling in the recent turn of events when he arrived at the strip mall.

Walking across the parking lot, he saw Mr. Abernathy's beat-up Datsun pickup truck in its usual spot and was looking forward to seeing him. The shop had been especially quiet, and he had missed the company. He enjoyed how he could never anticipate what impulsive and erratic thing Mr. Abernathy might do or say next.

Evan unlocked the door and entered the shop, reassured to see the light coming from the back office that Mr. Abernathy practically lived in.

"Good morning!" Evan called out as he closed the front door, then headed toward the counter to hang up his jacket and scarf.

"Is that you, Evan?"

"Yup. Just getting ready to open up."

Mr. Abernathy was an older man, likely in his late sixties or early seventies. He was rather short with the tanned skin of someone who spends a lot of time outdoors, with his arms sporting plenty of freckles. Atop his head he had a crown of fluffy white hair around a growing bald patch and a spectacular handlebar mustache. As usual, he wore beige slacks and a short-sleeved white, button-up collared shirt, complete with a bow tie. Today, he was wearing his red one with white polka dots.

Wearing his usual reading glasses and trademark smile, Mr. Abernathy emerged from the back of the shop, carrying a large cardboard box with a plastic grocery bag balanced on top. Evan watched as he carried the precarious stack to the counter and set them down.

"I came back with some wonderful new items for the shop," Mr. Abernathy said with a sparkle in his eyes. "When you have some time, would you mind setting these up?"

"Sure thing." Evan opened the box to inspect its contents.

Inside, he found a small group of beautiful geodes, both big and small, with sparkling purple and blue crystals encased in layered stone. There were eleven stones in total, ranging from the size of a golf ball to as large as a football. Evan took a glance around the cluttered shop, trying to imagine where he would find the space for them all.

"Um, where do you want these to go?" he asked.

"Up front somewhere," Mr. Abernathy said as he waved one hand in the general direction of the front of the shop. "I'm sure you'll find a good place for them. Though you'll need to price them first."

Evan looked down at the stones and sighed. This would take some creative reorganizing if they were going to be in the front of the shop. As for pricing, he didn't have a clue what geodes of this size and variety would typically sell for. They had never carried them before, so he had no reference.

"Uh, about pricing," he said. "How much should I sell them for?"

"Whatever you think is appropriate," Mr. Abernathy said as he turned one stone over in his hands to examine it.

"Um, okay... How much did you pay for them? I'll start there."

"Oh, I have no idea; I just had to have them." He set the stone on the counter and patted Evan on the back. "I'm sure whatever you decide will be fine."

"And what about these?" He ruffled the plastic bag. "What are they?"

The elderly man's face lit up again as he rooted through the bag, pulling out items wrapped in tissue paper.

"I met this wonderful artist from Sedona who did the most marvelous work with turquoise. These are some of her creations. Aren't they sublime?"

As he explained, he pulled out several pieces of handmade jewelry and a small stack of business cards from the artist. Evan had to admit they were beautiful and well crafted. Most of the designs included swirls and curves, which, combined with the blue-green of the stones, reminded him of the ocean. He could see their appeal and guessed that they would likely sell quickly. Luckily, the jewelry all had their original price tags still attached to them.

"Would you like me to price these, too?" Evan asked.

"Or just leave the tags on." Mr. Abernathy smiled, then headed back to his office, waving over his shoulder. "Whichever you think is best."

Evan often wondered how Mr. Abernathy made any money at all, let alone be able to afford to pay him. But he had never failed to give Evan his check on time, so he quickly shrugged it off.

He found a home for the jewelry in the crowded case under the front counter. After marking them up, Evan rearranged the other jewelry to create a separate space for the new pieces.

Before he could address the stones, however, the door opened, and the small bell chimed, announcing a new patron. As Evan had predicted, the shop was busy that day, with many regular customers visiting now that Mr. Abernathy was back.

It wasn't until late afternoon that the shop finally quieted down, and Evan could focus on finding a home for the geodes.

After an extensive survey of the front of the shop, he found a promising shelf that currently held three sets of custom handcrafted tarot decks. Each deck was themed for an ancient mythology: Egyptian, Greek, and Norse. Evan recalled from a few months earlier when Mr. Abernathy told him to move the cards to the front because no one had inquired about buying them in years. Evan knew why no one had purchased them, though, and moving them to the front of the store wouldn't help.

It wasn't the quality. Each one came with a ten-inch square wooden case with a glass window for a lid. Visible through the glass were three example cards and a booklet describing the lore, how to read the tarot, and some information about the artists. There was no doubt they were valuable, with over seventy-five gorgeous, hand-painted cards in each set.

The problem was their price. Few people could afford

to pay $700 for a deck of tarot cards, even ones as masterfully crafted as these. Evan had once suggested that they lower the price, but Mr. Abernathy had remained unusually stubborn on the matter. So, they had sat at the front of the shop, needing to be dusted often, as very few patrons even looked at them because of the bold price tag stuck to their glass.

Evan took the case with the Norse cards and headed into the back of the shop. With a little rearranging, he could create space near the other, more reasonably priced tarot decks. After placing the Egyptian deck, Evan was headed back with the Greek set when one card caught his attention through the glass case, causing him to stop mid-step.

The Death card stared up at him with a beautifully painted Grim Reaper on its front. The skulled figure wore a black hooded cloak and held within its hand a threatening-looking scythe. The weapon was complete with a black shaft and a broad silver blade. Roses were painted behind each shoulder, and they enclosed the figure in a series of green, thorny vines and black lines, making the entire image resemble a stained-glass window. A label across the top read "Death," but at the bottom, painted across the framed lines, was the name "Thanatos."

Deidre's voice echoed through his mind from the night before: "Well, hello there, Thanatos, having a nice evening stroll, are we?"

And again, near the end: "Oh look, Thanatos—here comes your hero!"

Looking down at the card, chills raced down his spine. He stared at it for a few minutes, his mind resisting the apparent connection. Thanatos. Hana.

"Everything okay there, Evan?" Mr. Abernathy asked, leaning out of his office, and Evan realized he must have stood motionless for some time.

"Yes, sir. Sorry," he said as he snapped out of his reverie.

Evan finished his task, setting the new merchandise on their display and returning to his place behind the counter just as the bell for the front door rang and more customers arrived. As he worked, Evan's thoughts kept returning to the Death card and the scene from the park the night before.

It was a dream, wasn't it? Didn't it have to be a dream? It couldn't have been real, right?

He wasn't so sure anymore.

The store slowed down about an hour before closing when Mr. Abernathy announced he was leaving for a cup of coffee and a snack.

"Would you like anything?" he asked.

"Uh, no, thank you. I'm fine."

As soon as the door closed, Evan headed to the rear of the shop for the book on Greek Mythology he had referenced for his essay. Back at the counter, he checked the table of contents for Thanatos and flipped to that page. The section on Thanatos was near the back of the book, much farther than he had skimmed when writing his essay.

"Thanatos, God of Death," he said, reading aloud. "Son to Erebus, the primordial God of Darkness, and Nyx, the goddess of the night. Twin brother to Hypnos, the God of Sleep and Dreams. Thanatos was responsible for securing the souls of the dead and ferrying them to the underworld."

The section continued to describe the stories of

Thanatos, Heracles, and Sisyphus. It was standard Greek mythology material: a quest, a great misdeed, and a curse. There was nothing that struck him as particularly useful.

Then he saw the author's note at the bottom of the page.

"Thanatos is a fairly lonely creature in Grecian lore," he read. "Unlike many Greek Gods, no mention is made of any loving relationship surrounding him. Mortals fear him, and his presence fills them with dread. While powerful in his own domain, he is ever alone. Surrounded only by death, the dying, and the dead. Though he was born of two of the most powerful gods in ancient lore, Thanatos appears to have no friends or rivals among the other gods, other than a close connection to his brother, Hypnos."

Evan flipped to the entry for Hypnos.

"Hypnos, God of Sleep and Dreams," he read. "Son to Erebus, the primordial God of Darkness, and Nyx, the Goddess of the Night. Twin brother to Thanatos. Lived within a cave in the underworld on the isle of Lemnos, surrounded by the Lethe River, where all those who drank from it experienced absolute forgetfulness. Often portrayed as lounging on his soft couch surrounded by his many sons and his Oneiroi (demigods of dreams)."

The rest of Hypnos's section contained several stories of his many escapades and multiple marriages. It wasn't quite Zeus-level, but Evan got the sense that Hypnos got around.

Curious to see if the tarot deck included Hypnos, he brought it back to the counter. It wasn't a card he could see under the glass lid, so Evan carefully opened the case and pulled the set of cards out of their velvet bag.

He handled the hand-painted cards with special care, slowly turning over each one in the deck and stopping when he came to the Five of Swords. The image was that of a scared young boy with short black hair. He sat huddled on a bed, with a bright red blanket wrapped around him and spilling onto the floor. Looming behind the bed was a large shadowy form with arms extended wide, hands ending in long black claws.

At first glance, the child appeared terrified, but as Evan leaned close, he could see that he didn't look scared, but menacing. His head tilted down slightly, and the pupils peering from the tops of his eyes had an evil glint to them. Along with the unsettling glare, he wore a one-sided smirk. Looking at it this way, the red blanket resembled blood running off the bed, pooling on the ground in front of it.

As Evan looked closely, he decided that the little boy looked far more terrifying than the looming shadow behind him. The evil smirk and shadowy monster reminded Evan of the girl from the night before and the monsters she summoned. The name on the bottom of the card was "Phobos and Deimos."

According to the book, Phobos and Deimos were the gods of fear, panic, terror, and dread. They were the sons of Ares, the God of War, and they would follow him onto the field of battle, spreading terror into the hearts of Ares's enemies. After staring at it for a few moments, Evan shuddered and quickly put the card back, continuing his search for Hypnos.

Eventually, Evan came across The Moon. At the bottom, the card was named "Hypnos."

The image was of a night sky with a large full moon. Lounging on a soft, cushiony couch was an angelic-looking man with long, curly dark hair. Above each ear, a set of small red wings poked out of the tangles of hair. The man wore a loose toga draped across his body. He looked relaxed and on the edge of sleep.

Resting at the foot of the couch was an assortment of animals. There were rats, possums, raccoons, dogs, and cats, each with a set of black wings emerging from their back. While Hypnos looked away, drowsing, the animals all looked forward, staring directly at Evan.

The artistry was amazing, and each card evoked a powerful reaction as he looked at them. Zeus was mighty and regal, the thunderbolt in his hand almost crackling off the image. Aphrodite was unbelievably beautiful and seductive, the glint in her eyes almost inviting you to step into her arms. Ares was fearsome and bestial, a maniacal grin stretching across his face as blood dripped from the blades of the sword and ax, one in each hand. Evan found a new appreciation for the quality of the cards and reconsidered whether they were overpriced.

Evan looked over a few more of the cards, not really seeing them before he carefully returned them to their velvet pouch and glass case. As he was placing them back, he recognized the name "Nyx" on the Four of Swords.

Within the stained-glass frame of silver and gold, stood a beautiful older woman. Her eyes were closed, and her face slightly tilted down with a restful smile. Her arms were spread wide as if she was waiting to give a loving embrace. Her dress was the night's sky, resplendent in stars, galaxies, and nebulae.

In one last spurt of curiosity, he looked for Erebus, but he didn't find a card dedicated to him.

Evan quickly finished putting away the deck and

mythology book and returned to his post behind the counter. By the time Mr. Abernathy returned, Evan was occupying himself with a game on his phone. While his fingers absently followed the motions and colors of the game, his mind was far away, contemplating ancient gods and a very talented tarot artist.

While he must have looked relaxed to any onlooker, inside, Evan was a swirling mass of emotion. He couldn't shake the thought that he had witnessed a battle between the Greek gods of death and fear. It seemed impossible, yet it explained the unbelievable events he had witnessed the night before. The more he thought about it, the more certain he became.

"Hey, Mr. Abernathy?" Evan asked as he closed the shop. "Do you think that the Greek gods were real?"

The elderly man sipped his coffee and considered for a moment. "Well, that's an interesting question."

"Or any of the old gods, for that matter," Evan said. "You know, Egyptian, Norse, Hindu..."

After a few moments of careful consideration, Mr. Abernathy finally answered. "What do you think?"

"I don't know."

"That's a good answer," Mr. Abernathy said. "How can we ever really know? But I can say this: they are no less real today than when they ruled the hearts and minds of men."

Evan sighed. He didn't know what he had hoped to hear from a quirky old man who thought he could see the future in glass balls and funny cards.

"Thanks, Mr. Abernathy. Good night." Evan waved as he grabbed his jacket and scarf and went home.

"Good night, Evan."

Evan's mind was still spinning by the time he approached the park near his apartment. On any other day, Evan would have cut through it without a thought, but today he paused at its entrance, filled with a sense of foreboding. He suddenly wasn't sure he had the courage to enter it again. *Maybe I should walk around*, he thought to himself.

As he stood there with the sun setting behind him, he nervously fiddled with his scarf and could barely wrap his head around the concept that his almost-girlfriend was the Grim Reaper. It seemed completely ridiculous, but another part of him already believed. Even discounting the crazy battle in the park, there were too many parallels to ignore. Like the way she creeped everyone out, how she described her home life, and the bizarre things that had been happening to him since she arrived.

However, his biggest dilemma was what it would mean if it were true. Could he stay friends with such a person? From his minimal research into Greek lore, mortals who got wrapped up with the gods never fared well, usually ending up screwed over, cursed, or worse. The sensible thing to do would be to walk away now while he still had the chance.

Even now, he wished he was with her, talking, laughing, or picking up where they left off in the changing booth. If he was going to cut Hana out of his life, it wouldn't be over his overactive imagination or fantasies. He needed proof.

He continued into the park with determined steps, heading directly for the lamppost where it had all started the night before. The light buzzed to life as he approached, making him hesitate, but there was no scary little girl and her bag of nightmares tonight.

At first glance, everything seemed normal. The bench he had smashed into was free of blood or stains. He saw no piles of fluff or remnants of fabric nor any evidence that a battle of magic and monsters had taken place here a little less than twenty-four hours earlier.

He sat down on the bench and looked at the night sky.

"I must have dreamed it after all," he said to the empty park, a sense of relief washing over him. Leaning back, Evan relaxed and enjoyed the cool evening breeze.

He sat there for several minutes, watching a few clouds roll by as stars appeared in the increasingly dark blue sky while the trees and bushes swayed playfully in the wind. He felt silly for worrying so much over something so ridiculous. With an enormous sigh of relief, he stood up and was about to leave when something caught his attention.

Across from the bench was a line of leafy bushes, set side-by-side near a children's swing set. He had seen them countless times but had never paid them any heed. As he looked at them now, though, he realized something odd about their shape. His curiosity piqued, so he got up and walked over to get a better look.

The top third of one bush was missing, cleanly sliced at an unusual angle. The damage had been recent, with newly cut branches and partially sliced leaves scattered across its top. Now that he was closer, he could tell that it had happened in a single slice across the plant as if a giant blade had cut the bush nearly in half.

A blade... or a magic scythe.

With an idea of what to look for, Evan turned and surveyed the park again. His earlier reassurance that it had all been a dream crumbled away as he could see dozens of instances where the plants around the park had received collateral damage from the previous night's battle. Walking to the approximate spot where Hana had battled the monstrosities the night before, Evan felt certain that all the damage to the surrounding flora had originated from this point. While surveying the terrain, a new chill ran through him that had nothing to do with the cooling temperature.

The memory of the silvery arcs of light flying from Hana's scythe came unbidden. Standing in the battle's epicenter, he could easily picture the blades of light slashing through the monsters she had fought. Once through the stuffed creatures, they had cleanly cleaved leaves and branches as they flew into the dark recesses of the park.

As he stood there in the face of overwhelming evidence, he still resisted the reality of it all. He desperately wanted to believe that it had all been a dream and that none of this was real. As he stood and looked, he realized that there was one piece of evidence from last night that couldn't be explained by any other means and headed off toward the bushes he had hidden in the night before.

A few feet from the spot where he'd been, he found what he was looking for. On the concrete path leading to where he had spied on the two girls were four sets of parallel gashes, several inches deep. Squatting, he ran his fingers down smooth grooves, remembering the terrible rending sound from when the monster's claws had gouged them. As he examined the cuts, his back spasmed in remembered pain. Goosebumps erupted all over his body, and he felt the ghost of the terror from the night before.

"It was all real," he breathed. "It wasn't a dream."

Leaves crackled behind him, and he whirled around, suddenly terrified that some horrible stuffed monster was bearing down upon him. Or, worse, a Greek god in the form of a cute little goth girl with a maniacal smile. But the park was deserted.

As his pulse gradually slowed, Evan stayed crouched over the damaged concrete path for a few moments before standing back up, feeling dizzy and nauseous. He staggered back to the bench and fell into it heavily.

As he sat there, his mind began replaying all the other bizarre events he had experienced since meeting Hana. He recalled how much it had hurt when he'd run into her on her first day, as if she was so strong that running into her was the same as running into a brick wall. Or how he fell asleep so unexpectedly while in her living room, sitting across from her sister, Hypnos. She was good at everything she tried to do, quickly picking up things like bowling and golf, even on her first attempt.

Then there were other oddities; things like how pizza, malls, and video games were foreign to her, as if she'd grown up not in another country but in another world or time. Besides her effortless skill and unfamiliarity with modern life, there were the unnatural reactions nearly everyone had toward her. As if they instinctively knew that she was dangerous, something to avoid and despise.

His musings eventually came around to their visit to Thousand Oaks and Mrs. Richardson. He had been saddened to hear of her death that night but had thought little of it other than wondering if he had been the last person to talk to her alive. Only now did he remember he hadn't been the last person. In fact, he had been out of the room, fetching her glasses, and it had been Hana who had been leaning in, befriending the elderly woman, listening to the stories of her past.

The realization struck him like a physical blow, knocking the wind out of him and causing him to slide off the bench, falling to his knees. There were no doubts now about who or what she was.

He had fallen in love with Death.

Chapter Twelve

Misunderstandings

The next morning, Evan could barely focus his eyes on his way to school. Sleep had evaded him the night before, his thoughts fixating on Hana and what he should do. When he met up with his friends at their usual corner, Katie and Oliver exchanged concerned looks.

"Hey, man, are you okay?" Oliver asked.

"Yeah, are you feeling all right?" Katie added.

"I'm fine." Evan sounded lifeless, even to his own ears.

"Really?" Oliver frowned. "'Cuz you look like crap."

"I said I'm fine, didn't I?" Evan said, grumbling. "I just didn't sleep well—that's all."

He hoped that would be the end of their questions—questions for which he didn't have any answers. He had turned over the situation all night and was more conflicted now than when he'd first discovered her secret. The three of them walked in silence for a while, and as they rounded a corner, Evan kicked a nearby rock out of frustration, flinging it down the road.

"Dammit!" he mumbled under his breath.

Carefully, Katie reached out and grasped his forearm lightly. "Evan, what's wrong?"

The unexpected touch caught Evan by surprise, and he yanked his arm away from her without thinking. A wave of embarrassment compounded his sour mood.

"I don't want to talk about it, all right? So just drop it."

Before she could react, Evan sped up and put some distance between himself and his friends. When he was sure they wouldn't try to catch up, he resumed his usual pace. A few minutes later, his anger subsided, leaving only guilt for overreacting.

Looking back over his shoulder, he saw the two of them walking several feet behind, neither of them talking to each other. With a half-turn so they could see his face, he stopped walking and waited for them to catch up. Seeing their guarded, wary expressions as they approached made him feel even worse.

"I'm sorry," he said when the others arrived. "That was uncalled for."

"No problem," Oliver said as he smiled and wrapped an arm around Evan's shoulder. "We've all had those days. Don't sweat it."

A quick look at Katie showed she wore a smile of her own, silently offering her support for whatever was troubling him. Evan's mood brightened in the warmth of their friendship, though he couldn't shake his worries about Hana.

How might his friends react if they found out that his sort-of girlfriend was the Grim Reaper? Would they be as freaked out as he was? Or worse... would they be in danger?

When he finally got to his desk, all his thoughts circled around Hana, who would walk into class any minute. It wasn't long before she arrived, books in hand

and a smile on her face. As she approached her desk, she spared a glance in Evan's direction, a searching look in her eyes.

Evan broke out into a cold sweat when their eyes met. At that moment, he must have failed to mask his inner turmoil because while he had intended to smile back to reassure her, whatever she saw on his face had the opposite effect. Her smile vanished, and she quickly took her seat without looking back.

Evan watched as Katie greeted Hana warmly, and a chill ran through him at how familiar his childhood friend had become with Death. What was he going to do?

The rest of his morning classes passed in a blur, and it wasn't long before Evan sat down for lunch at his usual spot. Lost in thought, he methodically pulled his lunch from his bag and began eating without tasting it.

"Okay, dude, spill it." Oliver poked Evan hard in the shoulder to get his attention. "What's wrong?"

"What?" Evan tried to remember what they had been talking about and had no clue.

"What is going on with you?" Oliver asked. "You're totally out of it and not in a good way."

"Nothing. I'm just tired." To emphasize his point, Evan leaned over and pinched the bridge of his nose. "I didn't get any sleep last night."

"Uh-huh." Oliver sounded unconvinced.

Evan's mind returned to fixating on his dilemma while they ate, quickly getting lost in thought again. At the end of the lunch period, Oliver finally broke the silence.

"Are you working tonight?" he asked.

"No," Evan answered automatically. "I'm not scheduled again until later this week."

"Cool," Oliver said with a smile. "Wanna come by my place tonight so we can study for the math exam coming up?"

"Math exam?" Evan said, confused, while silently berating himself for being so distracted that he couldn't even remember that they had a test coming up. "Yeah, sure, I'll swing by tonight."

He seriously doubted he could concentrate but decided to at least try to help his friend. The details were ironed out, and the two of them separated for the rest of their respective school day.

That night, Evan visited Oliver's house to study. When they got to Oliver's room, Evan pulled out his math book and began flipping through the pages.

"Remind me again what chapters the test is on?" he said, unable to remember anything about his math class.

"Holy cow, you're really messed up, aren't you?" Oliver asked, his voice thick with concern.

"I just don't remember the chapter, is all," Evan said as he waved dismissively.

As he flipped through the pages, trying to remind himself what they had last reviewed in class, Oliver's hand slapped down on the book, startling him.

"Dude!" Oliver said. "We don't *have* a math test coming up."

Evan looked up, blinking in confusion. "What?"

"There is no math test. I just said that to get you here." Oliver shook his head. "I can't believe it actually worked. Like anyone would believe that *I* would suggest a study session."

A wave of dizziness passed through Evan as he looked into his friend's eyes, his exhausted brain struggling to comprehend. Oliver carefully took the book from his hands and slipped it back into his backpack as he watched in confusion.

"So, what's up? Problems with Hana?" Oliver said as he plopped on the edge of his bed.

"Why would you automatically assume it has something to do with Hana?"

Oliver laughed loudly. "Are you kidding me? Of course it has to do with Hana. I mean, come on. Have you stopped thinking about her for even a minute since she showed up? I may be an idiot, but I'm not stupid," he said while continuing to chuckle.

Evan sighed, running his hand through his hair as he tried to calm himself. He needed to pull himself together. Just because Oliver could tell that his current distress involved the girl he was crushing on wasn't rocket science. He needed to stop freaking out over every little thing.

"You know what's funny?" Oliver asked.

"What?"

"We went through all of middle school and halfway through high school, and you never showed the slightest interest in anyone. Now, when the weirdest girl in Riverview shows up, you lose your shit," Oliver said as he laid back on his bed, staring up at the ceiling.

"That's not true. I haven't lost my shit," Evan said, feeling slightly offended. "And she's not the first girl I've liked since middle school."

"Oh?" Oliver sat up. "Who else then?"

"Debbie Warner," Evan said matter-of-factly. "In seventh grade."

Oliver looked at him with his eyes narrowed. "Who?" Then, a look of comprehension replaced his confusion. "Do you mean the chubby girl who sat behind you in math?”

“Yes, her. And don’t be mean. She was really cute and super sweet,” Evan said firmly.

“Okay, you’re right.” Oliver raised his hands in surrender. “I’m sorry. But seriously? You had a crush on Debbie Warner?”

“Yes.”

Oliver’s eyes widened at the revelation. “Did you ever tell her?”

“Yes,” Evan said sharply before turning away. “Well, kind of.”

“Kind of?”

“I gave her a valentine that year.”

Oliver blinked a few times before shaking his head. “Okay, Romeo. Then I take it back. But it’s no secret to anyone that you have a massive crush on Hana. And I would bet money that she likes you back.”

“Well, mutual attraction isn’t the problem,” Evan groaned.

“All right then, what is?” Oliver asked in an uncharacteristically serious tone. “What’s going on?”

Evan sighed and leaned back while he thought for a moment. He considered telling Oliver everything but worried about the repercussions of Hana’s secret getting out. Besides, he wasn’t certain that Oliver would even believe him.

“I found out that she’s been keeping a huge secret from everyone,” Evan said after a moment.

“What kind of secret?”

“I can’t say. Sorry,” Evan said while avoiding his gaze.

“You know you can tell me anything, right? It will be just between us, I swear,” Oliver said earnestly.

"I... I can't," Evan said in defeat.

Oliver reached out and placed his hand on Evan's shoulder. "It's cool, dude. If you can't say, you can't say. Don't sweat it."

"Thanks." Evan smiled back in relief.

"So, you found out something bad about her, and it's got you all messed up?"

"Yeah."

"It must be pretty bad..."

Evan thought about it further. He could still barely believe that the gods were real. That he had watched first-hand as two teenage girls flew up thirty feet high, jumping dozens of feet without a care and summoning monsters and weapons out of thin air. Most of the stories of the gods made it sound like they were all but invulnerable, except to each other or magic, and it made him feel truly powerless. What if that horrible little girl took out her anger at their school, or a hospital, or the mall? Could anyone stop her? The fact that Hana was just as strong, if not stronger, made his head swim again. He could barely grasp the implications of it all.

"Yeah, it's bad," Evan groaned again.

"Are we talking 'call-the-police' bad or 'hide-your-wallet' bad?"

"More like 'build-a-bunker-in-your-backyard-and-lock-yourself-in' bad," Evan said.

"Seriously?" Oliver asked, eyes wide with disbelief.

"Well, maybe." Evan shook his head again and shrugged. "I don't know. It's super confusing, actually. I don't really have a handle on it just yet, to be honest."

"I have to say, man, you have me super curious about what you found out about her..." Oliver said, raising his hand to forestall Evan from interrupting, "but I respect you don't feel you can't tell me right now. So, let's approach this differently. How do you want this to end? What do you want to happen?"

"That's a good question." Evan groaned with no immediate answer. He could barely wrap his head around who or what Hana was, and he hadn't even considered how he wanted it resolved.

A significant part of him wished he had just done as she'd asked and gone home when she'd told him to. Though the longer he dwelled on that, the more he knew he was lying to himself.

"You know what I think bothers me the most?" he said. "I think I'm less upset about her secret and more that she had to lie about it, you know? I feel... betrayed."

"Well, that's understandable. You can't have a friendship without trust, and if she's been lying to you the whole time..."

"So, what do I do?" Evan asked, looking back at Oliver.

Oliver stared back for a moment, blinking a few times before shaking his head. "I don't know. Have you tried talking to her about it?"

"No," Evan said while lowering his head.

"Well, then I think you have two choices; talk to her and get it all out in the open, or bail."

"Bail?"

"Well, yeah. If she's got this awful secret and has been lying to you the whole time, then maybe it's just best to cut and run. If there's one thing my parent's divorce taught me, it's that you shouldn't stay in a toxic relationship for any longer than you have to. If you can't work out your issues, then it's better for everyone if you just end it cleanly," Oliver said, with none of his usual joviality, as he sat on the edge of his bed, his hands folded in his lap.

Evan stared at his friend as his advice sank in. It made sense, but ending his friendship with Hana sounded unpleasant and painful.

"But, before you go do anything stupid, you should figure out what you really want, and talk to her," Oliver said. "Oh, and when I say end it cleanly, I mean that you need to tell her straight up. Don't drag your feet and draw this whole thing out longer than necessary, otherwise you'd be the one keeping secrets and lying. And that's messed up."

Evan considered Oliver's advice for several minutes before his friend interrupted his musing by pulling out a pair of GameBox controllers.

"Up for a few rounds?" Oliver asked, holding out a controller with a wide smile on his face.

"Sure." Evan smiled back, more than willing to forget his problems for a little while. "And thank you for the 'study session,'" Evan added in air quotes. "I really appreciate it."

"Of course," Oliver nodded. "Now, prepare yourself for some real pain!"

They both laughed as Oliver started up the game.

The temporary distraction had helped, and on his way home, Evan felt relieved that he wasn't without options with Hana. Oliver was right that he needed to get his head on straight and face the situation. As he considered his choices, the idea of abandoning Hana pained him, but there was a genuine possibility that there wouldn't be any way around it.

He thought about how he could approach her and what he would say as he walked. How do you tell someone that you think they're secretly a god? And what if he wasn't supposed to know? Her entire family seemed to be trying desperately to keep it all a secret. What might happen if they knew he'd found out?

The more he thought about the problem, the more he felt like he was overlooking something important. As he walked, he tried to think of what it could be.

It didn't help that every time he thought about her, the merged sensations of that first dream, mixed with the kiss from the changing booth, colored his thoughts and confused his senses. Despite knowing Hana's true nature, he still found himself drawn to her, wishing he could hear her laugh again.

Then it struck him, causing him to stumble and nearly fall as he arrived at the corner convenience store. Evan reached out a hand and steadied himself on a light post as he sweated despite the chilly evening. As he stood there, the ramification of his epiphany caused him to pant, his heart pounding in his chest.

His parents and aunt hadn't just been unlucky, in the wrong place at the wrong time. Their deaths had been intentional, planned. They had been killed, and Hana—or someone like her—had done it. And they would do it again.

She wasn't *just* a mythical god dressed up as a teenager; she was the incarnation of Death. All of the suffering he and his family had endured could happen to someone else—and by her hand.

Evan's knees grew weak, and he felt himself slowly slide to the ground. Suddenly, crashing waves of grief hit him. The quiet, scarred wound of the loss of his parents and aunt tore open with a vengeance.

The image from the tarot card of a skulled figure under a black cloak came to him, but this time from the edges of its face, he could see waves of shimmering silver hair flowing out with a vicious silver and black scythe in hand. Suddenly he was back in his aunt's hospital room, recalling the last time he'd visited her, mere minutes before she died.

The vision morphed further, and instead of standing alongside aunt Elaine's hospital bed as she struggled to catch her last few breaths, it was Aunt Maddie, her brassy brunette hair in a wad under her head, pale and sickly while the monitors beeped ominously. It was far too easy to imagine Maddie dying and Hana casually strolling up to end her life.

"Are you here for me?" Mrs. Richardson's words echoed through his mind, but in Maddie's voice, sending shivers down his spine.

"No!" Evan screamed into the night. "No, no, no!"

What had he done? He'd literally invited Death into his life and into the lives of his friends and family. It was clear from the night at the park that the gods of old were very real, and they didn't seem to have much reservation about killing anyone. He couldn't fathom why he'd been spared, but that didn't ensure Hana wouldn't change her mind at any moment and murder Oliver, Katie, Ellie, or anyone else if the mood struck her.

Oliver was right; he had to end it with Hana. Immediately. Though he needed to take care not to tip his hand that he knew her secret, possibly endangering everyone even further. This wouldn't be easy.

By the time he arrived home, the only decision he'd come to was that he would simply try to avoid her for now. He would remain friendly when he had to, but he'd keep her at arm's length. Oliver had told him to end it cleanly, but there could be dire repercussions if he screwed it up, so he needed to ensure he was doing the right thing before acting.

For the rest of the week, he put his strategy into practice. In the morning, he would smile and welcome her to class if they ran into each other, but unless one or more of their other friends were around, he would keep his distance.

It did not surprise him when his phone chirped on Tuesday during lunch:

Hana: Hey Evan, how are you doing?

Evan didn't know what to say, electing to set his phone aside to continue talking to Oliver, intending to answer her later. At the end of lunch, she sent him a second message, though he still procrastinated on any kind of reply.

Hana: Well, I hope you have a good day.

Her last text message to him for the week arrived on Wednesday while he was in study hall.

Hana: Can we talk? Please?

He knew he shouldn't just ignore her, but what could

he say? He'd wracked his brain all week, and the best thing he'd come up with still sounded terrible: *Hey Hana, so can I ask something? Did you know about those obscure Greek Gods in your essay because they were your next-door neighbors or something?*

Everything else in his head quickly turned dark. He didn't know whether to admit that he knew her secret, potentially risking the safety of everyone, or accuse her of being responsible for the loss of his parents and aunt. Every time he tried to consider what he would say, he would become emotional, feeling equal parts confusion, betrayal, and anger.

Luckily, she didn't text him after that, though as he ate dinner Thursday night, his phone buzzed in his pocket as Hana called him. He declined the call without pause and sent her to voicemail. A minute later, a chill ran down his spine when he saw the icon light up at the top of his screen, indicating she had left a message.

After dinner, he retreated to his bedroom and opened his phone, pressing the voicemail icon with trepidation.

"Hello, Evan," Hana began, her voice soft and tentative. "I tried to text you a few times, but I guess you haven't seen them. I hope you're doing well. I would really like to talk. I'm sure you're confused about what happened last week, and I'm sorry. I really should have talked to you last Sunday, but I was too nervous."

There was a long pause where Evan thought he heard her sniff away from the phone a couple of times before she spoke again. "I just want a chance to explain, so... please call me?"

After a shorter pause, the message finished. "All right then, bye."

She sounded so uncertain, almost as if she was afraid

of *him*. He listened to the message three times before pulling up her contact on his phone. His finger hovered over the call button for several long seconds as he contemplated pushing it. If nothing else, he wanted to hear her voice again and assure her everything was going to be all right. But it wasn't, and he doubted it ever would be again. Finally, he gave up, turning off his phone in case she called again, and went to bed early, though he wouldn't fall asleep for several hours.

When the week finally ended, they had exchanged fewer than a dozen words with each other. Several times he had worked up the courage to talk to her, but each time he'd envision her as the grim reaper, with a long flowing black cloak and skull-shaped face. His resolve would waver, and he would chicken out with some lame excuse.

The worst part was that he missed her terribly. He was acutely aware of her, even while keeping as much distance as possible. He had noticed that by the end of the week, she wasn't smiling anymore and no longer looked for him at the beginning of class.

He knew Katie suspected there had been a falling out, but to her credit, she didn't insert herself into his troubles other than to offer support if he wanted it. While Oliver remained cordial around Hana, exchanging pleasantries and acting completely normal all week.

When the weekend arrived, Evan hated himself for his indecisiveness, though he was still unsure of what he should do. *Maybe if I continue to avoid her, the problem will solve itself. I just have to forget about her and get on with my life.*

Unfortunately, that was easier said than done, and as he folded clothes Saturday morning, his thoughts were still swirling around Hana when there was a knock at the front door.

"Ellie, go see who that is," he said as his heart jumped into his throat. "And if it's Hana, tell her I'm not here."

Ellie balked at him. "What? Why?"

"Please?" he implored. "I can't explain why, but I can't talk to her right now, okay?"

"Did you two have a fight?" she asked.

"Go!" he urged as he hid in their hallway.

A second later, Ellie opened the front door, out of view from Evan.

"Hello?" Ellie said in an inquisitive tone as if she didn't recognize the visitor.

"Hi. Is Evan here?" Evan heard Hana's voice, causing his stomach to drop as a wave of guilt washed over him.

"One second," Ellie said, making Evan's heart seize in panic.

When Ellie came around the corner, he grabbed her by the shoulders. "What are you doing?" he demanded. "I told you to tell her I'm not here."

"Yeah, but that's if it was Hana," Ellie said, annoyed. "It's someone else."

"What?" He could swear he'd heard Hana's voice from the front door. "Who is it?"

"I don't know. She's pretty, with black and red hair."

"Mara?" Evan poked his head around the corner without thinking.

Mara stood in front of the open door, in a form-fitting purple crop top, with a sheer, black overshirt accompanied by a pair of blue, ripped jean shorts and black tights. She finished her ensemble with a pair of red platform-heeled sneakers. She was watching the inside of the house, waiting for Ellie's return, and when Evan's head popped around the corner, she smiled triumphantly and raised her index finger, bending it toward herself in a motion that she wanted him to follow.

Evan quickly spun back around the corner, but it was too late. She had definitely seen him; there was no way he could have Ellie pretend he wasn't home. Not once had it occurred to him that Hana might send her sister to deal with him—not after the fiasco from the study session. Regardless, she had seen him, so he had to deal with her.

He ran a hand through his hair to settle himself and walked around the corner with a sigh. "Hey, Mara," he said casually. "What's up?"

"I need pants," she said while looking him in the eye. "Take me shopping."

Evan stood dumbfounded for a moment. "What?"

With a roll of her eyes, Mara looked back at him, exasperated. "I said, I need pants. So, you need to take me shopping."

"Why don't you just go on your own?"

"Because I don't want to. So, get some shoes on so we can go."

Evan frowned. "Look, Mara, I'm not going to take you shopping, okay? I'm busy. You'll just have to go on your own or find someone else."

"That's not acceptable," she said while shaking her head. "You need to take me shopping."

"Have your sister take you."

"She's busy," Mara said. "And since it's your fault, you have to take me."

Without warning, Mara reached out and grabbed Evan's wrist in a vise-like grip. He instinctively pulled back, which threw him off-balance, and instead of pulling him out of the house, she pushed him inside.

Once inside, she reached down and grabbed a pair of Ellie's sandals and shoved them into Evan's stomach.

"There. Shoes. Can we go now?" She began pulling him out the door.

"Wait, Mara! Wait!" He planted his feet and resisted as hard as he could. Just like her sister, she was much stronger than she looked, further reinforcing that the sisters were not mere mortals.

She looked back with a determined, almost angry expression on her face. With the way she was forcing him around, Evan was certain that Mara would drag him along, whether or not he wanted to go. If he continued to struggle, would she just pick him up and carry him? How would he explain that to Ellie? Was she about to get dragged into this nonsense too? He couldn't let that happen.

A glance into the apartment showed his worst fear. Ellie was still standing a few feet into the kitchen, watching his interaction with Mara with a confused expression on her face.

"Fine! I'll take you shopping," he said in defeat, rubbing his wrist a moment later after she released him. "Just don't expect me to pay."

"No problem, I have this." Out of her pocket, she pulled a credit card emblazoned with a red-winged foot superimposed over a silhouetted mountain.

Sighing, Evan returned Ellie's sandals and grabbed his sneakers. "Hey, Ellie, I'm going to go shopping with a friend."

"Uh, okay. When will you be back?" she asked, her eyes darting rapidly between Evan and Mara.

"A couple of hours. I have my phone if you need anything."

"Who is she?" Ellie whispered, leaning in close as he tied his shoes.

"Hana's sister, Mara."

"Wait, why are you taking Hana's sister shopping? Does Hana know about this?"

"Don't worry about it, it's fine, all right? I'll be back later," Evan said as he abruptly stood and rushed out the door, hoping to avoid further questions and locking the door behind him.

Mara was leaning against the balcony railing, arms crossed, an air of triumph about her.

"Okay then," Evan sighed. "Let's go get you some pants."

"And shirts," she added as they headed down the stairs.

Evan groaned, resigned that it was pointless to resist the whims of a god. He regretted not having spent more time researching Hypnos. The brief description he remembered hadn't hinted at anything violent about their lore, so he doubted there would be anything like a reenactment of that night in the park. But who knew? Whatever was about to happen was best kept away from his friends and family, that was for sure. There was a slight chance that she really did just want to go shopping, though he highly doubted it.

Evan tried to be strategic in his choice of shopping

destinations. It had been exactly one week since he had visited the Bainbridge Mall with Hana and the others, and as he returned there with Mara, he had a very different agenda. He wanted to make the trip brief and painless. Being the largest shopping mall in the region, there would be many other people around. Hopefully, it would discourage her from bringing up any awkward conversations about gods, magic, or monsters. And with her aversion to crowds and strangers, it would likely shorten the trip, getting it over with sooner than later.

He felt bad for manipulating things and intentionally making her uncomfortable, but he had to use any advantage he could. Who knew what she had in mind for him?

Before they had even arrived, however, he lost faith in his clever scheme. As they boarded the bus, Evan grew nervous when he noted that the entire back half was completely empty. If Mara sat back there, it would be easy to hold a private conversation without the risk of being overheard. As he followed her onto the bus, however, she nestled herself between a pair of seated passengers at the very front rather than heading for any of the seats near the back.

With a growing sense of uncertainty, Evan chose a seat across from her, next to an older woman who was actively knitting something that looked vaguely like a hat. As the bus began moving, Evan watched Mara as the scenery passed by. She appeared happy and perfectly comfortable around complete strangers, easily engaging in several conversations as they crossed town.

When the bus finally came to a stop in front of the mall, Mara said goodbye to the three people she had been chatting with and stepped off the bus with a spring in her step. Evan followed behind, a sense of apprehension slowly building as they stood outside the broad glass entrance to the mall.

"I thought you didn't like crowds," Evan said, annoyed.

"Why would you think that?" Mara asked, narrowing her eyes for a moment before shrugging her shoulders. "So, where do we start?"

More lies from Hana. He really knew nothing about her.

"Let's see." Evan adjusted his strategy and focused on keeping the trip quick and efficient. While he had a good sense of the store selection and layout of the mall, he still referenced the mall directory to find the closest store that would carry something appropriate.

While there were a couple of closer locations that might work, he decided on a shop partway down the mall that was more likely to have a selection that would suit Mara's tastes. Feeling confident in his choice, they headed off.

As he had expected, the mall was full of other shoppers, and he had to slow his pace to keep from having to weave in and around them. This also meant that he had to walk closer to Mara than he wanted, which was yet another wrinkle in his masterminded plot.

As they passed by a women's lingerie store on their way to where Evan was guiding them, Mara stopped abruptly, captivated by a risque nightgown displayed in the window.

"Ooo, that's pretty," she purred.

Evan scowled. "I thought we were here for pants..." The idea of entering the shop with Mara filled him with a newfound dread.

"What?" She replied with a sly look. "You want me to wear pants without panties?"

"No, that's—" he said as he blushed furiously. "That's not what I meant."

"You're quite the pervert, aren't you?" Mara smirked. "C'mon, if you help me find something pretty, I just might let you see me in it." She started inside.

Evan had no intention of following Mara into such a place, especially not with so many witnesses around. In steadfast defiance, Evan crossed his arms and shook his head.

"There is not a chance in hell I'm going in there with you!" he said. "If you want to go alone, be my guest. I'll wait here."

Mara stared back, blinking in surprise. A wave of accomplishment flowed through him as her expression turned from one of mischief to disappointment. However, his euphoria quickly faded as her look of dissatisfaction magnified, and her lower lip trembled. He recognized her new tactic a moment too late as the first set of tears fell down her face, accompanied by a heavy sob.

"Don't you even care about me anymore?" she wailed melodramatically. "You promised you'd help me, and now you want to abandon me?"

In an overly dramatic fashion, Mara's sobbing grew louder, her whole body shuddering as she cried into the palms of her hands. Passersby shook their heads and scowled at the scene of an overbearing boyfriend berating his girlfriend to tears. Evan wanted to escape, but Mara wasn't finished and continued to get louder, making things far worse.

"I thought there was something special between us!"

She let loose another massive sob. "What did I do? Won't you even tell me?"

The crowd grew rapidly, murmuring their support for Mara's plight. Evan had to act quickly before things got totally out of control.

Reaching out, he grabbed her upper arms and stepped closer. "Mara, please! You're causing a scene!"

"Is that all you care about?" She pulled her head out of her hands, showing the crowd of onlookers an unobstructed view of her bloodshot eyes and tear-streaked face. "We have to do everything *you* want? Everything *you* say? My feelings don't matter? My needs mean *nothing*?"

Evan knew he was defeated. He was outmatched, and if he dragged this out any longer, he would likely have to answer to mall security or the angry mob. He had to end this farce.

"Okay. Fine. I'm sorry. I'll go. I'll go," he relented.

Mara's expression changed completely from one of dejected misery to ecstatic joy. "Okay!" She grabbed his hand and pulled him into the store, leaving the crowd behind.

As they entered, Evan watched the throng of people around Mara's performance dissipate nearly as fast as they had gathered. Many of them looked confused as if they weren't sure what they had just witnessed.

Evan could have told them what happened, though: he'd tried to match his will against a headstrong teenage girl—not to mention a Greek god—and had been summarily destroyed. It didn't bode well for the rest of his afternoon.

It took a moment to notice that they were walking farther into the lingerie shop than he thought necessary, and he took stock of his surroundings. They had breezed past the selections of everyday cotton undergarments and were headed directly toward the more revealing and intimate selections the store offered.

"Wait, where are you taking me?" he asked.

"To get me some undies."

"There are plenty back there!" He pulled on her hand, hoping to drag her back to the more reasonable parts of the store.

"But I want something pretty," she said as if it was an entirely reasonable argument.

"Who cares if it's pretty?" He hoped he could somehow talk some sense into her. "You're the only one who's going to see it!"

"How can you be so sure of that?" She flashed a flirtatious smile.

Evan felt the heat rise in his cheeks at her insinuation while Mara's eyes sparkled in delight. His stunned silence was all the opening she needed, pulling him deeper into the store.

"Come on," she said while pulling him. "I need your help."

"No, you don't!" He objected to no avail as she dragged him into his own personal hell.

Several hours passed in a similar fashion. Evan dreaded whatever enticing thing might lurk in the window of the next shop, knowing that if Mara found it intriguing, she would insist they had to go in, and he would have to go along.

In every shop, she tried on a wide variety of clothing, both reasonable and outrageous, and showed it off for him every time. She delighted in making him uncomfortable. And after the fifth lingerie modeling,

Evan wondered if his face would be permanently red from all the blushing.

After a couple of hours, Evan wasn't certain Mara had an alternative agenda other than the shopping trip and torturing him. She didn't mention her sister once but seemed singularly focused on their visits to each shop and the various articles of clothing that she "needed." He had also decided that his role in the whole affair was simply comic relief because she continually ignored any input he gave, often choosing the exact opposite of any advice he offered the few times she asked his opinion.

It was nearly one o'clock when Mara called a halt to it all.

"I'm hungry," she announced. "You should take me to lunch."

"Did you know that you're very demanding?" Evan struggled to add the latest pair of shopping bags to the others he was already carrying, his hands sore from their collective weight digging into his palms.

"I know what I want," she said with a shrug. "Should I just wait around, hoping you'll guess what I need without giving any clues? Or would you rather I defer to you in all things? Ask your opinion before I tell you what I desire?"

"No, I suppose not." He agreed it was her right to express herself but still wished she were more polite about it.

Looking around, he noticed they were rather close to Ellie's favorite diner and ice cream parlor. They themed the entire place after the 1950s with a checkerboard tile floor, padded red booths, and raucous classic rock-and-roll music. Though the best part was that it was close, and he wouldn't need to travel far to sit and shed the collection of bags he was carrying.

"Let's go there." He pointed with an elbow. "They have some great food."

Mara agreed readily, and they entered a few seconds later, Evan struggling to manage his burden without hitting any of the other patrons as they made their way to an open booth.

"Interesting place," Mara said as Evan stuffed the purchases under the table. "I need to pee, so order me something yummy, okay?"

With that matter-of-fact statement, Mara walked away toward the bathrooms.

Evan had no idea what Mara liked, so he ordered some of his favorites, a large basket of french fries and two malt milkshakes—one vanilla, one chocolate, so Mara could have whichever she preferred.

With the bags tucked away, he slid into the farther bench, glad to be off his feet for the first time in hours. He wondered where else she might want to drag him to afterward—probably on the other side of the mall. He rubbed his hands, hoping she was nearly done. His arms felt like cooked spaghetti, and he didn't know how much more he could carry.

As he waited, it surprised him to find that he was enjoying himself. Despite being a little pushy—okay, *very* pushy—Mara was fun to be around. She was spontaneous and entertaining while still being polite and personable to the staff of every store they had visited, though that courtesy rarely extended to Evan. She had a good eye for fashion, and while he still blushed at the memory of some things she'd purchased, he thought that the lessons he learned could prove helpful for the next time Ellie wanted to go shopping. He had finally relaxed a little, not thinking about Hana or his dilemma since the first shop.

"I'm back," she announced upon her return. "Miss me?"

Rather than sit across the table as he expected, she sat down next to him, shoving him into the farthest corner of the booth, pinning him against the wall. It must have looked to the other patrons that they were an item, though Evan tried his best not to think about it or just how close she was.

The server arrived with their fries at that moment, placing them on the table in front of them and walking away.

"What's that?" Mara asked, leaning in and inhaling the aroma.

"They're french fries," Evan said, unsurprised that she had no exposure to the food. "They're sliced potato, deep-fried and salted."

While Mara grabbed a french fry for a close examination, Evan poured a generous amount of ketchup on the plate, looking forward to the combination of sweet and salty.

"So, what happened between you and my sister?" Mara asked as Evan shoved a handful of fries in his mouth, causing him to cough in surprise.

When he was sure he could talk again, he answered. "Why do you think something happened?"

"Because little miss perfect's been acting funny all week," Mara said as she put the fry in her mouth and chewed happily. "She's been all moody without her usual annoying cheerfulness, and it's only gotten worse. She's also been keeping herself really busy every night, studying or practicing or doing something until bedtime.

It's annoying. Even more than usual, and she always acts this way when she's upset."

"Why do you think that has anything to do with me?"

"Because she likes you, moron. Duh."

"What?" A thrill ran through him, despite his determination to set his feelings for Hana aside. "I mean, uh, why do you think that?"

"Because I know my sister. And I know what she's like when she's crushing on a boy."

Evan didn't have a clue what to say. He had avoided Hana all week precisely for this reason, and now Mara had him trapped in a public place. She stared at him, waiting for an answer. Suddenly he felt incredibly stupid for thinking that he controlled the situation. From the moment she'd appeared at his house, he'd been doomed.

Evan turned back to the fries while he tried to analyze his feelings for Hana. He liked her, there was no doubt about that, but he just couldn't reconcile her two sides. While his mind despised the very concept of what she did, his heart longed for her, delighting every time he saw her and lamenting when she wasn't around. The previous week had been successful in terms of keeping his distance but utterly miserable for him. And now it sounded like she was hurting too, which made it so much worse.

"So?" Mara took another fry. "What happened?"

Evan sighed, uncertain how he could talk to her without revealing that he had discovered their secret. He still wasn't sure if there would be consequences for knowing and wanted to avoid tipping his hand, especially to Mara.

"There was a fight," he finally said, wording it carefully.

"You two had a fight?"

"Sort of."

Mara frowned. "So what? She and I fight all the time."

"That's different—you're sisters. You're supposed to fight."

She shrugged. "So, you two had a fight, you lost, and now you're all butt-hurt?"

"Why do you think I lost?" he asked.

"Because she's Hana," she said with a shrug. "And you're... you."

"Thanks," Evan grumbled. "But it wasn't like that."

"Then what was it like?"

Evan shook his head, trying to get his thoughts in order. Mara's rapid-fire questioning and talent for picking the perfect words to get under his skin had him flustered, making it difficult to form a coherent answer.

"Why are you asking me about this?" he asked, trying to deflect her questioning. "Shouldn't you be asking Hana?"

"I tried, but she won't talk to me." Mara shrugged and shoved another fry into her mouth absently. "For some reason, she doesn't like to confide in me. We rarely talk about anything personal. Normally, I'm just fine with that. She keeps to herself and doesn't bug me much, which is cool.

"This is different, though," she said, looking away. "I can't remember the last time she broke down crying, not since we were little kids."

Evan's heart lurched.

"Then yesterday, I overheard her talking to Mom about moving back home," Mara said. "So, I figured I'd ask you what made my sister cry and want to move away. Especially since she's the whole reason we moved here."

Evan leaned back in his chair, his mind racing to process what he'd heard. He knew that distancing himself would be unpleasant, but he hadn't thought about what it would do to Hana, and he'd never expected it to affect her so strongly. She's a super-powerful Greek god, right? The image of Hana in tears—brave, strong, confident Hana—made him want to hold and comfort her. He questioned all his decisions from the past week.

And to make matters worse, Hana was asking about moving away? The idea of never seeing her again struck him like a blow, and he had to remind himself to breathe.

"I... I had no idea," he said meekly.

"I figured."

Despite his sense of regret over Hana's pain, an after-image of Aunt Maddie dying in a hospital bed, just like Aunt Elaine, steeled his heart. Why should he spend even a moment worrying about Hana's feelings when her whole reason for existing was to cause suffering and pain in others?

"So, have you talked to her?" Mara asked after a few seconds.

"No."

"Really? Why not?"

"Honestly? I don't know what to say."

"So, you've just been ignoring her?" Mara scowled.

"Yeah," he said, embarrassed.

She gave him a withering look. "That's messed up."

Before Evan could formulate a response, the server returned, placing two tall milkshakes in front of them, complete with whipped cream, sprinkles, and topped with a bright red cherry.

"What's this?" Mara eyed the two glasses suspiciously.

"They're milkshakes," Evan said. "Trust me; you'll like them."

To demonstrate, he reached for the nearest one—the vanilla—and scooped a large spoonful into his mouth.

He watched Mara as she cautiously pulled the chocolate shake toward herself and poked it with the spoon experimentally. Slowly, she raised a small spoonful of ice cream and examined it, sniffing at it cautiously. Turning the spoon on its side, she watched with trepidation as the ice cream slowly oozed off the spoon and plopped back into the whipped cream topping.

"It's good. See?" He reached past her, taking a small spoonful from her milkshake and eating it, showing her they were delicious.

With much more caution than she'd had with the french fries, Mara took a much smaller spoonful of ice cream and put it into her mouth, closing her eyes at the last second in anticipation.

The instant her mouth closed around the spoon, her eyes shot open. Surprised ecstasy painted her face as she rapidly plunged her spoon back into the tall glass for another, much larger scoop.

"Oh, mah gawds..." she said through a mouthful of milkshake and cream, sending a few droplets flying. "This is amazing."

"I told you." Evan smiled. "But you'll want to slow down a little."

"Why?" She shoved another huge spoonful into her mouth.

"You'll give yourself brain freeze."

Mara looked at him confusingly while taking another

enormous bite. Then, as if on cue, her expression changed from pure joy to agony.

Evan couldn't help himself from chuckling as Mara grabbed the side of her head, squinting at the sharp pain from too much ice cream, too fast.

"Don't worry," he said. "It'll pass soon."

He was right, and within a few minutes, Mara was back to enjoying her frozen treat, albeit a little slower. Evan watched her delight as she enjoyed every spoonful of her very first milkshake. It reminded him of Hana's first time eating pizza and how much enjoyment she had with the new food and games afterward. He missed Hana terribly, and watching her sister caused his heart to ache anew. He had to remind himself that she was the Angel of Death and that he needed to walk away before anyone else got hurt.

When Mara finished licking the glass as far as she could reach to capture every drop of ice cream, Evan slid the rest of his milkshake to her and smiled. When she had polished off the rest of his glass, Evan paid and picked up all the shopping bags.

"Where to next?" he asked.

"Home," Mara said plainly.

"Really?" Evan asked in surprise, looking down at what they had already bought, noting that with all her purchases, they had yet to buy a single pair of pants.

"Yeah, I'm getting sleepy and got everything I wanted," she said.

"Um, okay." Evan shrugged as they headed back to the bus stop. Despite how he had dreaded the trip initially, it surprised him that he was disappointed that it was over.

While waiting for the bus, Evan considered picking up

their conversation from earlier when Mara leaned over and rested her head on his shoulder, falling asleep immediately. He sighed as a few passersby smiled at the two of them sitting on the bench together in what must look like a cute couple enjoying their Saturday. He thought about waking Mara up or at least moving her off him, but she seemed so comfortable he didn't have the heart to do either.

As Mara snoozed against his shoulder, Evan wondered what her goal had been in literally dragging him out of his house. She seemed pleased to gain a bunch of new clothes, but he guessed that the lunch conversation had been her actual goal.

She really was a wonderful sister, even if he hadn't thought so at first. He wondered if Hana had any idea about the extent Mara had gone to for her today and doubted it.

The bus ride home was a time for quiet reflection as Mara continued her nap on his shoulder. Evan sat with his phone in his hand, the first line of a message to Hana on its screen.

"Hana," it began, with a blinking cursor waiting for him to continue.

He just couldn't find the words. His thoughts ran in circles as he sat there, looking at the expectant phone. He didn't want her to go and yet, didn't know how he could continue a friendship with her either. What could he say? What could he ask? And worse, would her answer even matter?

When the bus finally arrived at their stop, he closed the phone in defeat and gently woke Mara.

"Hey, Mara, we're here." He shook her lightly.

"Mmmm?" she mumbled, slowly becoming alert.

"Come on," he said, pulling her up and guiding her toward the exit. Mara was slow to wake up and stumbled more than once on the brief trip off the bus.

Once outside, Evan turned her in the right direction and continued to escort her home. Within a dozen steps, however, she was fully awake.

"I got this," she announced suddenly, pulling the bags out of Evan's hands.

"I don't mind helping you get home," he said.

"No need. See you later!"

And with that, she turned and headed off at a brisk pace, leaving Evan behind without a second glance. He was sure that his trip with Mara was without Hana's knowledge, and for some reason, she wanted to keep it a secret. With a shrug and more to think about than ever, Evan headed home.

By the time he arrived at his shift at the bookstore on Sunday morning, he still didn't know what to say. He knew he needed to talk to Hana, and soon, or he would miss his chance entirely.

He had devised a plan to treat the problem as a school assignment and write out all the things he wanted to say or ask. Unfortunately for him, the shop was busy that morning, and it wasn't until nearly 5 pm. that it quieted down long enough for him to pull out his notebook and consider what he wanted to say.

With pen in hand, Evan stared at the blank page. The whole situation was so ridiculous. Was he really going to ask a seventeen-year-old girl if she was an ancient God of Death? Even writing it down on paper was crazy. And even if he could get through that somehow, what could he possibly say about the whole killing people thing?

"Hey there, Evan, whatcha doing?" Mr. Abernathy asked, surprising Evan, who hadn't heard him approach.

"Oh, um, studying."

"Really?" He looked down at the empty notebook on the counter and the textbooks still stuffed into his bag. "I'm not an expert, but I believe books work better when they're open."

"Oh, uh, yeah," Evan said.

Mr. Abernathy winked to make it clear he'd been teasing. "So, what's bothering you? You haven't been yourself this weekend."

"I'm having some trouble with a friend," he said.

"A female friend?" Mr. Abernathy asked with a knowing smile.

"As a matter of fact, yes."

"I thought so. Have you tried apologizing?"

"But I've done nothing wrong."

"Women like it when men apologize," Mr. Abernathy smiled. "Besides, are you so sure you haven't done anything wrong? Sometimes we make mistakes, even when we have the best intentions."

Evan thought about his entire conversation with Mara at lunch and had to admit that he had some things to apologize for.

"Yeah, okay, maybe you're right," Evan said. "But that's not going to help much, trust me."

"Would you like to talk about it? Believe it or not, I've had a lot of experience with ladies over the years."

"Not really." He didn't know how to share enough

details without Mr. Abernathy thinking he was insane.

Mr. Abernathy turned to face him directly and crossed his arms behind his back. "Evan, my boy, do you like this girl?"

"Yes. Quite a lot, actually. But that's besi—"

"All the more reason to work things out, then."

Evan sighed. "Mr. Abernathy, I appreciate the advice, truly, but I don't think we can just 'work out' what happened."

"Goodness, that sounds serious."

"Yeah, it is." Evan sighed, feeling demoralized.

"I know!" Mr. Abernathy said enthusiastically. "How about a tarot reading? You can ask the cards what you should do, and if we're lucky, the universe will provide guidance."

"You know I don't believe in all that stuff."

"Really? You don't think that maybe, just maybe, there is a little bit of magic out there?" Mr. Abernathy's eyes sparkled. "Enough to help you out when you really need it?"

The old man's comment gave Evan pause. With what he'd learned about Hana and the Greek gods, he wondered if he'd been unfairly closed-minded about tarot and fortune-telling. And it wasn't like he had anything better to guide him.

"All right, sure. Why not?"

"Excellent!" Mr. Abernathy beamed in excitement. "I'll go get my best cards."

Evan chuckled as the elderly man nearly ran back to his office in his excitement. Who knows? Maybe the cards might provide some guidance and show him a way out of this mess. As he leaned over, sliding his notebook into his bag, the door chimed, announcing a new visitor.

"Welcome to Silver Linings," he announced with false cheerfulness as he stood up. "How can I—?" his words caught in his throat, and suddenly his heart felt like it might beat out of his chest.

Hana stood in the doorway, looking at Evan with a guarded expression.

Chapter Thirteen

Soul Searching

They stared at one another, neither speaking for several long seconds.

Finally, Hana stepped in and walked to the counter. "Hello, Evan," she said as she arrived.

"Hey, Hana." He swallowed nervously. "So, uh, can I help you with something?" He fell back to his customer service role.

"I was hoping we could talk."

"Right," he said. "Well, I'm, uh, working right now." Immediately, he worried his tone sounded dismissive. "I get off in about an hour, though. Can you hang around until then?"

"Of course," Hana said as she fidgeted. "Um, any suggestions of where I should wait?"

As Evan considered nearby locations, Mr. Abernathy returned from the back of the shop, his favorite deck of tarot cards in his hand.

"Did I hear a customer come in?" he asked excitedly.

"Um, not really," Evan said. "This is my friend, Hana. Hana, this is Mr. Abernathy. He's the owner of the bookstore."

"Pleasure to meet you," Hana said.

"Believe me—the pleasure's all mine." Mr. Abernathy beamed his whitest smile at her. "Can we help you with something, dear?"

"Thank you, but no. I just came to see when Evan was getting off work."

Mr. Abernathy glanced between the two of them, a look of comprehension spreading across his face.

"Well, if you and Evan need to talk, then he can go now," Mr. Abernathy said unexpectedly.

"What?" Evan asked, surprised.

"Go ahead." The elderly man waved a hand toward the front door. "It's dead in here, anyway. Go spend time with your friend. I'll cover the shop."

Evan couldn't help but cringe at his unfortunate choice of words, but luckily Hana didn't seem to notice.

"All right. Thank you," Evan said. "I'll be right out then," he told Hana as he gathered his belongings.

"Thank you, sir," Hana said to Mr. Abernathy. "I'll just wait outside."

As Evan locked the register, Mr. Abernathy put a light hand on his forearm.

"You should definitely apologize to that one," he said with a grin. "She's something special. Don't let her get away."

"Thanks again, Mr. Abernathy."

Evan took a deep breath and headed out.

"Your boss seems like a very nice person," Hana said as the two of them began walking home.

"He is," Evan said. "A little eccentric at times, but he has a big heart. I enjoy working for him, though I often wonder why he keeps me around. We are very rarely busy. I guess he just likes the company."

"I'm sorry for just showing up," Hana said. "I went by your house, and your sister told me where you worked and... I hope I didn't get you in any kind of trouble."

"No, not at all. We haven't had a customer in over an hour, so I'm happy to get out of there early."

"Oh, good," she said as they passed an elementary school playground, complete with a swing set, basketball court, and jungle gym. When she spotted it, Hana stopped and pointed to a group of tables just beyond the playground.

"Can we sit and talk?"

Evan knew they needed to discuss a variety of topics, but nervousness raced through him at the prospect.

"Sure." He agreed, despite his desire to continue walking and avoid the inevitable.

They sat down opposite each other, with Evan stashing his backpack under the table. He didn't know what to say, so when Hana began, he was more than happy to let her talk.

"I'm really, very sorry about what happened last weekend," Hana said. "I expect you have some questions, but the reality is... complicated. I just wanted to let you know that we're moving back home. I know I've made things very uncomfortable for you, so you won't have to worry about seeing us ever again."

Evan wanted to contradict her. He wanted to tell her he didn't want her to go, but the words caught in his throat.

"But before I go, I want to thank you," she said. "I

will always cherish my time at Riverview, especially meeting you and all of your friends. I'll never forget the pizza, bowling, mini-golf, and the wonderful times we had together, even if it was for just a few short weeks. I'm very glad you ran into me that first day, believe it or not."

Tears welled at the corners of her eyes as she delivered what Evan suspected was a prepared speech. It pained him to see her suffering, though he shoved that aside and reminded himself of what she truly was.

"I'm so sorry you got dragged into everything," she said. "I never meant for any harm to come to you. Please believe me."

Evan sat there quietly, stunned and unsure of how to reply. Mara had warned him they were considering moving away, but he had assumed it would take some time to organize. Hana made it sound like they would be packed and gone tonight, and considering who they were, that was likely exactly what was about to happen.

Despite being warned, it still shocked him to hear it directly from Hana. His heart ached at the idea of her walking out of his life, even if her exit would solve a lot of problems.

He began fidgeting with his scarf. A powerful part of him wanted to tell her to stay—that the grim reaper stuff didn't matter to him—but he couldn't. The implications were just too great and not something he could ignore.

An onslaught of emotions overwhelmed him. He couldn't think straight and knew he needed to say something, but nothing would come out. He looked down at his scarf as he tried to sift through it all.

Every emotion was as sharp as a knife and cut deep; the unexpected excitement he felt at being so close to her after a week of avoidance, her basic admission that his concerns over her true nature were right, and of course, the pain of losing her so abruptly. The thought of her leaving hit like a sledgehammer, causing him to wince in pain.

It was the wrong thing to do.

Hana's tear overflowed and fell down her cheek, chased by another. She stood up after a quiet moment, wiping the tears onto her sleeve.

"Goodbye, Evan," she whispered with a hitch in her voice as she began walking away.

Watching her leave finally spurred Evan to break his silence. He would never have another chance to talk to her. And a single, burning question had repeated itself over and over.

"How?" he asked, still looking down.

Hana turned to face him with sorrow painted on her face and fresh tears on her cheeks. "What?"

"I know who you are. I figured it out," he said. "It's crazy and impossible, but I know you're not a normal teenage girl. You're Thanatos from Greek legend, aren't you? And Mara is Hypnos, and your mom is Nyx. And I'm pretty sure that the creepy girl who attacked us is Phobos."

The look of anguish on her face tore at him anew, causing his own eyes to tear up, blurring his vision. She started to speak, but he raised his voice to finish before she could interrupt.

"I don't understand it exactly, but I'm certain I'm right," he said. "What I don't get is how. You seem like a good person. You're kind and sweet... unless that's all an act. Despite that, how can you be the God of Death?"

Hana took a long time to answer. "It's just who we

are, Evan," she said. "We all have a role to play—a job to do. It has to be done whether we do it or someone else does."

The ease with which she admitted her nature with a clear conscience left him stunned, stoking the fires of the anger that had been slowly burning since his revelation of who she was.

"But how can you do it?" he asked. "How can you run around *killing* people? Sure, people die; it happens. I can almost understand the old or sick, but what gives you the right?"

Hana stiffened, her eyes growing wide. "What?"

"How can you make the decision that all of a sudden, for no goddamn reason, some young couple needs to die in a car accident?" he hurled at her, unable to remain seated and standing in challenge. "How can you turn their two young children into orphans? Take them away so early that their youngest child doesn't have a single memory of how they looked or sounded?"

His volume grew increasingly louder as he spoke. With his fists clenched in a rage, his tears began to flow. Years of pain and sorrow poured out of him without warning.

"How can you take a wonderful, kindhearted woman cherished by her family and friends and give her cancer in her forties?" he yelled. "What right do you have to make us watch her suffer in agony as the disease ravages her body and then finally breaks her spirit, making her wish for death?

"How the *hell* do you have the right to tear a family apart over and over again? And why? Because it's your *job*?"

Hana's expression of shock and surprise at Evan's

sudden outburst changed to one of compassion and sorrow. She took a step toward him, raising her arms and opening her mouth to speak. But his courage waned suddenly, and he didn't want her any closer. He quickly backtracked from her advance, and she stopped abruptly, dropping her hands to her sides as a fresh wave of tears fell down her face.

Evan stood there, looking at her, and could easily see the depth of her regret and sympathy. Her hands twitched as if she desperately wanted to reach out and comfort him. The tears that fell from her face felt like a punch in the gut. Along with his rage and sorrow, a sense of guilt built, adding fuel to his pain.

As he stood defiantly, his rage leaked out of him. He wanted to be angry and demand answers, but as he looked at Hana, his heart betrayed him, warming at the mere sight of her. His anger calmed, leaving behind a chasm of loss and betrayal.

"And why did it have to be you?" he asked through a sob. "Why couldn't it have been someone else? Someone I don't care about? Someone I hate? Someone I didn't fall in love with?"

"Oh, Evan." Hana shook her head. "I'm so sorry."

"Why did it have to be you?" he asked desperately, as the last of his anger evaporated, leaving him weak and spent. He fell to his knees, his head dropping into his hands as he sobbed uncontrollably.

Suddenly she was there, her warm, smooth hands reaching out and caressing his wet cheeks. The two of them remained there while Evan's pain poured out of him, Hana staying at his side, slowly caressing his tears away as they fell. After a time, she lowered her head to his, and they remained forehead to forehead until he calmed. With a feather-light touch, she encouraged him to raise his head to look at her.

He stared deeply into her brilliant and sorrowful mercury eyes, and a fresh wave of pain struck him.

"Please give me a chance to explain?" she pleaded.

Evan nodded, not trusting that he could form words. He was drained, and any resistance he might have had toward her was long gone.

"You..." Hana took a deep breath. "You're right about some of what you said. I am Thanatos and Mara is Hypnos. Our mother is Nyx, and Erebus is our father. And, yes, the girl from the other night, Didi? She's Phobos, daughter of Ares and Aphrodite. That is all true."

Evan shook his head from side to side in disbelief. He didn't doubt her, but it was utterly insane to hear it out loud.

"But..." Hana sniffled. "Evan, this is really important, okay? I don't kill people. I don't decide who lives or dies, or how someone dies, or even when."

"But..." he said. "But isn't Thanatos the God of Death?"

"Yes, and no," Hana said. "Thanatos is the *harbinger* of death. We ferry the souls of the recently deceased to the underworld. We arrive shortly before someone's death to make their passing into the afterlife quick and painless, but we don't end their lives. That falls in the realm of the Fates."

"But you're the Grim Reaper..."

"Thanatos and the Grim Reaper are not the same," Hana said. "Legends of the Grim Reaper likely originated with Thanatos, but I don't end anyone's life. If I had to, I could never have agreed to take up the mantle of Thanatos."

"Mantle?" Evan blinked in confusion.

"Will you let me try to explain?" she asked gently.

Evan desperately wanted to believe in her. He desperately wanted them to be together without fear that she was the manifestation of death, a herald of pain and suffering. He hoped that something she might tell him could make everything all right, clinging to the sliver of hope that there was a way out of this mess.

Slowly, Hana rose to her feet, gently pulling Evan with her. She led him back to the table, and they returned to sitting across from each other, still holding hands. Her eyes were big and bright as she looked at him, and he could sense the deep sincerity that flowed from her.

"My sister and I are a part of the most recent generation of the Olympian gods, as you have guessed. Our divine purpose is to serve the mortal world and perform whatever role or task we are born to do."

"But you said that you agreed to it? You don't have to be Thanatos? You can just be a normal teenager if you want?" Evan asked, hopeful for the first time since that night at the park.

Hana sighed and slowly shook her head. "The time to decide has passed. I've already agreed, and the powers have already been bestowed upon me. There is no going back now."

"Oh."

"May I continue?" she asked carefully.

Evan nodded quietly.

"As I said, Thanatos's role is to collect the spirits of those who have recently passed and to ensure they make the journey to the afterlife quickly and painlessly. I don't take the life of the living, nor do I have any influence on their death."

"So, if you don't kill people, what do you do?"

"Well," Hana smiled cautiously, "when a person comes to the end of their life, their bodily functions cease. They stop breathing, blood stops flowing, and the brain stops working, but the soul is often trapped. It's bound within the body, helpless to escape. Thanatos has the power to separate the soul from the body so the spirit can move on to the afterlife."

"What happens if someone dies and you aren't there to collect their soul?"

"It depends." Her smile slipped a little. "Most of the time, they're stuck until the body decomposes. But it is an unpleasant experience: caged, unable to get free but sensing what is happening around them. Once they are free, they normally find their own way to the afterlife."

"So, there is an afterlife?"

"Yes." She raised a hand to forestall his next question. "But before you ask, I am forbidden from speaking about it. And to be entirely honest, that part is still mostly a mystery to me. It will be one of the last things I learn about."

"But you know when someone is going to die, right?"

"No, I don't." Hana shook her head. "Looking at you, for instance, I don't know when or how you will die. But I can sense when there is someone nearby is nearing their end."

"Is that what happened with Mrs. Richardson?"

"Yes. When Annette recognized me, I knew she was very close. It wasn't really my responsibility to be the one to collect her, but she asked me, and I eventually agreed."

"Seriously?"

Hana nodded again. "When she asked if you were there for her, she was actually talking to me. She sent you away to fetch her glasses so we could talk in private."

"Oh." Evan slowly realized that's why she'd been vague about where the glasses were; she was trying to delay him.

"While you were gone, she told me she was terribly lonely and in a lot of pain. She'd lost her husband several years earlier, and her pain treatment had stopped working a few months ago, but she had told none of her doctors."

"Seriously? Why?"

"Apparently, she hated how the pain medication affected her," Hana said. "She told me that when it was working, she couldn't think clearly and often had trouble remembering things like the names of her children and where she was. Her choices were to endure the agony but remember who she was or to live in a fog of confusion with a lot less pain. When she recognized me for who I was, it relieved her that her suffering was about to end."

"I... didn't realize," Evan said.

"At first, I refused," Hana continued. "I told her someone else was coming. She insisted, but when I told her I wasn't allowed, she asked if I'd listen to her story. So, I sat, and we talked."

"About what?"

"Everything," Hana said. "She told me all about her life. About her husband, Lloyd, and her children, Gerald and Victoria. She had a lot of marvelous stories." She frowned, saddened. "But the last few years have been awful for her. Her son moved overseas years ago, and her daughter is busy with her own children, one of which is grown with a child on the way. Annette hated feeling like she was a burden on them and knew she was losing her battle with cancer."

Evan nodded; he knew what that was like.

"By the time she was done talking, her time was up," Hana said. "Another Thanatos arrived, but I asked if they'd allow me to take her. She was very sweet, and I wanted to be the one to carry her on." She exhaled. "To be honest, she's only the third soul I've ever taken."

"Really?"

"My sister, Mara, and I are not full-fledged gods yet. We're still young with a lot to learn and for some of our powers to develop. My time will come in a couple of years, but right now, I'm just a high school student."

"Aren't Thanatos and Hypnos both guys, though?" Evan asked a question that had bothered him since he'd looked at their images on the tarot cards.

"In classic literature? Yes," Hana nodded.

"Then why aren't you a guy?"

"Why aren't you a girl?" she quipped.

"Um, I don't know. I guess I was just born that way?" he shrugged.

"It's the same for us. I was born in a girl's body, and I'm comfortable that way, so I'm a girl," she said with a smile. "And who knows, perhaps the Thanatos and Hypnos of old were actually women, and the poets of ancient Greece and Rome just preferred to portray them as male since all the old stories were written by men," she said as she shrugged. "Though I have met other Thanatos, and many of whom are male."

"There are more of you?" he asked before remembering that she had already mentioned a second

Thanatos attending to Mrs. Richardson.

"Yes, there are many of us."

"Why?"

"Well, there are a lot of people in the world, Evan. One person would be hard-pressed to deal with every dying person if they had to take care of everyone. Even a god. That's why new gods are born from time to time, to properly fulfill our divine role."

"So, how old are you?" He asked another of the questions that had bothered him in the past week.

"Seventeen. My birthday was in March."

It was a lot to absorb, and Evan considered everything carefully. It was an incredible relief to learn that she didn't *take* the lives of the living, and he wouldn't need to worry if she would run off to inflict the same pain he had endured on another innocent soul. But the fact remained that she was a real-life god. He had been so caught up in the thought of her being a murderer that the greater implications of gods truly existing and living among people had been an afterthought. With a few moments to ponder, he found the concept difficult to absorb and could hardly guess at the ramifications it would have.

"Can I ask you a question?" Hana said tentatively.

"Sure," he said. "Go ahead."

"How did you figure out who I was? And the others?"

"Well, I kind of got lucky there," Evan said. "That night at the park, that creepy girl, Deidre, called you Thanatos a few times. Then the next day, when I was working, I came across that name again."

"You mean at the bookstore?"

Evan nodded. "Mr. Abernathy has a set of really nicely painted tarot cards, where each of the cards represents a Greek god. I was moving it around the store when I saw a card with an image of the Grim Reaper on the front. It represents the Death Card, and across the bottom, it has the name Thanatos. It seemed like too much of a coincidence with your scythe and all, so I looked it up in the book I used for our mythology assignment a couple of weeks ago.

"The book entry mentioned Hypnos, Nyx, and Erebus on the page for Thanatos. Later, I went through the rest of the Tarot cards and found one for Phobos and Deimos. At first, I thought I was insane, but I went back to the park and saw the aftermath of your fight: damaged bushes, trees, and the gouges Deimos made in the concrete." He shrugged. "It was really hard to believe, but nothing else made sense."

Hana was quiet for a time, a look of thoughtfulness on her face.

"Is it a problem? That I know?" Evan remembered his earlier concern that there might be consequences for learning the truth.

"Perhaps, but I don't think so," she said. "There are rules that we have to follow while we live among mortals. And one of the most important is that we don't reveal our true selves."

"Oh!" Evan's eyes widened as he worried about what would happen now that he knew the truth.

"Relax, it's okay," Hana said quickly. "They don't expect us to keep the secret from everyone. We just need to keep it from getting out to the public. So, we can't go showing off in front of a grocery store or in the middle of school."

"That makes sense, I guess."

"Does it?" Hana asked, raising an eyebrow.

Evan smiled back and nodded, but as he continued to consider everything, he converted his nod to a shake. Hana chuckled while motioning with her hand that he was free to ask whatever questions he wanted.

"You said there were rules?" Evan asked. "Like what?"

"There are several," Hana said. "Mostly based around keeping our existence a secret. So, we can't use our powers in public, use our real names, or run around telling everyone the gods exist. Additionally, while living in the mortal world, we have to pass as a mortal and live with the same limitations."

"What do you mean, limitations?" Evan thought back to the battle between Hana and Deidre and couldn't imagine that anything he had witnessed was remotely possible by a mortal.

"We eat, drink, sleep, buy clothes, pay rent, that kind of thing," Hana said. "We live like mortals do, for the most part."

"Wait a minute, does that mean that you don't actually have to eat or sleep if you didn't want to?"

"Well, technically, no. When I was young, I enjoyed eating and sleeping, so I often did. I just didn't *have* to."

The idea fascinated Evan. "Can you choose not to sleep or eat here if you wanted?"

"I suppose so." Hana shrugged. "Though it would become uncomfortable after a while. And it's against the rules."

"Hold on. If it's against the rules to expose your true self to mortals, then what was the deal about Phobos attacking me in the park? Didn't that break the rules?"

"Technically, yes," Hana said with a look of chagrin. "But if she had killed you, then the secret would have been kept safe."

"Killed me?" Evan balked. "Wait, wait, wait! Letting people know your secret is against the rules, but killing innocent people isn't?"

"No," Hana said, looking away and fidgeting in her seat. "Killing innocents without cause is also against the rules. Especially in large numbers. But killing someone who found us out before they could leak our secret... that's kind of a gray area." She shook her head. "I don't think Didi was trying to kill you. She just... gets carried away."

"Oh, that's reassuring," Evan said sarcastically.

"The intent is to keep ourselves hidden," she said. "Didi may have gotten into a bit of trouble, but she would likely only have been reprimanded if she had killed you to keep our secret safe. Especially considering who her father is. Some gods can be rather callous and put little to no value in individual humans."

"That's fucked up!"

"I agree!" Hana nodded vigorously. "They're wrong to think that way."

Evan thought back to the fight with Deidre, and a fresh wave of goosebumps erupted, knowing that he had nearly died at the hands of a homicidal middle-schooler and her giant monster.

"So, I didn't just imagine that thing slicing up my back?" he asked. "That wasn't just a dream or anything?"

"No, I'm afraid not." Hana sounded remorseful.

"How did I get better?" Evan asked. "Did you do that?"

"No, it wasn't me. I don't have the power to heal. I called my mother, and she tended to your wounds and clothing."

Evan supposed it made sense that a God of Death wouldn't have the power to heal the living, but it made him curious about her mother and what role she played in the modern era. He recalled she was the goddess of the night, but he didn't remember any details about her other than being the mother of several of the old gods.

"While we're on the subject, why is Phobos here anyway? Isn't she supposed to follow Ares into battle or something?"

"I... I don't know, actually." Hana said, looking away. "I haven't seen her since that night in the park."

After learning about Deidre's true nature, Evan asked another question that bothered him. "Do you know why she'd be running around tearing up graveyards and assaulting people?"

"I'm sorry, what?" Hana looked back at him, her eyebrows furrowed in a look of total confusion.

"The Graveyard Smasher." Evan blinked. "Why is Phobos digging up the dead? Is that a part of her whole 'fear' thing?"

"No." Hana shook her head. "Didi isn't the one who's been vandalizing those graves. I'm quite certain she has nothing to do with all of that."

"Really? But—" the rest of Evan's question was cut off by a piercing alarm from Hana's watch.

"Dammit..." She winced as she reached across and silenced it.

Curious, Evan looked at his own watch and noted that it was 6:18. *An odd time for an alarm*, he thought to himself.

"Does that mean you have to leave?" he asked.

"Kind of, yeah."

Obviously, whatever the alarm signified was

important. While Hana remained seated, she was antsy and on edge, shuffling her feet and looking at her watch every few seconds. Evan still had a load of burning questions, but they'd resolved the biggest problem.

"We can pick this up later," he said, "if you're around."

"Is that what you want?"

As Evan thought about it, there were so many unknowns and unasked questions, and he still wasn't sure how much of it he fully believed. He was willing to give it more time, though.

"Yes," he said. "Yes, it is."

At his answer, Hana visibly relaxed and smiled. "Okay."

Hana's watch sounded again, this time in a much louder, more urgent tone.

Hana was out of her seat in a flash, spinning around, her skirt flaring out in a blur. In the same motion, she reached across and conjured her gleaming scythe as he had seen her do that night in the park.

"What is it?" Evan asked as he looked in the direction Hana faced, nearly falling off this bench at the sight of what was coming toward them.

Chapter Fourteen

Death Incarnate

From across the playground, the most horrifying thing Evan had ever seen was barreling toward them. The creature was long and dark, with a thick, snake-like head several feet wide and a pair of bright, burning eyes set in a distorted face. It was easily thirty feet long, with a sleek, elongated body and dozens of human arms and legs sprouting from its belly, like some sort of giant disfigured centipede. Its skin looked like flowing liquid, oozing across its length in a disgusting combination of black, green, and blue. As it moved, small bubbles formed on its body, bursting in a thick gray ooze that mixed in with the rest of the sludge coating the beast.

"What the hell is that?" Evan cried out.

"*THAT* is the Graveyard Smasher!" Hana growled.

"That... thing?" Evan croaked. Hana answered with a single forceful nod.

As he watched in horror, the creature collided with a metal jungle gym halfway across the playground. The monstrous thing didn't take any notice of the obstacle, running right through it, the metal melting and sizzling wherever it touched, its many arms pushing on the various pipes and joints, twisting and distorting it with unbelievable ease.

"Run!" Hana yelled as she moved forward.

She swung her scythe in a wide arc as she stepped, summoning a sickle of light and slinging it toward the creature. Evan watched as the light sliced into the sludge and was completely absorbed with only a small wisp of smoke as evidence that she'd hit it. The monster continued to flow toward them at a terrifying speed, altogether unperturbed by her attack.

"Evan! *Run!*"

The urgency of Hana's voice finally spurred him to action. He climbed out of the picnic bench and staggered away just before the creature smashed into it, sending his backpack flying high in the air, with small wisps of smoke sizzling off it upon landing. Unable to think clearly, Evan's mind grasped onto Hana's single instruction, and he turned and ran. He sprinted toward the back of the school, eyes darting back and forth, scanning for someplace safe.

Glancing back as he ran, he saw Hana continue her assault, hurling several more arcs of light toward the creature, each ending in small puffs of smoke. Feeling more terrified than ever, he put his head down and willed his legs to greater speeds.

As he sprinted toward the nearest school building, he thought about the small catalog of monsters he could recall from Grecian lore. Nothing he could think of came even close to describing this thing. The long body suggested something snake-like, but the many human arms and legs, oozing sludge, and large, almost human-like eyes conflicted with anything remotely natural.

Evan caught sight of the beast barreling down on him out of the corner of his eye, just in the nick of time.

Planting both feet into the thick grass, he threw himself backward onto the sod, dodging the massive beast by mere inches.

As it slid past, Evan could smell the cloud of stench surrounding the monstrosity. It reminded him of raw sewage, so pungent that it nearly caused him to double over and retch.

Realizing that it had missed its prey, it turned in a wide arc to make another pass as Evan scrambled to his feet. The monster was surprisingly fast for its size, and Evan began to frantically look for a new avenue of escape. He needed to get something between him and it if he was going to stand a chance. Hana was nowhere in sight, and Evan feared the worst.

Choosing a path between two nearby buildings, Evan began running again, hoping he could make the narrow gap before it caught him. He dared to look behind him as he ran, and his heart sank at how fast the creature was closing. Suddenly, out of nowhere, Hana fell from the sky, scythe coming down in a broad slice. Her blade cut deep into the monster, slicing down from the crown of its head and across the side of its face, cutting across its right eye. The orange orb exploded in a shower of black ooze.

The creature reared back and roared in pain. Evan shuddered at the sound of a dozen voices crying out in a chorus of agony and rage. A fresh wave of fear raced through him, causing him to stumble and fall to the ground just as he arrived at his hiding spot. Crawling on his hands and knees, he hid behind a dumpster where he could watch the fight unfold.

Now that Hana had struck a solid blow, the monster approached her more cautiously, keeping her at a distance while it swayed back and forth. Hana pressed her advantage and lunged forward, swinging for its head again. The beast was prepared and pulled back this time, snapping viciously as she closed. As its head retreated, its long body twisted unexpectedly and whipped its tail around with a counterattack.

Hana dodged the worst of the surprise attack, but the tip of its tail dragged across her side as she spun away. As it struck her, a glob of black sludge stuck to her hip and thigh, the fabric of her clothes erupting into a cloud of smoke where it touched. Hana cried out in pain and jumped backward thirty feet in a single bound. The sludge fell off as she landed, and the grass below her sizzled briefly before the sludge dissolved.

A good-sized section of her blouse was gone where the sludge had been, her skin bright red and inflamed, as if she had been badly burned. While she stood at the ready, her grimace gave evidence of her pain.

Evan swallowed hard. If that slime could hurt a goddess, what would it do to him? He didn't want to find out. At least it seemed to have forgotten him for the moment.

Hana and the monster faced each other across a short distance. Its head shifted back and forth while its tail swung in anticipation, reminding Evan of a predator stalking its prey. Hana remained perfectly still, feet wide apart, her muscles tense and eyes glued to the monster with single-minded determination.

For a moment, all was still.

Then Hana lunged at the beast in a cloud of dust. She instantly closed the distance between them, seeming to teleport herself forward, swinging in a wide arc at its head as she closed the last few feet.

Surprised at the speed of her attack, the creature barely avoided being decapitated. Pulling back its head at the last moment, it sacrificed its long body to her attack in order to protect its head. Her wicked blade connected solidly, cutting across its chest and opening a wide gap.

The beast roared again in its unnerving multiple voices as light poured out of the massive wound. The creature swung its tail in retaliation, forcing Hana to jump away before she could follow up on her first blow with another. Evan watched in horror as the sludge oozed across the creature's body, closing the wound as if it had never been there. In the span of a few seconds, he couldn't tell where she had struck the thing.

Well, THAT's not good. Evan thought. *If the thing can instantly heal any damage Hana does to it, then how can she possibly defeat it?* He had to trust that Hana knew what she was doing as she continued to battle the weird creature.

Hana had the advantage in the wide-open field of the school's playground: with her incredible speed, she could move in, strike, and retreat before the monster could dodge or retaliate. There was nothing to limit her movement, and the monster struggled to anticipate where her next attack would come from.

She danced in and out, repeatedly cutting deep gashes across its body. He could tell she wanted to end it quickly with a blow to the head, but the monster was cagey and protected itself fiercely. So instead of a single killing blow, Hana had opted for a strategy of attrition. She was settling for repeated blows to the body, wearing the monster down.

Each time Hana slashed the creature, Evan caught glimpses of a bright light shining from the wound before the sludge reformed again. It was hard to tell if Hana was making much progress, though the toll the fight was taking on her was obvious.

After several minutes of pitched battle, she looked

awful. Her skirt was burned in half a dozen places, with a sizable hole along her left hip. Her blouse was barely hanging on where the creature had landed a solid blow, the sludge eating away the fabric across her right shoulder, exposing most of her back and one bra strap.

She was panting, air plastered to her face as her skin glistened with sweat. She looked tired, though it was tough to tell how the beast was doing. Evan thought it looked weaker, as the sludge seemed to slow as each fresh wound took longer and longer to close where it had been nearly instantaneously earlier. He hoped she was winning and about to finish it off.

The creature must have had a similar thought when it lunged again with more speed than Evan thought possible. Instead of attacking, however, it turned toward the nearby street and fled, exploding through the chain-link fence that surrounded the school.

Its unexpected flight caught Hana by surprise, but she recovered quickly and gave chase, following its trails of devastation around a corner and out of sight.

Now that the coast was clear, Evan staggered out from behind the dumpster and looked at where they'd gone. This was his chance to escape. He could grab his things, run home, and maybe even call Hana's house to tell them what was happening.

As he pulled his phone out of his pocket and began thinking about what he'd say, the image of Hana came to mind. Her exhaustion was setting in, and her clothes were nearly falling apart from the damage she'd taken. This wasn't like that night in the park. This was far worse. The monster wasn't playing a game; it wanted her dead, and if it ambushed her, it just might succeed. The thought of Hana dying drove him forward as he pocketed his phone and sprinted across the decimated playground, following as fast as he could.

He couldn't see the monster or Hana, but the swath of damage they had left behind gave him a clear path to follow. He realized that maybe the monster was more injured than he had previously guessed as its passage meandered, bouncing off walls, parked cars, and light poles. It looked like a drunk driver had careened down the road, sideswiping everything in its path. As he followed, a few curious heads popped out of their front doors, looking up and down the street.

Evan made another quick turn, and for a moment, he caught a glimpse of the beast flowing up and over a faraway house, vanishing from sight nearly a block away. Hana followed, jumping on top of a light pole at the far end of the block, then leaping off in pursuit. She flew dozens of feet into the air before falling back down, out of sight behind the row of houses.

Evan could hardly believe how far they'd gone so quickly. He ran as fast as he could, causing a few pedestrians to cry out in surprise as he raced by. Had no one noticed the teenage girl leaping from building to building in pursuit of a giant black snake monster? He would have expected screams of fright or cars squealing to a stop to catch a better glance, but no one reacted. They appeared completely oblivious to the battle raging around them.

When Evan got to the end of the street, there were no new clues about where they had gone. The road was quiet, with a few people walking lazily past and a handful of parked cars. He scanned each direction until he noticed a cat at the end of a far corner, its hackles up, hissing at something out of sight.

Following his instincts, Evan raced in the cat's direction. By the time he reached the corner, the animal was long gone. Scanning the neighborhood, he noticed the entrance to a large, old graveyard close to where he stood, and something inside of him told him that's where they'd gone.

Evan hurried across the street, causing the driver of an oncoming car to slam on their brakes while blaring their horn. Once inside the graveyard, he took a moment to get his bearings. The place felt ancient, with rows and rows of headstones and statuary placed haphazardly across an overgrown terrain of rolling hills and large trees. It didn't appear that anyone had bothered to cut back the grass or weeds in months. Many of the shorter grave markers and paths between them were heavily obscured, and there was no way he could run through such a place without tripping over them. With growing anxiety, Evan jogged as fast as he dared, looking for Hana, certain that she and the monster had come this way.

The sun was setting, and as Evan worked his way further in, the area grew darker as large sections were cast in long shadows from the surrounding trees. The place was much more menacing than the entrance, and it quickly became treacherous to run with all the overgrowth. Evan worked his way in as fast as he could, moving past row upon row of gravestones, watching his steps carefully to avoid tripping and falling. The place was far larger than he had imagined, and it was several minutes of careful searching before he found any sign of them.

As Evan rounded another corner, he came across a large marble gravestone with its top half cleanly sliced off, the remnants of the stone laying in a pile of rubble on the ground. Close to the sliced stone, he came across a small statue where some of the ooze from the beast must have splashed onto it, as its entire left side had melted, with a deep hole at its base.

The trail of destruction led farther into the labyrinth of stones and pathways, and he followed it as fast as he dared. Finally, he caught the sound of Hana's whirling scythe and stone crashing into stone nearby.

Evan slowed his pace and moved toward the sounds of battle carefully. As he crested a small hill, he finally caught sight of her, and a fresh wave of fear washed through him.

Hana was at the end of a long row of graves with her scythe held limply in one hand while the other wrapped around her side, blood slowly seeping down her arm. Her skirt was nothing but tatters, and somewhere in all the chaos, she'd lost a shoe. She was panting heavily, with minor scrapes down her left cheek and a few thin rivulets of blood slowly dripping down her neck. Despite her apparent fatigue and wounds, she looked focused and determined, ready to spring into action as her eyes darted back and forth, peering into the dark recesses of the graveyard.

If Hana had the advantage in the playground, the monster had the advantage here. The confined space with rows of gravestones, shadows, and blind corners limited Hana's movement, giving the monster places to hide and potentially ambush her. She couldn't make good use of her speed here, and now she had lost sight of the monster entirely.

Evan's heart thudded in his chest. Hana was backed into a corner with little room to maneuver, with a plethora of hiding and striking locations for the creature to attack from. To make matters worse, this part of the graveyard was heavily shadowed because of a large building along its southern edge, limiting what little sunlight remained and cutting off any escape routes other than the way they'd come.

Despite his better judgment, Evan worked his way down toward her, his only thought being that he had to get her out of there. As he moved, he worried she was too injured to get out of the dead end on her own. His only thought was to sneak up to her and help her retreat to somewhere more open where she wouldn't be at such a disadvantage.

He crouched down and slipped between several headstones as quietly as possible, slinking ever closer. As he moved, he listened intently for any sign of the monster, though the only thing he could hear was the sound of Hana's breathing. It was labored and wheezing, heightening Evan's sense of urgency to get her out of there. In a few brief moments, he was close to where she stood.

"Hana!" Evan whispered.

"Evan?" She looked at him in shocked surprise. "What are you doing here?"

"Come on! You have to get out of here before that thing comes back." He motioned urgently for her to follow.

"You shouldn't be here! Why did you follow us?"

"There isn't time to talk," he said, scanning the immediate surroundings, still hoping to escape before the monster returned.

She hadn't started moving yet, intensifying his suspicion that she was severely injured. He thought he might have to carry her out when the ground exploded around him, filling the sky with flying dirt and debris as the horrifying monster erupted from a nearby row of graves. It threw several headstones and coffins into the air, but Evan felt an arm wrap around him before the debris fell, picking him up and tossing him to the side.

He landed heavily, bouncing and rolling as he hit the ground, looking back in horror as a headstone crashed to the ground where he had been a moment earlier. As he came to a stop, he looked back to see the oozing beast towering nearby, its head swinging from side to side, looking for its prey.

Evan spotted Hana, and his shaky breath caught in his chest. One row over, she lay on the ground, eyes closed, as a torrent of blood flowed out of a deep gash on her temple. She had sacrificed herself to save him, and it would all be over if the beast spotted her.

As quietly as he could, Evan scrambled to Hana's limp form. Relief flooded him as he turned her head and felt her breath on his cheek, while his heart sank when he saw the severity of the gash. Pulling off his scarf, he quickly wrapped it around her head, hoping to stop the flow of blood.

"Hana!" he whispered urgently. "Hana! Wake up!"

As he crouched, lightly shaking Hana to rouse her, his ears picked up the sound of the monster moving toward them.

Evan looked around in a panic. He couldn't see it, but it was close, lurking somewhere nearby. With how fast the monster had flown down the street, he knew he had no chance of escaping on foot, and he wasn't willing to abandon Hana.

In his search, his eyes fell on the silver-and-black

scythe lying on the ground at the foot of a gargoyle. A wild image formed in his mind of using the vicious weapon to hold off the beast long enough for help to arrive. Hana said there were others, right? Someone *must* be coming. He just needed to buy them time. Regardless, with no chance of escape, it was fight or die.

The sight of Hana lying on the ground, helpless and bleeding, chased away all fear. He knew he was no match for the creature, but he had to do something.

The problem was speed. He had seen just how fast the monster moved and knew he would never reach the weapon if he didn't have a head start. Looking around, he spotted a large, jagged piece of rubble with a glistening wet spot where it had most likely struck Hana. A wave of anger flooded through him, and he grabbed the sharp stone, hurling it as far as he could, away from the two of them and the scythe.

He cringed at the loud sound of it ricocheting off another headstone, but the distraction worked. The beast lurched away from him, giving him time to act. Without a moment's hesitation, Evan lunged for the sinister blade.

The creature didn't remain fooled for long, and before Evan had run a dozen paces to the weapon, it had already turned on itself and was racing back.

Evan reached the scythe and bent to pick up the menacing-looking weapon, adrenaline pumping through his veins. As he went to stand and ready himself, he nearly fell over when the weapon refused to budge. It was unbelievably heavy—easily fifty pounds—and it took all his strength just to pick it off the ground.

With no time to waste, he spun around, grunting at the effort it took to raise the blade into the air, ready to defend himself. To his surprise, the monster didn't attack but paused, standing on top of several headstones, watching him intently.

It approached slowly, keeping its one good eye solidly glued to Evan as it snaked from headstone to headstone. Evan kept himself at the ready, though the incredible weight of the weapon strained his protesting muscles.

"Come on!" he grumbled. "What are you waiting for?"

Evan knew he couldn't hold the weapon up much longer, already feeling like his arms were being pulled out of their sockets. He considered lunging toward the creature before his strength gave out, but it was still too far away. He couldn't cross the distance and carry the weapon effectively. As if that wasn't bad enough, the tight confines of the rows of graves made moving treacherous. He knew he had only one shot, so he had to make it count.

The monster continued its slow advance and was nearly in range when it paused. Raising its head, it sniffed the air and then turned in Hana's direction.

"Hey! Come get me!" A new shot of adrenaline pumped through Evan at the thought of the thing attacking Hana in her unconscious state. Exerting himself further, he kicked a large piece of rubble as hard as he could; the stone struck the side of the creature's head, sizzling before bouncing off harmlessly.

The beast hardly noticed, ignoring Evan completely while slithering toward Hana's prone form.

"No!" Evan threw himself at the creature with the scythe held high as he raced down the row of graves, the awkward weight of the weapon making it difficult not to stumble. He swung downward as he closed the distance, hoping to connect with its one good eye.

He was far too slow.

As he swung down, the creature reared up and away from his strike with ease. The blade sank into the soft earth and stuck fast. Evan tried to pry the weapon from the soil for a second strike, widening his stance and using all his strength in a mighty pull, to no avail. The weapon seemed to resist him, almost as if embarrassed at the failure of his one attempt, refusing to be wielded by someone so inadequate.

While his strike hadn't landed, it confused the beast, which backed away to a respectable distance. There it lurked, watching Evan intently, seemingly hesitant to act too rashly.

Breathing in ragged gasps, Evan knew he was spent. His arms and legs were weak, his muscles screaming. He grabbed the scythe's handle and tried one more time to free it from the ground, pulling with everything he had.

"Come on!" he groaned as he pulled.

The thing wouldn't budge, feeling even heavier than it had before. Finally, his strength gave out, causing him to fall heavily backward onto the ground. Aching from his efforts, he stayed there, waiting for the beast to strike.

"I'm sorry," he mumbled, thinking of Hana, his family, and friends. He had failed them all and now would pay the ultimate price. A macabre laugh escaped him as he remembered that night he returned to the park and the thought that mortals who get involved with the gods never end well.

The creature reared back, preparing to attack. With a strange sense of calm, Evan watched as the beast towered over him, its long body stretching high into the air with its singular eye focused on him. A small part of him thought it was fitting that it would all end in the middle of a dark and lonely graveyard. He had literally courted death, and this was his reward.

He watched, transfixed, as his death approached with blinding speed, and suddenly—Hana was there.

If he had blinked, he would have missed it. She appeared out of nowhere, feet planted in the soft earth in front of him, throwing up a cloud of soil and grass, her arrival causing a slight breeze to wash over his face.

In one fluid motion, she tensed to leap, reaching out with her good arm and pulling the scythe free from its earthly prison. The weapon gleamed in anticipation, impossibly sharp and ready to bite into the flesh of its enemy. Before the beast could change course at her sudden appearance, she kicked off the ground and launched herself toward it, throwing up even more dirt before the initial cloud had time to fall back to earth.

She flew up to meet the beast on its inexorable path, swinging her blade up as she went. The blade sank deep into its underbelly and sliced down the length of its long body.

Hana's momentum carried her from its snout to its tail, opening the monster from underneath and flooding the graveyard in a shower of blinding, bright light.

As she fell back to the ground, the wound continued to spread open, the light spilling out, discarding the sludge-covered ooze like a snake shedding its skin. To Evan, it was as if the black, tar-like sludge had been a coat that had been unzipped, the acidic slurry bursting into a cloud of smoke and vapors as it fell away, evaporating into the evening dusk.

Hana stood triumphant with her head looking up at the bright light that was the beast's core as it condensed and shrunk, rapidly morphing into the figure of a man, resplendent in pure, blinding light, translucent and beautiful.

Exhausted, Hana set her scythe aside, leaning it against a nearby headstone as the glowing figure drifted down, floating like a feather in the wind. When it finally reached her, Hana stepped forward, catching the figure and cradling him tenderly in her arms.

"Hello, Mr. Richardson," she said, speaking gently as a mother to her child. "It's a pleasure to finally meet you."

Evan sat stunned, barely able to comprehend her words. What had been a fifty-foot-long horrifying monster of sludge, with a hundred spindly arms and legs, had transformed into the glowing form of a man he had seen in the pictures in Mrs. Richardson's room.

"Annette is waiting for you," Hana said to the man as she held him. "Would you like to go see her?"

The man smiled up at her. His mouth was moving in a whisper so faint Evan couldn't be sure if he was speaking or not.

With another smile, Hana reached down with one hand and folded the image of the man onto itself. It was as if he was a long piece of cloth that she carefully layered back upon itself, repeatedly, with each pass reducing his size by half. Within a dozen gentle folds, she had reduced the full-sized body of a man to that of a small marble, then pressed her hands together to condense it even further.

She then produced a small silver locket from around her neck, which she carefully opened and deposited the brightly glowing ball inside. After closing the locket, the light dimmed, only visible as a faint glow around the clasp.

Evan watched, amazed and dumbfounded.

Chapter Fifteen

New Beginning

Wordlessly, Hana retrieved her scythe and set it into her leg, where it became a tattoo once more. With the fabulous weapon secured, she returned to Evan, who hadn't moved from where he sat watching in awe.

"Are you hurt?" she asked as she squatted down next to him.

"I... I don't think so," he said as he blinked. "Is it over?"

"Yes," Hana said. "It's all done. The lost soul has been secured. I will return him to the underworld later, where I'm sure his wife is waiting for him."

"Lost soul?"

"I'll explain later, okay?" she said as she smiled. "Let's make sure you're all right, and we can go somewhere safer and warmer."

Evan nodded and accepted her help standing up. A quick check showed that he hadn't sustained any serious injuries. There were a few bruises and minor scratches from his efforts, but nothing requiring medical aid. On the other hand, Hana was a sight: she was covered in a series of minor cuts, with the entire right side of her head caked in dried blood. Besides the battle wounds, her clothes were in tatters, having been eaten away in dozens of places, barely holding together.

Evan removed his jacket and wrapped it around her.

"Oh, thank you," she said.

"Of course." He smiled. "I should look at that." He pointed to the side of her head and the scarf still wrapped around her wound.

Wordlessly, she turned her head to the meager light from a distant streetlamp. Evan leaned in and carefully removed the scarf, watching Hana closely for any flinching or signs of pain. She seemed fine as he removed the makeshift bandage and was amazed when he finished, as the wound had shrunk considerably. It looked like she had suffered a slight cut a week ago rather than a massive gash only a few minutes earlier.

"Holy cow!" he gasped.

"Is it Okay?" Hana asked with a note of concern.

"It's almost gone!"

"Oh, that," she said. "I heal very fast. We all do, actually. In fact, by morning, you won't even be able to tell I was hurt at all."

"You really are amazing," Evan said, thinking that his own assortment of scratches and bruises would take at least a week or two to heal. If he had taken the level of abuse she had, he'd need to be admitted to a hospital. Her fast healing aside, he was still amazed at everything he'd witnessed.

"Thank you," she whispered, blushing as they walked.

They continued making their way out of the graveyard when Hana stumbled, Evan catching her before she fell.

"Are you sure you're all right?" he asked as he steadied her on a nearby tree.

"Okay, maybe I'm not *entirely* fine," she said sheepishly. "I'm still a bit dizzy."

"Here, let me help you." He slid an arm around her waist, supporting her as they walked.

"Thank you."

They headed out of the graveyard, taking a meandering path to work their way out of the devastation.

"So, what was that thing?" he asked, trying to distract himself from thinking about how close they were and how underdressed she was under his thin jacket.

"A lost soul," Hana said. "You would call them ghosts."

"That didn't look like any kind of ghost I've ever heard of." Evan shivered, remembering its terrifying body, acidic sludge, and multitudes of arms and legs.

"Most of the time, they are totally invisible," she explained. "When people see them, they appear as transparent versions of their former selves or indistinct, vaguely humanoid wisps. But a lost soul doesn't stay pure forever...

"See, when someone dies, and their soul lingers, it becomes a kind of emotional sponge. They slowly absorb the feelings that living people give off around them. So, if they linger around people who are sad or lonely or in pain, they can become polluted with an excess of negative energy."

"And that thing was Mrs. Richardson's husband?" he asked.

Hana nodded, stumbling slightly as they walked. "I imagine Mr. Richardson stayed around to keep his wife company after he died. And while the facility your aunt runs treats its guests with love and care, it's still a place with a lot of pain, grief, and loss. When Annette died, I'm guessing that Lloyd's soul became distressed, searching for her around the neighborhood. I think he's been 'looking' for her this whole time and was drawn to the graveyards in his search."

"So, he was the Graveyard Smasher? I was certain that it was Deidre." Evan shook his head.

"Why would you think it was Didi?"

"Because she was mentioned in one of the news reports, and the police wanted to talk to her."

"Oh," Hana said with a giggle. "I suspect she was looking for me. She knows I live around here somewhere, but not my actual address or phone number. I bet she learned that the local graveyards were being destroyed and thought I would investigate, so she hung around, hoping to see me."

"She wanted to see you? Or kill you?" Evan asked, shivering again at the memory of her murderous smile and apparent delight at his near-death.

"Ah, well..." Hana wrung her hands. "Didi can be, um, excitable, you could say."

"Excitable?" Evan blinked at her, his tone dripping with sarcasm. "That's an understatement! She tried to kill me! I still don't get how you can consider her your friend when she's totally cool with randomly murdering people."

"She's not normally like that. Didi is Phobos, the God of Fear, and her role is to follow Ares into battle to spread terror everywhere she goes. She's been raised not to think about mortals as people, or at least not as anyone who matters. If you knew about her upbringing, you'd understand." Hana looked away. "Her father is the God of War, and her mother, well, let's just say that she's very passionate. They both have very skewed perceptions about mortals and behave more like the gods from the stories. You know, treating people more like playthings than individuals.”

“Great,” Evan mumbled.

“I know it didn’t look like it, but she’s actually really sweet. Believe me.”

“Well, maybe.” Evan shrugged.

“I’ve never known her to be so ready to fight or kill, though. In battle, she spreads the fear of people’s mortality to spur them into action or retreat and cease fighting. I’ve never known her to actually want anyone dead before.” Hana grabbed Evan’s arm and squeezed for emphasis. “I’m still worried for her. I don’t know why she showed up that night, but I think she might have run away from home. I’ve known her since we were kids, and she isn’t naturally that violent. She only lashes out like that when she’s really upset over something. I’m worried she’s in trouble, and I want to help her.”

Evan struggled to separate the psychopathic little girl from the old friend Hana remembered. He wanted to give Hana’s childhood friend another chance but secretly hoped he wouldn’t have to deal with her ever again.

“So, if it wasn’t Phobos who trashed the graveyards, you think it was Mr. Richardson’s ghost?” he asked, intentionally moving the conversation away from Didi.

“I suspect so. He was probably looking for his wife, and the longer he searched in vain, the more distraught he became. His fear, anger, and loss grew, magnified by all the negative energy he had accumulated over the years. Eventually, he became the monster that attacked us.”

“So, anyone who dies can become one of these lost

souls and start terrorizing the living?”

“I’m afraid so,” Hana said. “In fact, that’s exactly why I agreed to become Thanatos. If one of us is present shortly after someone dies and gathers their soul, they won’t linger and become a danger to others.”

“Oh.” Evan marveled. “So, you need to be there every time someone dies, then? Well, Thanatos does I mean.”

“Not necessarily. Not everyone who dies requires attention,” Hana said. “Most spirits will naturally find their way without help. But if someone dies with a lot of unfinished business, or if their death is especially traumatic, then there is a good chance they’ll try to stick around. And we have to deal with them.”

“How do you keep this all a secret?” Evan looked around at the destroyed graveyard. “I mean, that thing was huge, and look at the mess it left behind!”

“Mostly, what I am and what I do is invisible to people. People fear death and will ignore me most of the time,” Hana said. “Also, Lloyd was a rather extreme case. He was by far the largest and strongest lost soul I’ve ever seen. Normally, they are much smaller, and we can take care of them quickly with little effort or disturbance.”

She noticed him looking at the broken gravestones.

“Don’t worry about all the damage,” Hana said. “We can leave that to someone else. I’ll let my mother know that we tore up the graveyard and the school’s playground, and I expect they will send someone to fix it up by morning.”

“It’s hard to believe that this stuff goes on all the time and no one ever notices,” Evan said, noting the extent of the damage.

“It’s all my fault. Things wouldn't have gotten out of hand if I was better at my job."

"What? Nonsense!" Evan said emphatically. "You were amazing! I've never seen anything like that!"

"Thank you," she said as she smiled. "I'll do better next time."

For a time, they walked quietly, Hana leaning on Evan as they went. By the time they exited the graveyard and headed back to the school to recover Evan's bag, the streetlamps were lit, and a cool breeze ran through town. Hana shivered, and Evan pulled her closer, hoping their shared warmth would keep a modicum of the night's chill away. He couldn't do all the cool god stuff that she could—not even remotely—but he could do this.

The cool evening air chilled Evan as they walked, and he kept talking to distract from the growing cold.

"Hey, so, I was thinking. You said that you and Mara used to look like each other, but then you got sick. Is that true?"

Hana stiffened under the coat briefly before looking down at her chest. "No. I'm sorry. That was another lie."

"It's Okay. But can you tell me the real reason you don't look alike? Are you actually twins?" he asked, regretting his bluntness but still curious.

"Oh yes, we're honest to goodness twins. We have a few pictures from when we were kids, and you can hardly tell us apart. But in the last few years, I've started to... change."

"What do you mean?" Evan blinked.

"My skin has gotten pale, and of course, this." Hana flicked a length of her long, silver hair. "It began a few years ago as a slightly lighter brown, and I stopped tanning in the summers. Now I look more like a ghost than my sister or mom."

"Do you know why you've changed?"

"Mom says that some gods do that. They take on the characteristics of their job, and so... I look more like a skeleton," she said with a sigh.

"Oh." Evan regretted his question even more.

"It's not just me, though," Hana continued. "The red tips in Mara's hair? That's relatively new, as is her napping all the time. She used to be the active one, if you can believe that. Now it's hard for her to stay awake for more than a few hours."

"Oh, that sounds rough." Evan nodded, thinking about his afternoon with her and how they had spent most of the morning and afternoon together. He wondered how much of an effort that trip had truly been for Mara, even though she had passed out on the ride home.

"Well, I think you're beautiful," Evan mumbled, feeling the heat in his cheeks as he turned his head away, hoping she couldn't see him blush violently.

"Thank you," she said quietly, turning her head.

By the time they retrieved Evan's things from the playground, they were exhausted. They decided to take the bus home rather than walk the entire way and sat down together at the nearest bus stop. Evan was sure they'd get some odd looks from the bus driver, but he didn't care. *Let them gawk and wonder*, he thought.

"So, what happens now?" he asked as they waited.

Hana took a deep breath. "I guess that depends on you."

"Me?" Evan asked.

She nodded slowly, looking away from him. "I still wonder if it would be better for my family and me to move away. All I seem to do is bring you pain and hardship. So..." She took another deep breath. "If you want, I'll leave."

"And if I don't want you to leave?"

Hana brightened and looked back at him, blushing when he returned her smile. "Then I'm uncertain what comes next, to be honest. This is all very new to me."

They sat there quietly, each lost in their own thoughts. Slowly, muscles protesting, Evan reached out and put his arm around Hana's shoulders. She stiffened for a moment, then immediately relaxed. As they sat, she leaned her head against his shoulder, and he rested his chin against her silver hair.

Whatever it was, they'd figure it out together.

It wasn't until the bus lights appeared around the corner that Evan broke the silence. "Can I ask a favor?"

"That depends on the favor."

"You know that paper you wrote for Mr. Hanson? The one he said was fiction, and you got in trouble for?"

"Sure."

"Can I read it?" he asked. "I think it would help if I knew more about how things really work and less about what the classic literature says."

"Sure." She smiled mischievously. "But it will cost you."

"Oh? What do you want for it?"

"How about another date?"

Chapter Sixteen

Epilogue

Hana watched as Evan walked around the corner toward his apartment. A warmth spread through her as she reflected on the day. The outcome would have been unimaginable earlier that morning, but it was a tremendous relief that she would stay and that the boy who had stolen her heart truly cared for her in return—the real her.

Smiling broadly, she stepped into her house and closed the door. As she turned around, it surprised her to see the tall figure of her father, sitting casually at their kitchen table, legs crossed, sipping a cup of coffee.

"Daddy!" she called out and raced to embrace him.

With a smile of his own, he stood, arms open wide as she jumped into them as if she were still a child.

"Hello, sweetheart," he said in his resonating voice.

"What are you doing here?" Hana asked after giving him a fierce hug.

"Your mother said you were moving back to Olympus, so I came to help," he said as he smiled.

"Oh, right," Hana said, looking around at the boxes scattered around the house that were already partially filled with their belongings. "I'm not sure that's necessary anymore," she added sheepishly.

"Mmmm," he said. "I had a feeling that might be the case. Why don't you sit down and tell me about it?"

Hana's father guided her to take a seat at the table, and as she sat, he strolled to the kitchen and returned with a damp washcloth, holding it out for her as he reclaimed his chair.

Hana took the washcloth and began wiping her face while considering how much she should share.

"If you're not going home, then I must assume that you and that young man made up?" her father said after she remained quiet too long.

"Uh, yes." She swallowed nervously, uncertain about her father's reaction to Evan's knowledge of their secret. She'd been honest about the need to keep their existence hidden, but it was also accurate that a select few could know the truth. "We finally got to talk and worked it all out."

"Well, that's good," he said while shooting Hana a grin. "Is that all?" he asked, pointedly looking at the blood-soaked washcloth she was fidgeting with.

"Oh, yeah. I also finally found the lost soul that's been tearing up the graveyards. I have him here." She showed him the locket, which was still glowing.

"Very good. I must assume that it was the lost soul that did this to you, and not that young man?" he asked in seriousness.

"Evan would never!"

Hana's father erupted in a fit of laughter at his daughter's incredulous reaction. It took only a moment for Hana to catch on that he had been teasing her and began laughing along with him, the stress of the afternoon easing in his calming presence.

"I'm sorry, I couldn't resist," he said. "Are you all right?"

"I'm fine," she said. "I guess I should work a little harder on my combat training."

"How about you go get cleaned up, and then we can start unpacking," he said, wiping a small tear from the corner of his eye.

Hana bounded up the stairs and returned dressed, washed, and happy after a few minutes. The two of them worked quietly for a while before her father started talking.

"I must say, I'm relieved that you're happy here. I was a little worried when you told us you wanted to live among the mortals, with their natural aversion to you and all. I was concerned that you wouldn't be able to make any meaningful friendships."

"Oh, I love it here!" Hana gushed. "I wish you could meet my friends, Katie, Sarah, and Evan. You'd also get a kick out of Oliver; he's funny."

"I'd love to meet them," her father said. "Though, I'm rather surprised that of all the people you could befriend, it would be that boy, Evan. Considering it was the car crash that took his parents' lives that we watched all those years ago."

Hana stopped dead in her tracks as her heart stopped and her hands went numb.

A vase she had unwrapped and was carrying across the room slipped from her grasp, falling hard on the tile floor, exploding into thousands of tiny pieces.

"Oh, your mother's not going to be happy about that," her father said, looking around at the shattered remains.

"What did you just say?" Hana asked.

"Well, that piece was from your mother's childhood.

She's not going to be pleased that we broke a three-thousand-year-old vase."

"Not about that!" Hana snapped her head around to glare at him. "Who cares about an old piece of pottery?"

"Your mother does, that's who," he said with a chuckle. "Maybe I can ask Hephaestus to fix it?" he mumbled to himself.

"What did you say about *Evan*?" she demanded.

For a moment, her father stared back at her blankly before answering. "Don't you remember? It was right before your eighth birthday, and after learning about Thanatos, you told your mother and me you didn't want to be one.

"So, after we talked a bit, I asked you to let me show you the role Thanatos plays so you could see firsthand how their job is merciful rather than cruel."

Hana thought back to that day so many years ago and recalled how frightened she had been to face her parents. It's not easy to tell two of the most powerful beings in the cosmos that you don't want to be a god. She simply couldn't allow herself to become a creature that took the lives of others, and while it crushed her to disappoint her parents, she knew she couldn't do it.

Her mother and father had been very patient and understanding with her, listening to everything she had to say and agreeing that she could never be so cruel. Then her father took the time to explain the true role of Thanatos and the soul's journey after death, taking care to explain what a lost soul was and how awful it is for a spirit to be trapped.

Hana had remained stubbornly unconvinced until her father suggested a field trip to the mortal world. He offered to personally show her why Thanatos was so important, eventually winning her over with his earnestness.

They visited a large human city, where her father took her to a busy street corner, with cars and trucks flying past as they came and went on their daily routines. Thinking back on it, she could remember the beautiful sky and fluffy clouds as Evan had described them, though she had forgotten that detail until now. She had been frightened to see someone die and had only been brave enough to watch because her father held her hand so tenderly, assuring her that what was about to happen was both inevitable and merciful.

The accident happened so quickly that she barely registered what had occurred. One second, cars were flying past, and the next, there was a terrible screeching noise followed by a loud collision as a car struck the steel pylon for an elevated train.

She remembered that a little boy had been thrown from the crash, landing far from the rest of the car, which wrapped itself around the metal beam. She had initially assumed that it was his death they were there to witness until Thanatos arrived and strode purposefully toward the remnants of the car, completely uninterested in the child.

The harbinger of death was resplendent in a classical long, flowing black robe, complete with a cowl and a bright white skull. In his left hand dangled a long, curved blade suspended from the end of a gleaming silver chain—a variation of the standard scythe for which their kind was known. Even with the voluminous outfit, he was the thinnest person Hana had ever seen. And while she knew there was an adult underneath, she privately wondered if they weren't a skeleton outside of their ceremonial garb.

Once he arrived at the wreckage, Thanatos leaned in with the tenderest of care, pulling forth the mother and father's spirits from within the tangle of metal and glass. Not long after he reached in, the two souls were removed and standing alongside him. For a moment, the three of them stood still, the two spirits looking around, confused and disoriented, before the mother's gaze fell on the body of her young child.

The nearby doctor's office staff began frantically working on stabilizing Evan. His mother rushed to his side as they worked on him, falling to her ghostly knees and wailing. His father was next to her a moment later, urging the medical staff to do a good job and save his boy.

Thanatos glided over, following the pair patiently. As he arrived, he reached out tenderly, pulling the two spirits away from the living who were working to save their son. The parents initially resisted, though Thanatos persisted kindly and patiently. Although he had the power to manipulate the spirits in any way he desired, he didn't use force, instead choosing to encourage the two souls calmly.

Hana remembered watching in awe as he talked to them for several minutes, unable to hear their conversation but touched by Thanatos's care and sensitivity for the parents. After a time, he finally convinced them to move on to the afterlife and leave their children behind, unburdened by a pair of ghosts haunting their days. After a last farewell to their child, Thanatos gently collected their souls as Evan was loaded into the ambulance, stabilized and in good hands.

Then, without a word, Hana's father lightly pulled on

her hand, and the two of them walked around a corner, out of sight of the other onlookers, and into the darkness in which Erebus is supreme. When they arrived back at their home on Olympus, Hana had changed her mind. She wanted to show the kind of compassion and caring Thanatos had shown the two young parents and swore that she would treat everyone with the same tenderness and love.

Her mind returned to the present, and as she stared back at her father, tears ran down her face.

"I thought you knew," he said.

"I had no idea those were *his* parents!" she said. "He told me about his accident, and I thought it was an odd coincidence that we had witnessed something similar all those years ago. But I never, for a second, thought that it was the *same* accident!"

Her father remained quiet, a look of sympathy on his face.

"How is this possible?" Hana asked. "Did you send us here on purpose? Did you know he was here?"

Erebus shook his head slowly. "I didn't know he was here when you asked to move to the mortal world. We followed your friend, Hermes, remember? I never imagined that you might run into the same boy from our trip. You have my word."

Hana suddenly felt weak, wobbling where she stood, her legs threatening to give out from underneath her. With a gentle hand, her father guided her into the nearest chair before she collapsed.

"How do I tell him?" she asked, looking up at him.

Her father remained quiet, leaving Hana to her thoughts as he turned back to the methodical task of picking up the pieces of shattered pottery.

Acknowledgments

Any piece of work is the culmination of a journey, and mine started with the words, "Follow your dreams." Even though it was said as a half-joke at the time, it inspired me to do just that. I had no idea what I was getting myself into when I started and would have given up many times if not for the support of a wonderful group of people.

To Erik Scott de Bie, your guidance on my first draft and the inspirational feedback you provided has stayed with me all these years. To this day, your encouraging words come to mind often. Your enthusiastic support despite all its shortcomings continues to drive me to push through the challenges.

To Will Horner and Tiana Povenmire-Kirk, I cannot express the depth of gratitude I have for your guidance in helping me craft the best version possible of this story. Truly, it wouldn't have come to fruition if not for the two of you. I look forward to working with you for years to come.

And to my wife, there is so much I could say about your endless support and encouragement that it would take pages and pages to express my feelings. But for here and now, I'll stick with thank you, and I love you.

And for all the others, Marlee, Tom, Aeron, Jim, Marie, Steve, Andrea, Pam, Vikki, Colleen, Sarah, Mallory, Jin Amber, Yulia, and countless others, thank you. This has been one of the most challenging things I've ever embarked upon, and it was with your support that it all came together.

Will Butler